THE SNOW GLOBE

BY

TONY FAGGIOLI

ATTICUS CREATIVE

For the six million women every year
who will be stalked.

CHAPTER ONE

IT WAS JUST BEFORE MIDNIGHT. Maggie Kincaid was wearing her favorite pair of cotton pajamas while seated comfortably in her plush leather chair, a worn book open in her lap. She had tried to read *The Magic Mountain* by Thomas Mann many times before. This time, she'd made it three-quarters of the way through without having completely lost interest. That was not to say she was engrossed by the novel—actually, she was horrendously bored by it—but this was supposed to be one of the best books of the twentieth century and she didn't want to feel as though she was missing out.

But now, once again, her mind had begun to wander. Forcing herself to read a book she didn't particularly enjoy reminded her of her school days. People often said those were the best days of your life, but Maggie often thought about how memory never lived up to reality. In your mind's eye, childhood was always such a special time, such an easy time, when in fact it wasn't all that great, really. It was just that over the years, in your need to convince yourself that at

1

some point in your life you'd had a better time at it than this, you willfully forgot all the name calling, all the insecurities and moments of humiliation—or worse. Your childhood had its happy moments, just like adulthood, but since it's human nature to be unhappy in the present, you spend your childhood wishing you were grown up and your adulthood wishing you could be young again.

Sex was the same way. You could be in the mood for something rather illicit one night, only to find that your partner wanted a little romance instead. The next time it would be the opposite. Either way, even when the mood or mechanics of the event felt right, you never really got the real deal. Love always escaped the boundaries drawn by passion and lust. It always came out untouched, and you always came out unchanged. It wasn't that Maggie felt that life was unfair; she simply felt something was wrong.

She gently closed the book and looked around. Her reading lamp was on but the rest of the apartment was dark, save for a small clock across the room that flashed the time in soft blue. Zossima, her cat, quietly slept on one of the white couch pillows nearby, the blue glow of the clock highlighting the outline of his shape. Besides Zossima she was, of course, alone, and she smiled as he opened his eyes and stared briefly at her before resuming his snooze.

It was funny, Maggie had no problem looking her cat directly in the eye, but she found it difficult to do the same with people. Maggie knew that people thought her beautiful. Her face was soft, with naturally pink cheeks that perfectly complemented her slight chin and firm cheekbones. Though her lips were thin they were naturally red, and she had a small mole just above them on the left side of her face. She had coffee colored eyes that, to Maggie's discomfort, had a way of making people stutter if they looked into them too long. This was especially true of men, but not entirely out of the ordinary for women, either. When she didn't return someone's gaze, often they would label her as a bitch or an airhead, depending on whether she was wearing pants or a skirt that day. No one seemed to notice her very light mustache, though—but it was a flaw she obsessed over. Even though it grew in blond, she still bleached it so that it would blend in with her pale skin.

Maggie shifted in her seat, put the book on the floor and stretched her back. The chair she used for reading was her sacred place and her salvation. A gift from her sister, Julie, she'd owned it since her freshman year of college. She'd placed it at an angle next to a window in the corner of the apartment so that she could retreat from the world without feeling entirely separated from it. No one else could use it, not guests or lovers. Not ever. For this reason, whenever company was coming, she stacked books or boxes on it so that no one would be tempted to try it out. But, truth be told, it had been a very long time since Maggie had any guests or lovers. The days of visitors and relaxed debates about life and boys and term papers were things of the past, before her life had become what it was now. Before Michael. Before the costs of things began to outweigh the gains.

Through the window she had a clear view of the one-lane street below that crisscrossed a quarter-mile up with Frederick Douglas Boulevard. It was a quiet street in a loud city, nestled in Harlem, and being three stories above it gave her the opportunity to spy whatever happened to be going on.

One night, while giving her eyes a rest, she had removed her reading glasses and glanced out the window to witness a couple making love in a parked car. After some time, they finished and then kissed for a while. It wasn't until after they hastily redressed and the girl stepped out of the car that Maggie recognized her. She lived in the apartment building across the street with a much younger man than the one she had just been with. This was surprising, because the few times Maggie had seen the young couple together, they had always seemed very much in love. He had probably been upstairs sleeping, expecting her home late from an important business meeting. For the girl to do this act, this close to home, and in this way, Maggie had found both amazing and, much to her shame, provocative.

The neighborhood was also blessed with an insomniac. Maggie had first noticed the old woman a week after moving in, walking aimlessly up and down the street with her newspaper tucked under her arm. It had been early in the afternoon and the woman, who she guessed was in her late seventies, was stomping down the curb at a rather sporadic pace, moving much faster than a woman her age was usually capable of before halting for a breath and going on again. She had a thick neck, and her pure white hair was covered in a black-net scarf that only old European women ever seemed to wear. She wore a heavy wool coat, which seemed odd for that particular day because it had been around sixty-eight degrees. A woman of quite some girth, with feet stuffed into brown loafers and hands that were pudgy and pale, her round face completed the image of a walrus; heavy cheeks hung past her jaw, and her nose was full and hitched below small, wrinkled eyes.

At the time, sitting there in her new apartment, trying to accept that she was once again in a new city, Maggie had barely given the old lady a second glance. But later, over the months, she began to notice her on the street all the time, during the evening news, or late night, after Maggie had finished watching Jimmy Fallon. The old lady hadn't truly scared her though, until one night when Maggie had awoken with the flu.

She had gotten up for a glass of water, her throat and eardrums painfully swollen, and while searching for a bottle of Tylenol—which was never where it was supposed to be— she looked out the living room window and saw her. It was

4

half past three in the morning and there she was, lurching up and down the street with that same newspaper tucked under her arm. The Walrus Lady's lips were moving, or at least they appeared to be. In the faint moonlight it was hard to tell for sure.

Maggie's imagination had overtaken her then, that or her fever had overridden her better senses, and she thought she could actually hear what the Walrus Lady was saying: *There are more things in heaven and earth, Horatio, than are dreamt of in your philosophy.*

Except she was saying it in Latin, and the translation wasn't quite so smooth. It frightened Maggie so much that she backed quickly away from the window, a chill running up the stairway of her spine, and retreated back to bed.

Through the window she also spied other things at different times of the day; people running groceries up the steps of their building while their cars were double parked in the street, the late delivery UPS man, the children wrapped in their parkas and knit caps, the occasional group of friends going out to catch a movie or a bite to eat on the weekends, and the always reliable blue Honda that had returned and was now ominously parked down the street on an almost nightly basis.

The world outside was like a play list of songs you'd never heard before. If you were patient enough to wait out the lyrics or drumbeats that just didn't quite do it for you, eventually, if you were lucky, you stumbled across a song that managed to bridge the chasm that divides all human beings from one another and be touched in some way. Suddenly, you'd find yourself humming along, and you would find a space between the noise that was all your own.

As if on cue, her cell phone chimed with Julie's nightly check-in text: "A STITCH IN TIME." Maggie smiled sadly and typed her reply: "SAVES EIGHT." Their secret code. Deliberately incorrect. In case Michael had finally gotten to her and tried to reply on her behalf.

She sighed and looked out the window again, trying not to think of such things, the lights and sky beyond the glass both beckoning and foreboding.

CHAPTER TWO

ONCE A SOUND SLEEPER, now Maggie barely managed four or five hours each night. And though, with a doctor's help, she tried a few prescription drugs in Chicago, she stopped taking them, as they made her slow and hazy, two conditions not meant for a life of looking over your shoulder.

In the morning Maggie dressed for work, a blue blazer over a matching blue skirt that was cut a healthy distance below the knee. She hated panty hose; they itched and suffocated her legs, and weren't exactly beneficial to one's foot odor, but at this time of year she needed all she could get to stay warm. Over her panty hose she wore socks and a pair of Nike's, her blue flats packed in her bag for when she got to work. She hadn't worn heels in years. Over her outfit she wore a heavy coat with a cotton liner and deep pockets that her mother had given her for Christmas the previous year. It was light brown, not quite beige, and fit her perfectly, leaving just enough room for a scarf. Today she had chosen a thick white one with a dark blue snowflake pattern.

On her way out the door she spilled some cat food into Zossima's dish and kissed him lightly on the top of his head. "Have a fun day, Zoss. I'll be home soon." He purred and swung his head quickly under her chin, the soft fur of his ears tickling her gently. She smiled, grabbed her keys and briefcase, and stepped out into the hallway.

Going down the stairwell she slipped twice, her Nike's almost giving way beneath her. Someone had already come in from the snow a few times and used the stairs, leaving staggered puddles the entire way down. She navigated her descent with more caution, hoping to God that she did not wrench an ankle.

The main entrance to the building was a pair of double doors, the first of which was unlocked and led to a small foyer lined with mailboxes. The second was a security door, which led to the outside. To enter the building, you had to scan a card. A modern amenity on this side of the city now, with the number of rapes and murders on the rise the way they were. After all, this was the twenty-first century and you didn't want people fumbling for keys anymore. It was easier and quicker to simply scan your card through the proximity reader.

At the bottom of the steps Maggie ran into the landlady, Mrs. Catherly. As usual, she'd found a reason to come out into the entryway to greet everyone on their way to work. A widow, Mrs. Catherly never had children and now it seemed that the closest she would get to being a doting mother were those moments when she could pester her tenants.

"Good morning," Maggie said.

"Well good morning to you too, Maggie," Mrs. Catherly replied, a warm smile crossing her face. Her teeth were yellowed by either too much coffee or brandy sours through the years, and she always looked like she had a cold, her nose congested and her blue eyes swollen.

"Ready for another day?" Maggie smiled back as she stepped into the entryway.

Mrs. Catherly was arranging the previous day's junk mail, lining everything up nice and neat in the lower bin of the boxes. "Oh child, my 'being ready' days are over. It's you that should be ready, you have a whole world out there waiting to take you on."

"How about if I don't feel like fighting?"

"Pretty girls like you gotta have spunk. Boys *like* spunk. Work is one thing, but if you ever—"

"Mrs. Catherly, please ..." Maggie smiled, rolling her eyes in anticipation of the coming sermon.

"—wanna find yourself a husband," Mrs. Catherly pushed on, raising the arthritic index finger of her right hand, "you're gonna have to go out there, find 'im, and haul his ass home."

Maggie laughed. "That sounds unbelievably romantic."

Mrs. Catherly stopped for a moment, a curious look crossing her eyes.

"Have I ever told you my six-year theory?" she began.

"No, you haven't, Mrs. Catherly, and I'm sorry but I'm late for work, so"—Maggie looked up to see an expression on the old woman's face that had the beginnings of hurt feelings written all over it—"if you make it fast I'll take notes," she finished, proud of her improvisation, but quietly mad at herself for delaying her exit. Now she really might be late for work.

"Well." Mrs. Catherly sighed, a measure of dignity and wisdom etched into her face. "A woman only has six good years to get a man. For some girls it's their early to mid-twenties, others blossom a tad later. Either way, you hear a lot of talk about a woman's biological clock— as if all we're good for is babies—but no one wants to talk about the clock that really counts."

Maggie was annoyed by what she guessed was going to be some painfully old fashioned viewpoint on life, but she was mildly interested as well. "Oh? Which clock is that?"

Mrs. Catherly tilted her head slightly to the side, her gray hair resting on her left shoulder and her lips crooked to hint at what she obviously believed was the cruel irony of what she was about to convey.

"It's the allure clock," she said with satisfaction.

"The allure clock?" Maggie asked, suppressing a laugh.

"Yes, and don't think I didn't notice that little smirk, young lady," the old woman huffed, a scowl crossing her face before she continued. "It's that short period of time when a woman can attract all the attention in a room . . . and still afford to ignore it. Times like that men are apt to lose themselves in every word she says and every smile she gives."

"Obviously not men from New York," Maggie replied. "They're too busy smiling and listening to themselves."

Mrs. Catherly rolled her eyes. "You've had less than a year here to size things up and already you're passing judgment? This, after coming from . . . where was it again?"

Maggie looked nervously at the ground. "Baltimore."

She hoped this lie was consistent with what she had told Mrs. Catherly when she first moved in. She had told her last landlady, the one in Virginia, that she was from Cleveland, and the one before that, in Miami, that she was from Baltimore."

"Yes, that's it. Didn't they teach you patience in Baltimore?"

"Make up your mind, Mrs. Catherly. First you're talking six year deadlines and now you're talking patience?"

Maggie noticed that the entryway smelled like an odd combination of wide open winter and closed in walls, the scents of molting leaves and snow-fresh air from the outside co-mingling with the indoor smell of old paint and rusty pipes.

Mrs. Catherly, who was a short distance away, turned and stepped forwards, her hand coming up to Maggie's elbow as a comforting smile spread across her face. Despite the smile, she looked both frail and sad.

"Honey, I may be a simple girl from Maine who didn't know any better than to follow her husband to the big city fifty-two years ago, but let me tell you something. You are as shining and bright as you will ever be, right now. I watch the boys outside walk you to the subway with their eyes every morning, and never—not once—have I ever seen you look back. You just keep on going out and coming in, every day."

"Thanks for the advice, mother," Maggie teased, uneasy now and just wanting to leave.

"Make fun all you want, but don't say I didn't warn you when you're my age and too old to do a hoot about it."

They exchanged good-byes and Maggie stepped outside and closed the door behind her, partly to protect Mrs. Catherly from the cold air and partly to escape any more lectures.

She was a sweet old woman who meant well, but Maggie wondered if her advice would be the same if she knew the other side of those six years. For some girls those six years start when they're fourteen, when they notice boys, and sometimes men, looking at them differently. Those years don't ever seem to end. Through all the boys in high school who have a crush on you, to the prom date you start falling in love with until his hands go places they shouldn't and he needs a finger in the eye to understand two-letter words like "NO" and who responds to those words by leaving you on the curb miles from home.

Allure was fine, for a short time, but after that it was like riding a taxi in a strange city; it could take you places, but usually the long way, and always at a steep cost.

As if in testimony to this fact, Maggie looked down the street and noticed the blue Honda was gone now. She allowed herself to hope for one brief moment that he was gone for good, but deep down she knew better. He was never going to go away. Not ever.

Mrs. Catherly was right. Boys might be walking her to the subway with their eyes each morning, but there was one of them waiting for the chance to get right behind her, and at that perfect moment when the train came racing down the rails, give her a good, solid push.

CHAPTER THREE

THE SUBWAY RIDE, as it turned out, was uneventful. She had a fifteen-minute ride before her stop and used this to peruse the front page of the paper she'd picked up from the newsstand on the corner. Another war in the Middle East. Boys and their toys. Never underestimate the male ego, she thought. Once you do you'll have a freakin' smart bomb doing the jitterbug right down your chimney.

She glanced at the weather box in the upper left-hand corner of the page: more snow tonight and tomorrow. This made her happy. Like most people from the East Coast she loved the snow and the joy of watching the seasons change. She had grown up in Virginia, but her mother and father lived in Napa, California now, and Julie had moved to Los Angeles a couple of months ago. Standing there in the cramped subway car, the stifling heat of too many bodies jammed into one place, the mixed smell of too much deodorant and perfume sifting through the air, she realized she missed her sister very much.

They had talked a few weeks earlier about living in big,

bad Los Angeles. Julie had told her that the men there were like dolls, big muscled and squeaky clean handsome, but also quite dopey and hollow on the inside. They'd both laughed then, remembering the time when, as children, they decided to secretly dismantle Julie's Ken doll. They started with his head, their fingers nervously clenching down on his ears and face as they wrenched it off his body, revealing the small mounting nub below. They shrieked in horror and glee, thinking they had found his penis. That night on the phone, reliving the moment as adults, they joked about how right they had actually been.

Her stop came along before she could get homesick anymore. Madison Avenue was just as crowded as the subway, but she made it to her office tower and up the elevator with seconds to spare. It was one thing being an ad rep at this agency and being late, but a late *receptionist* was another thing all together. An MBA from Georgetown, a misguided engagement, and this was her reward. No real home. No career. No saving for the future.

The job was only temporary, until Maggie felt comfortable enough to interview for something more up to her speed. But for a while it had been fun, when she thought herself free from him. The pay was okay and with her parents' help she was able to afford the apartment. More importantly the job had few responsibilities, and therefore she was rarely forced to stay late.

This left her plenty of time for her reading chair. It was there that she felt most at peace, sifting through the pages of new stories or rereading old classics, just to see if Boo Radley would still come to the rescue or if, with one last reread, she could gain any more insight into the last thoughts of poor Lennie, sitting there next to the river, George so very close by but about to become so very far away.

Every one of them, like old friends held dear yet soon

14

forgotten, were worthy of an occasional revisit, if only to remind yourself of how you used to be.

Once at her desk, she fell into the usual never-ending
grind of phone calls. You had to deal with either the attitudes of the people calling in wanting to know why the person they were trying to reach was not available, or the attitudes of the people they were trying to reach who were annoyed that they were being bothered in the first place. Voice
mail, that faraway purgatory for both caller and called, was
her only escape button from the deluge.

It took forever for 5:00 p.m. to come, and when it did
she wasted no time in heading for the elevator and catching
the subway home.

CHAPTER FOUR

As SHE ARRIVED HOME, Maggie was pleased that the Honda was still nowhere to be seen. Regardless, she took no chances. Once upstairs and safely inside her apartment, she immediately took an inventory of her surroundings.

First, she checked the small rug that covered most of the hardwood floor of the entryway to make sure that it was exactly as she had left it. That morning, upon exiting, she'd centered it perfectly with her foot and then tilted it slightly to the right. It had not been disturbed.

She transitioned into the living room next, checking the positions of a number of items: the neatly stacked coasters on the coffee table, the pillows on the sofa, the arrangement of the remote controls for the television and stereo. Looking across the adjacent hall, she could see the *Time* magazine propped up against the outside of her bedroom door. She'd also fixed a small mirror to the upper right of the bedroom door, tilted to the left so she could see directly into the bathroom down the hallway. Maggie always left the bathroom door open, flat against the wall, and hung clear plastic shower curtains. She looked into the mirror and was able to verify that the bathroom was also clear.

She checked her old-school answering machine for new messages, the outgoing message always being the generic robotic voice programmed into the machine, and saw that she had none, which relieved her greatly. He loved to leave messages, and they made her sleep even worse, but they also gave her recorded proof of his harassments.

She was hungry, so before changing she decided to quickly pop a bagel into the toaster oven and put the kettle on to boil some water for hot cocoa, a nightly ritual. Tea might've been the better choice, lavender and chamomile had been suggested to her more than once to help her sleep, but she hated tea for some reason, always had.

It was a cold night, and the walk to her apartment from the subway tunnel had been brisk. She'd made it to her building and to her mailbox in record time, finding a note from Mrs. Catherly mixed in with her letters and bills. It was no surprise that Mrs. Catherly had a mailbox key, nor was it altogether surprising to find that she used it without much embarrassment. The note said that she would be gone to visit her sister in Florida for the rest of the week. *Good for her*, Maggie thought. *At least one of us won't freeze her ass off tonight.* The building heaters were antiquated and worked just enough to prevent rigor mortis from setting in before sunrise.

She took off her coat, shoes and pantyhose and immediately went into the bathroom to wash her feet under the tub faucet. Then she changed into a pair of red sweats, heavy hiking socks and a large flannel shirt. In the silence she could hear the water boiling and decided to leave her hair down for now, the thought of warm chocolate too good to hold off any longer.

Making her way into the kitchen area, which was separated from the living room only by a counter-top and three barstools, she opened a packet of Swiss Mocha and dumped it into her favorite mug, which had a photo of John Steinbeck on it with a quote from *East of Eden*: "And this I believe: that the free, exploring mind of the individual human is the most valuable thing in the world."

Pouring the water into the powder, she noticed Zossima at her feet. Having decided to welcome her home, he danced his way between her calves and rubbed his back generously against them, purring loudly as he did.

Maggie lifted a foot and rubbed it against his head, smiling down at his lovely gray face and sky blue eyes. "Hello, sweetie," she said. Her hot chocolate ready, she popped the almost burnt bagel out of the toaster oven and covered it with butter, then headed for the living room to watch the news.

Afterwards, she turned off the television, sat up and stretched liberally. Zossima was curled up at the end of the couch and her movements had disturbed him. He shot her an annoyed glance before nodding back off to sleep. Making her way to her reading chair, she noticed heavy snowflakes were falling outside. The storm had arrived. The moon was buried behind the flurries, the streetlights below now dimmed by the blanketing white powder.

She was just beginning to feel lonely when she realized with dread that she needn't bother. There, at the end of the street, almost out of sight, was the blue Honda. He was back. Safely beyond the hundred yards of her restraining orders.

She shook her head. Life itself seemed like a storm, capable of becoming destructive at any moment. Boxed up down there in that car, his angst to the boiling point, God only knew what he was capable of. But Maggie was tired of running. How many restraining orders could she file, and in how many places? Time and again they were just paper notices sent to a man who could no longer see clearly enough to accept what he read.

He'd known all along what took her too long to figure out: it was all a ruse. The paper limitations and biblical warnings from men in black robes with too many cases to handle were served from within a justice system that could not walk you home at night. The police, sometimes annoyed by a call and other times sympathetic, only reminded her of their own limitations. Faith in the system was the first to go, followed shortly thereafter by hope, and what you were left with was the simple fact that you were pretty much on your own.

Maggie knew that now. She'd found out the hard way, after what he'd done to Staci in Miami. That was what haunted her worse than anything. That someone else had been forced to pay the price for her final realizations. She would never again involve an innocent person in an effort to protect herself.

Maggie hated him, more than she could measure. But a part of her had loved him once; his touch, his embrace. He had held her in a way that stilled her restless soul. And in making love to him, for the first time in her life she felt somehow liberated, as if a part of her had gone fugitive and was at last coming out of hiding. At least for a while. But then she couldn't make him let go, like she had all the rest. At first, it was hard to fault him for that. Love was a many-fingered thing, with a firm grip not easily broken, and a small part of her knew exactly what it was like to be completely taken with something.

One of her most vivid memories was of a day at her

grandparents' house, when she was a child. Her grandmother had been baking, the house immersed in the smell of cinnamon and warm bread, and she'd told Maggie to go keep busy outside. Instead, she crept into her grandfather's den and avidly scanned a bookcase of leather-bound treasures there, rows and rows of books, the titles embossed in gold and silver. She couldn't recall them all, but two stuck out in her memory: *The Odyssey* and *Paradise Lost*. She had flipped through the gold-leafed pages, incapable at the age of eight of fully comprehending the words but completely swept up in them nonetheless.

It was while glancing across the books that she stumbled upon a small glass ball perched atop a beautiful ornate stand. In the ball was a painted picture of a winter cabin on a snowy meadow, a deer in the foreground. Without even realizing it, she picked up the ball and turned it over in her hands. Suddenly, to her joy, white specks of captured snow began to dance around inside.

It wasn't really snow, of course, but at that age the difference was moot. The specks scattered and crisscrossed inside the ball, captured in a tempest created solely by her hand. Still in her Sunday church dress with thoughts flush from the morning's sermon, she had imagined that this was what it must feel like to be God. A smile broke across her face and a happiness she rarely felt again cut a swath across her heart. The cabin and the deer, trapped forever inside the ball in suspended animation, took on a beauty and a wonder all their own. It was a faraway place, of her own making, but all at once she was there in that meadow, her feet cold and her cheeks red.

Years later, after graduating college, her grandmother had thrown her a party. All her family and friends had come to wish her well, trade a few rumors and speculate on her future. Later, after most of them had gone home, she found herself in her grandfather's study again, after all those years. She didn't know how she ended up there; she'd been avoiding that end of the house all day. Her grandfather had been dead for many years by that time, and she still hadn't reconciled with that fact, but there she was nonetheless. The room was dark, lit only by the outside light that was beginning to fade with the setting sun, and she was overcome with an odd and distant sadness.

Then she noticed the snow globe, which she'd completely forgotten about it until that very moment. It was in the same place, as if it had never been moved in the fifteen years that had gone by. The deer and the cabin were caught up in the fullness of her imagination, each reflecting the images of the other and she smiled, the act of doing so oddly capturing the sadness in her heart instead of chasing it away.

CHAPTER FIVE

ZOSSIMA MOVED AT HER FEET, awakening her. She'd fallen asleep on the couch, her mug still in her hand, its contents somehow unspilt. The clock said it was just past 11:30 p.m. Yawning, she glanced lazily down at the street and noticed that the Walrus Lady, in full snow gear, was on patrol again, making her way down the sidewalk at that slow, labored pace, as if putting one foot in front of the other was less an act of will and more an act of resolution.

Maggie shook her head and was just about to look away when, to her shock, the old woman came to a stop. Right alongside the blue Honda.

Her arm actually extended out to its roof for support.

In a split second the entire street moved to within two feet of Maggie's face.

There was a sudden movement inside the car.

"*Get away!*" Maggie screamed in the silence of her apartment, jumping to her feet.

For what seemed like an eternity, the Walrus Lady

stayed frozen in place. The streets and sidewalks were covered in a blanket of snow, as was the Honda. Maggie debated throwing on some clothes and going down to the street, but at this point there was still a chance it could end well. If she went down there, that chance would be lost entirely.

Before she could consider it any further, the Walrus Lady pulled her arm away from the car, seemingly startled. She backed away and stared at the passenger window, then—amazingly—she actually leaned forwards to get a closer look through the glass. Maggie couldn't tell if someone was speaking to her from inside the car.

"Oh shit! Get away. Please!" Maggie screamed again, sending Zossima scattering into the bedroom. The snow began falling harder, obscuring her vision a little, but the Walrus Lady finally backed away from the car, pulled her hands up to her chest and immediately began to retreat towards her apartment complex.

Maggie focused her full attention on the Honda. She fully expected the entire nightmare to begin, right then and there; the driver's door would fly open and the man she once loved would simply unfold from its depths, intent on showing the old woman what kind of trouble a nosey mind can get you.

Instead, the taillights of the Honda came on, startling Maggie so badly that she dropped her mug. It shattered on the hardwood floor, dark cocoa splattering like blood against the drapes. The Walrus Lady didn't seem to notice the car, or the plume of exhaust that erupted from its tailpipe, as she was now diligently scaling the steps of her building. She didn't even look back as the car pulled away from the curb and drove off.

Maggie let loose a long, tight sigh. Her legs and feet were numb and her head was on fire. After watching the Walrus Lady make it safely into her building, Maggie walked slowly to her bed and sat down, feeling her heart clenched in her chest.

At that moment she believed she could run again—to Austin, or San Francisco, or Honolulu.

But it wouldn't matter; he would follow her and find her. He always did.

Overcome by exhaustion and drained by fear, Maggie crawled under the sheets and fell asleep.

That night she dreamed of heaven.

This dream had appeared infrequently throughout her life, but almost always, scene for scene, it was the same. In the dream she was in a small boat, floating across a radiant blue sea. She was seated at the bow naked, looking forwards, as the boat floated evenly along the water, leaving no wake.

The air was cool and exhilarating, like menthol. There was a gentle breeze that seemed to be coming from all sides, and the sea was covered in a light fog. The wind carried voices from a distant shore, the outline of which she could barely make out. Most of the people standing on the shore were indistinguishable, but some of them she recognized right away: her grandmother, her cousin Timmy, who had died of cancer when they were children, and her aunt Pat.

The shore was the edge of an island. Maggie did not know how she knew this, but she did. A wonderful odor occasionally wafted by, a blend of nutmeg and carnations. She felt a joy in the distance that emanated across the water to her but that she was not yet a part of. This made her anxious, and she rocked back and forth on the bow trying to hurry the boat along, the feelings inside her not unlike the excitement of a teenager heading to a party where someone they really like is going to be.

Tonight, though, the dream was different in two ways.

First, the boat, made of old wood and carved with odd-looking initials everywhere, drifted to a stop, the shore still vaguely in sight.

Second, and most startling, was the appearance of the Walrus Lady, her shape outlined in a shadowy white that was not quite gray. She stood on the shore at what appeared to be the water's edge, dressed in her usual attire but without her customary newspaper. The breeze had eased, but Maggie could still hear the Walrus Lady saying something. Something horrible, but in an oddly reassuring tone.

She said the words over and over again, speaking in Latin: *Persona non grata.*

Maggie was not welcome.

Not welcome in heaven.

Even in the midst of her sleep, Maggie dreamed she was in her bedroom, screaming.

CHAPTER SIX

THE NEXT MORNING, she awoke feeling unsettled and disturbed. After taking a shower and shaking off the memory of her dream, Maggie dressed and headed for work again. Stepping out onto the street, she noticed there was no Honda in sight and the snow was still soft and white.

It was an eight-minute walk to the subway. First she would go up her street, W. 144th, to Frederick Douglas Boulevard, where she would make a right and go past the corner deli, an express dry cleaners and the neighborhood pharmacy. A short distance later she would cross the street and make a left on 145th Street, passing a Popeye's and Bank of America along way, before finally advancing to the subway entrance at 145th and St. Nicholas.

She knew every step, every store, and every alcove along the way. Businesses, cars, buses were all around, but to her mind it was all simply a stage. Her focus today, as it was yesterday and as it was every time she left her apartment, was on only two things: people and reflections. She took measure of everyone in front of and around her, segregating first the males from the females. Once this was done she took note of any male that fit the one physical attribute that he could not hide: his height. She'd learned long ago that head hair and facial hair could be shaped a myriad of ways, as could clothing and mannerisms, but height was much tougher to disguise, especially when you were six foot four. If she saw any man that was near that height on her side of the street, either in front of her or behind, she immediately crossed over to the other side. On the other hand, if the person was across the street she either quickened or slowed her walking pace until he was in her direct line of sight.

Anyone on the street who did not fit his description became her immediate ally.

Over the years he had maintained only one consistency: he'd never attacked her in a crowded place. That made everyone, the woman in the beige business suit in front of her now, the balding man in the blue trench coat further up the street by the newsstands, the pair of old ladies in double layer jogging suits taking their morning walk together and passing on her left, obstacles between him and her. At this time of the morning on a weekday there were always people out and about, and the number of them only increased as she made her way closer to the subway.

From there, however, the game shifted in his favor, because down in the subway tunnels, from the pay booths through the turnstiles and even in the trains, there were too many people to keep track of, bumping into you or swiftly crossing your path from all directions, and they went from being her cover to his. Though he'd never attacked her in a public place, Maggie knew all too well now not to gamble too heavily, indeed to gamble her life, on the odds that he never would.

In her mind's eye she could see him in that crowded subway train with all those bodies crammed together like sardines. How easy it would be for him to sidle up behind her and stick a small knife directly into her kidney, twisting it with just enough affection to make her think that he still cared, before she worked enough air into her lungs to scream, then in the ensuing chaos that would follow he could simply drop the knife and at the next stop, with so many people exiting the train in so much panic, he could slip away, his revenge finally complete.

For this reason she usually left early for work, giving her first dibs on the seats of the subway car where she would immediately take her place against the back wall, facing everyone.

Besides people, her walk was defined by all the glass and mirror around her, or rather the reflections they offered. Apartment windows, store windows, car windows, the mirror-like images from the polished metal sides of the donut and hot dog carts on the corners, all of them reflected her immediate surroundings in clear detail.

She constantly glanced from left to right, gathering feedback from all the reflections like disjointed pieces of a jigsaw puzzle that stretched from her apartment building entrance to the subway tunnel. Each piece of glass or metal multiplied her vision so that at times she felt as if she were inside the eye of a fly, seeing a hundred different perspectives along the entirety of her walk, five or six of them available at any given time to fix not only her position on the street, but her attention as well.

Maggie could still remember what happened in Washington, DC one day when she'd exited the subway tunnel at Farragut West, late for work because the metro was held up in Arlington with some sort of rail problem. On a quiet side street, she let her guard down, for just a second, and while passing a delivery truck that was parked in front of a late model van, she failed to look between the two vehicles.

Her saving grace was the large mounted mirror on the side of the delivery van, which faced her and gave her a glimpse of something moving swiftly behind her. She spun around immediately and screamed, bringing her right hand up to defend herself, all her keys interlaced between her fingers, as she'd been trained to do in the rape prevention class she'd taken in Miami, and there he was, about fifteen feet behind her. Evidently realizing that his chance was gone, he smiled at her before turning immediately to walk in the opposite direction.

What amazed her was the way he played it off so well, as if he'd half expected it. He'd even shook his head as he walked away and made a comment to a few men that had stopped cold in their tracks further up the sidewalk.

"Lady's crazy," he said, motioning over his shoulder with his thumb at Maggie, who was still standing there defensively, glaring at him as he disappeared around the corner, her breathing shallow, her heart racing.

She was horrified when she looked up to see the two men still looking at her warily with her key-clawed fist.

As if they actually believed him.

CHAPTER SEVEN

IT WAS DARKER than usual that night when she arrived home from work, the last remnants of the storm dampening the twilight by the minute as she hurried down the sidewalk. She was about thirty feet from the steps of her building when she noticed the blue Honda was back again.

It had moved, and now it was only seven or eight cars away.

On her side of the street.

Her body tensed. Her left hand gripped hard on the apartment building key card, and instinctively her right hand reached into her jacket pocket for the canister of mace she always kept there. Her fingers fumbled around the cold metallic tube as she positioned it properly in her hand. She used her thumb to flick the trigger guard out of the way as her index finger slid comfortably over the button.

She froze. The driver's door was ajar, about six inches, and the enormity of this fact caused an onslaught of panic to rise in her body.

Oh my God, oh my God, oh my God.

She advanced swiftly down the remainder of the sidewalk, trying to stifle her panic, her head on a swivel, one glance to the car door followed by a glance at the bushes along the entryway of the building next to hers, a swift peak back at the car door, and sporadic glances all around.

He could be anywhere!

Her breathing growing shallow, she pushed on. She reached her building and took the stairs two at a time, balancing her feet, keeping her toes flat and pressing hard into the pavement to minimize the risk of slipping and falling. The entryway was before her, its wooden edges like a box around the double glass doors it framed. To the left of the doors and chest high was the security box, the small metal surface waiting to read her card.

Fear began to overtake her, because in climbing the steps she'd been forced to turn her back to the street . . . and the Honda. She sensed—*knew*—that her time was running short, and because of this she had to remain focused on the entire key card process, not sparing herself the time to glance over her shoulder. She could see him now, in her mind's eye, coming soon, racing down the sidewalk in long strides. If she could take the steps in two, he could take them in four, and then what?

Her hand brought the key card towards the box. Chills crawled up her neck, telling her he was already there now, just behind her, his hand reaching for her hair, yearning to yank her head back and slice her throat. Her fingers were around the card and it seemed like that moment—the time it took to swing her last three fingers out of the way so that her index finger and thumb could properly oppose one another to grip the edge of the card and slide it quickly but firmly through the scanner—lasted an entire lifetime.

31

But in reality the moment didn't last long at all.

It was cut short by a simple turn of events that left her dismayed and amazed.

She dropped the card.

It bounced, there on the pavement that made up the front porch of her building, like a dancing plastic nymph. Instinct was all she had left. She lunged at it with both hands, snatching it in mid-bounce with her left hand and then reaching back to fend him off with her right, not looking at where she was pointing the mace but preparing to push down on the trigger.

Her left hand came up to swipe again at the scanner but caught only air. On her second try she managed to scan the card correctly, falling against the door of the entryway simultaneously, not hearing its customary buzz as she swung herself around the door and slammed it so hard she thought all the glass inside it would shatter.

Then, she looked up to face him on the other side of the glass.

There was no one there.

The relief that washed over her was so powerful it made her sick, her hands trembled uncontrollably and soon her body was in on the act, awash in shivers and fits. *Fuck!* she thought, and this surprised her, because she rarely used this word; she found it vulgar and uneducated.

Maggie made her way through the second double doors with quite some effort, feeling so weak and tired that a nap, right there on the floor, would not be beyond her. She leaned on the stairwell railing for a few moments. Mrs. Catherly, sweet old nag that she was, would be a welcome sight now. But, of course, the one time Maggie needed her, the busybody had opted out for a Mai Tai and the Florida sun.

"Here's hoping she forgets her fucking sunscreen," she whispered into the empty air, again that special word sneaking into her vocabulary.

After a while, Maggie was steady enough to begin the walk up the four flights of stairs to her apartment.

The second floor was occupied by some NYU students, who had obviously picked tonight of all nights to have a little get together. The Stones were on full blast, Mick Jagger blabbering on in some narcissistic tirade about having someone under his thumb. She always hated that song, but was surprised that college kids nowadays still found The Stones party music material. She could hear a girl laughing loudly and another one shouting the lyrics. There were other voices, maybe six or eight in all. *So early, just getting started,* she thought.

The third floor was vacant, had been for a month now. The girl that lived there had moved out in a huff, Mrs. Catherly setting her out on her ear. The girl had been a mousy brunette with cropped hair and green eyes who had guests all the time that were not male, and Mrs. Catherly had noticed this quickly. She'd tolerated it until one of the female roommates on the second floor had gotten into it with her boyfriend, who had found her with Ms. Green Eyes in a compromising moment. A nasty quarrel had ensued, because it was one thing to find your girlfriend with another man, quite another to find her with another woman.

Even Mick Jagger might have a hard time with that one.

When Maggie made it to her apartment and unlocked the door the smell from inside rushed out to surround her. She'd made it safely home; on a stretch but still across the plate. All that awaited was for the umpire to make the call and the crowd to cheer.

She did her automatic inventory of the apartment and noticed that everything was in place, just as it should be—with one notable exception.

The bathroom door was half-closed.

As if someone was behind it.

CHAPTER EIGHT

KEEP CALM, keep calm. The desk. Get to the desk. Don't let him know you've noticed anything.

She feigned a firm voice and called out for Zossima, who came scurrying to her from beneath the couch. It was at times like this that she wished she had a dog, but it was simply too hard to find places in the city that were willing to allow them. Fighting against every instinct in her body, she forced herself to turn her head and eyes away from the bathroom door, relying instead on her peripheral vision to catch any movement from that direction. The entire apartment was silent. She could almost feel his eyes on her, looking at her through the crack between the bathroom door and the frame.

God. Please. Just let me get to the desk.

In one of the desk drawers was a small .22 pistol that her father had given her a few years back. She only had to make it about fifteen feet from the door to the desk, where the gun was hidden under a notepad. Instead of thinking too much she simply moved calmly in that direction, Zossima running alongside her.

Reaching the desk, Maggie opened the drawer with no hesitation and saw the notebook. As she moved it aside, for one brief instant she was terrified that the gun would not be there, but it was. Feeling his eyes on her, she turned her back to the bathroom, using her body to block his vision as she grabbed the gun, welcoming the sight of the blue metal barrel. There was weight to it, meaning it was loaded, and this scared away her last paranoid thought that maybe he had already found it. She exhaled with relief.

Instead of confronting him immediately, something inside her told her to wait. *Better to lure him out, make him come to me.*

Keeping her back to the door she moved around the desk and into the kitchen, relying on the hardwood floors of the apartment, which were creaky in many places but especially in the hallway between the bathroom and the living room, to warn her of any advance he tried to make.

Nothing. She heard nothing.

She turned to face the oven, which was on the opposite side of the desk wall, and this gave her an immediate view of the bathroom again. She kept her head down and let her hair slide forwards, just enough to partially shield her eyes, then stole a glance at the bathroom door again. It remained unmoved. The kitchen was designed for open access from either end of the small apartment, with one end nearest the door and the other end nearest the windows that looked out over the street. She rattled a pan and reached her free hand into the silverware drawer, her fingers haphazardly moving some spoons and forks around.

That's right, honey, I'm just making dinner. Totally clueless that you're here. C'mon, you bastard.

All he had to do was step out and commit himself to the open space between the bathroom and her place in the kitchen. Once he did that, he would have a couch and a table pinning him in on the window side of the apartment and the front door, now locked, pinning him in on the other. She would have eleven shots, and if there was one thing she was sure of by now, with all those visits to the gun range in New Orleans, she was a damn good shot.

Pinch off each round evenly, don't fire randomly, don't empty the clip. Make each one count. Chest shots. Aim for nothing but his core.

The silence of the apartment was unsettling. Zossima was meowing at her feet, expecting his evening treat. Without thinking, she kicked him out of the way, harder than she had intended but in no mood to be tripped up by her cat at this moment. She stepped further into the kitchen, sacrificing again her sight of the bathroom door, straining her ears for the slightest sound, hoping desperately that he would now feel her completely vulnerable and make his move. After a few moments, she again slid down the counter and rattled the pans to fake being busy. She looked up. The bathroom door remained as it had been, half-closed.

Shit!

She took measure of the *Time* magazine against her bedroom door, wanting to verify further that it was the bathroom he was in and nowhere else. She always folded the magazine down the middle, standing it on end and leaning it at an angle against the door, always nearest the hinge side. This way it would be utterly impossible to get into the bedroom, close the door and replace the magazine in its original position.

It had been the one trick that had saved her in Miami when she'd come home one morning after going to the gym and found the magazine propped up the wrong way, nearest the door knob side. She had fled the house immediately and called the police, who had escorted her back to her apartment to find the bedroom door now open and the magazine just lying on the floor, capsized.

But the magazine was unmoved. Sitting just as it was when she had left that morning.

Up to this point she'd managed to maintain her composure, carried more by the determination not to panic than anything else, but the fear in her body was beginning to rise again, an internal vomit of adrenaline sending goosebumps across her neck and down her back. She knew she could not stand here for very long and wait him out. She was tired of waiting, and there was no way she could bear much more of it.

I can't take it anymore. It has to end. One way or another.

Saying this to herself caused tears to well up in her eyes because, in many ways, this was a partial surrender. That's what this had all come down to; she was now even willing to die to end this. For herself, for her family, for her friends.

An inner debate broke out in her head.

Maggie Kincaid, don't start with that crap. No tears.

Why, why shouldn't I cry?

Because it will affect your aim.

She bit down hard on her tongue, the pain bringing her focus back. Tasting her own blood in her mouth, bitter and slippery, something in her gave way and the inner door that she kept barred and locked against all her hidden rage at what her life had become swung wide open.

Enough of this.

Stepping back out into the hallway, she brought the gun up to eye level and advanced swiftly towards the bathroom, waiting for the door to fly open with each step. He had no other option.

There's nowhere to run, you rat bastard, nowhere to go.

The floor creaked beneath her feet, and reaching the bathroom door, she decided there was nothing left to do. She squeezed off a single shot through the center of the door before kicking it in. A cascade of sounds greeted her: the flat echo of imploding wood as the bullet propelled through the door, the bang of the door handle as it struck the inside bathroom wall, the shattering of the shower tile as the bullet struck it and scattered shards across the porcelain tub, and Zossima's wail from somewhere in the living room.

The gray-black gunpowder smoke blossomed outward into the bathroom, carried by the force of the air that had been shifted into the room by the kicked-in door. Her eyes parsed the room like a computer, digitally splitting it into visual input bytes that her mind could quickly examine, dismiss and put aside. She looked at the towels hanging perfectly on the wall rack, her bottle of lotion on the sink, the bathroom scale on the floor, the hole in the shower wall, the dripping faucet. Other than that? Nothing. Zero.

The bathroom was empty.

Dread hit her like a stone.

He . . . baited me.

CHAPTER NINE

SHE IMMEDIATELY SPUN in panic to face the bedroom door, convincing herself that he had found a way around the magazine trick. It was still closed. She kicked the magazine aside.

He will expect me to go in carefully. He will expect me to be afraid.

She charged. With one hand twisting the handle, she threw her full weight against the door, using it as a weapon against anyone who might be standing behind it.

As she expected, the bedroom lights were on. She always left the lights on in the house, all day, the electric bill be damned. It was a small room, with a dresser against the wall near the foot of the bed. There were two nightstands, one on either side of the bed, and two hanging glass flutes over the bed, both filled with rocks and meant to hold water for floating candles but now dry and meant only as weapons of last resort. All her furniture was high-gloss Cherrywood, which was her favorite but which she also chose because it was very slippery. He had loved to tie her up when they were together, and when she imagined what his dream scenario was for her, it always included two things before he killed her: tying her up, and raping her. She had a small closet but she had removed the doors when she moved in and placed them down in her storage cage in the basement. He had no place in this room to hide.

But he wasn't here either.

She realized then that he wasn't anywhere in the apartment. At least not anymore.

Her mind finally wound down to a level that allowed her to think clearly. She remembered something else in the bathroom that had caught her eye for just a second—a piece of paper or something, hanging from the faucet in the tub. Maggie walked back to the bathroom and saw it again. It was yellow and red with a white box in the center, a tag of some sort. There was writing on it.

She fingered the bullet hole in her shower curtain before pushing is aside to grab the tag.

In clear block letters was printed: "WE CAME TO SERVICE YOUR PLUMBING TODAY." Below that were a half dozen check boxes listing the various scenarios for the effort put forth: UNABLE TO FIX PROBLEM, WATER TURNED OFF, CONTACT APARTMENT MANAGER, CALL SERVICE CENTER FOR SPECIAL INSTRUCTIONS, and PROBLEM FIXED. This last box had a check mark in it. Someone named Howard Oravitz with Cecil's Plumbing had signed the paper. Handwritten at the bottom of the slip were the words: "Problem was not in your unit."

She sighed disgustedly. "Son of a bitch!"

She brought her free hand up to her forehead and then rubbed her eyes, completely exhausted again, and walked out into the living room, feeling foolish and angry that Mrs. Catherly had not warned her that a service call had been made. She'd left strict instructions that no one was ever to be allowed into her apartment without her being present, even promising Mrs. Catherly that she would take a cab from work on a half hours' notice if necessary. How did this happen?

As quickly as she asked the question, she answered it: Mrs. Catherly was out of town. That meant the building owner or a management company would be in charge while she was away. Passing the desk, she looked down at her answering machine. The message light was blinking.

A new feeling of dread came over her.

She pushed the message button, prompting the machine to display the number of messages she had. Three. She held her breath. His voice could be hiding in any of them.

The first message began to play:

"Mrs. Kincaid, this is Janice Phelps with Paragon Management. We are the company that oversees your building for the owner. As you may or may not know, your apartment manager, Mrs. Catherly, is out of town. We just received a call this afternoon from Apartment 101 that there is a bad plumbing leak, and we have sent a representative from Cecil's Plumbing out to check on it. We tried to reach you at your work number but you weren't in, and your unit may have to be opened to determine where the leak is originating from. We apologize for any inconvenience this may cause you. We will try to reach you again if we have to enter your apartment."

Maggie shook her head, the gun still in her hand, unsure whether to feel relieved or angry.

The second message was more of the same, with Janice Phelps notifying her that her apartment would have to be entered because the leak was severe and the plumber could not figure out where it was coming from, but not to worry because a "representative" of Paragon Management would come out to the building to let him in and that Cecil's Plumbing was fully insured and bonded, and so on and so forth.

"Great. Great for Cecil's," Maggie whispered.

She sat down on the floor next to the desk, feeling the cool wall against the back of her head. She felt as if she were on fire. No doubt the last message would be Janice Phelps calling to apologize for the fact that someone from Cecil's Plumbing had stolen a Pepsi from her refrigerator and missed the toilet while they were taking a piss.

But the next message was not from Janice Phelps. Nor was it from anyone at Cecil's Plumbing.

The tone beeped and there was silence.

Maggie snapped her head up, her eyes widening as she strained to hear.

Something.

No.

Anything.

Please.

Silence.

It's a wrong number, that's all. That's ALL!

But the recording did not click to end the call.

There was a hissing sound, like a light whistle.

You bastard.

His trademark call. Just enough noise to keep the machine taping.

Maggie began to cry. It was all happening again. The same way it always happened.

First, the car would turn up. It had been a red Mustang at the beginning, but that one had been impounded so he had switched to a green Focus when she had begun to run. He switched cars in almost every city once she got the restraining order, so the police would have no proof that he had violated his hundred-yard restriction unless they caught him point blank and in person. The last two towns it was the blue Honda. Whichever car, she knew they all belonged to him whenever she saw the Greenpeace bumper sticker. Each time, she would hope that it was just another Greenpeace supporter, another "save the whales" freak and not him. Those damn bumper stickers were all over the country. It didn't always have to be him.

But it had been. Every time. It was his way of telling her and her alone that he was back.

Then, after the car, would come the calls. First at home, and then at work. Which was always worse. In the car, he was a thing walled off and distant. But the calls made him more of a presence, more a thing that had transcended her physical space and was now a violator of her mental space.

Only then did the game really begin, because after the calls it was always different. Maybe he would mail her something or send her flowers. Maybe he would follow her. In Boston, where she had owned a car, he had slashed her tires and written vulgar things on the windshield. And then there were the other things, much worse, which she did not want to think about right now.

After a few minutes the hissing stopped and the message ended, the closing beep of the machine careening around the hollow shell of the apartment, reinforcing her solitude. As if to comfort her, Zossima crawled into her lap as she rocked back and forth crying softly, the hard floor beneath her pressing painfully against her bones.

No matter how hard she tried to wish it away, it was no good.

The game was about to begin.

All over again.

CHAPTER TEN

As THE NIGHT outside went from charcoal gray to pitch black, Maggie sat staring down at the gun that now lay in the open palms of her hands. She remembered the day her father had given it to her. It had been a sad day, even though it was her birthday, because by then everyone knew the mess she was in, but they had no idea how to help her.

The problem was, they knew, but they didn't really *know*. Her aunts, uncles and cousins might have been aware that she was having boyfriend problems, but it was too hard to explain that someone was actually trying to hurt her. As the situation with Michael had escalated, Maggie had always figured her father to be her ace in the hole. She allowed herself the comfort of that thought, as she imagined almost all daughters did, no matter how old they grew. Whenever the shit hit the fan, Daddy would be there. He'd told her as much when she started getting the threatening letters. An avid gun collector and competitive sharpshooter when he was younger, he had made more than one passing remark about taking care of the situation "the old-fashioned way," which sounded very Al Pacino and out of place for a third-generation Irishman who had taught high school history for twenty years. And yet, at the same time, he sounded sincere.

But then came the cold, autumn day when he had taken the dog for a walk. He told everyone later that he never saw it coming. One moment just walking the dog, minding his own business, and then suddenly a feeling that something wasn't quite right, followed by a dull pain and then a numbing in his mind that froze both his perception and perspective. He was falling—in a detached sort of way, but falling nonetheless—in the neighbors' yard, face first into a pile of weekend-raked leaves that had not yet been bagged or burned. For the longest time he just lay there, gasping for air, sucking up the smell of mold from all those rotting leaves, moaning for help. After fifteen minutes the neighbor, drawn outside by her dog's persistent barking, had finally found him.

That had been three months before Maggie's birthday. But as she stood there and watched her family eat cake and talk about college costs for her youngest cousins or the ongoing drug rehab for one of her uncles, her father had sidled gently up alongside her and tickled her rib.

"W-w-w-we've g-gotta t-t-t-alk, kiddo," he said, and even the last word had come out sounding more like how a Japanese tourist would say it: "keeedo."

The stroke had slurred his speech and left him with a stutter, the mobility on his right side left somewhat weakened, too. He could still get around but at a much slower pace, and she had witnessed him earlier that day struggling to hold a half-gallon carton of milk in his right hand as he made his morning cereal, his arm shaking in little earthquakes.

He led her down the hall and into the basement, where he kept his gun collection in a series of glass display cases. On one of the cases she noticed a small black leather pouch. He motioned for her to sit down on one of the two barstools that were nearby.

"Dad, what's going on?"

Sitting down next to her, he picked up the small leather pouch. "H-h-honey, I want you to h-h-h-have this," he said, nodding his head repeatedly as he spoke, as if forcing the words to come out.

He reached out and gave her the case, and when she took it from him her fingers touched his hands and she realized now how wrinkled they were, these hands that had cupped her childhood cheeks while he smiled down at her and encouraged her after every soccer practice. They had been strong hands, with fingers that lent themselves to a firm grip and yet a soft touch. These same fingers that had taught her how to stretch pizza dough one day, when she had stayed home sick from school and he'd taken the day off from work to watch over her, were now old and frail.

"Dad, this isn't necessary . . . Really, I mean . . ."

He simply shook his head and motioned for her to open the case.

She unzipped it, and the gun inside slid out into her hand. She was surprised to see how small it was and how cold the steel felt.

"You s-s-see that clip?"

She nodded.

"It h-h-h-h-holds t-t-ten bullets plus o-one in the c-chamber. It's a .22 Beretta, not vah-vah-very powerful from f-far away but good up c-c-close."

"Dad, please, I don't know about this, it—"

"That w-w-w-ill be en-enough f-from up close. They w-will bounce a-around in h-him."

She had looked up then, from the gun in her hands that had momentarily fixated her attention, to her father's face.

Maggie was not prepared for what she saw there.

That precious face. Daddy's face. Reduced now to a sullen and almost tragic thing. He looked at her with eyes full of shame, as if at that moment he were somehow admitting a sort of personal defeat. It was one thing to survive the stroke, and to endure the physical therapy that had followed, but that moment there in the basement, and that single act of handing her a weapon to fend for herself, was a sort of final admission, as much to himself as to her, that he could not protect his little girl anymore, no matter how desperately he wanted to. His eyes that day had been like flat clay, soft and dull, clipped with wetness at the edges.

She had started to cry but he reached out and grabbed her arm, squeezing it tightly.

"No tears," he said, with so much conviction that the stutter had no room to impede.

"Okay, Dad."

"You r-r-remember," he continued, looking deep into her eyes, "if the m-m-oment ever comes, u-u-use it."

Nodding, she reached up with her free hand to wipe her eyes.

Maggie did not have the heart to tell him that she had already bought a gun, down at Piccolo Pete's south of the city, with a friend who had also been worried about her. Worried enough to help her shop for it. She had bought a snub-nose .38 revolver because, as silly as it seemed to confess it that day to her friend, those were the guns used by some of the detectives in the *87th Precinct* novels by Ed McBain she'd grown up reading. It was the only gun caliber she knew of, or remembered.

She had the urge to hug her father, and when she did she noticed that when he hugged her back, it had been his right arm, the one affected by the stroke, that was hugging her the tightest.

CHAPTER ELEVEN

THE PHONE EXPLODED above her in the dimly lit apartment, snapping her out of her memory and back into reality. She looked at the clock. It was just past 8:00 p.m. Zossima jumped in her lap and she comforted him. "It's okay, Zoss."

She waited for the machine to pick up, expecting whatever came.

"Mags? Are you there?" came a concerned voice.

It was Julie.

Maggie leaped to her feet and picked up the phone. "Hello, hello?" she said.

"Hey there, what's up?" Julie asked.

You don't want to know. "Nothing. Nothing at all."

"You didn't respond to my text or answer your cell!"

"I'm sorry. I dozed off." Maggie sighed, bringing the hammer of the gun up to her forehead and using it to scratch the edge of her hairline.

Julie sounded relieved but angry. "Not. Cool."

"I know. I suck."

"I'm just glad you're okay. Shit."

"Hey. Jules. It's okay. I'm fine."

"Yeah." One word. Followed by a long exhale.

Maggie moved to change the subject. "So, what's goin' on?"

"Well. I texted the usual, then I also told you to call me when you got a chance because I had big news."

"What's the news?"

"I landed that new job," Julie replied, with very little enthusiasm.

"Hey!" Maggie forced a smile, hoping it would help her feign the sincerity she needed to avoid tipping Julie off to what was truly going on. "That's great, Jules! I'm so happy for you."

"Yeah. Big money. Company car. The works."

"Yay!" Maggie said weakly as she made her way into the kitchen, putting the gun down long enough to give Zossima a can of wet food.

Julie sifted out her tone immediately. "Mags. What's wrong?"

"Nothing. Jeez. So when do you start?"

There was a long pause before Julie answered. "In two weeks. I've got product classes, and some IT training to go through. But I'll live."

"That's so cool. Have you told Mom and Dad yet?"

Again, a chunk of silence. "Maggie . . ."

"Julie. Everything's okay."

"Are you sure?" Her sister's voice was wavering with emotion.

"Hey. C'mon."

"You scared the shit out of me."

"Look. I missed a text. I didn't mean to, but . . ."

"I still don't get it. You need to get out of there. Come to LA and stay with me, or go stay with Mom and Dad for a while."

"Julie, we've been over this so . . . many . . . times."

"I don't care. It's stupid to be out there all alone."

"I have to live my life, Jules. I can't just sit around . . . I can't just hide and run and hide some more." And now Maggie's voice was beginning to crack.

"You swear you haven't seen him?"

She hadn't actually seen him, and bringing up the car would cause a chain reaction of calls and panic—her mom, her dad—that she just couldn't deal with right now, so Maggie took the wiggle room she had in the question and gave up a white lie. "No."

"I can't believe you're not tired of New York yet, anyways."

"Julie . . ." Maggie said with a sigh.

"Just sayin', no need to get defensive."

"I wasn't going to get defensive."

"I know that tone, young lady!" Julie replied in a perfect impersonation of their mother, a trick she'd mastered in her teen years.

Maggie laughed. "Jules, you can stop busting my balls here."

"Young lady, do I need to remind you that you don't *have* any balls?" Julie barely got it all out before losing their mother's slight Massachusetts accent and laughing.

The chill between them had been warmed away.

"Ha, ha. Very funny. Anyway. I'm doing fine. New York is amazing."

"If you say so. Is the job going good?"

"Yep. Keeps me busy. I've made a few friends there. Did you ever go out with that Kevin guy again?"

"Yeah, but only for lunch."

"Uh-oh. Two lunches in a row? That's not good. Why hasn't he earned himself a dinner yet?"

"I dunno. I'm definitely calling for a retreat on him. He's just too boring, and . . ."

They spent then next half hour talking about poor Kevin, with Julie coming up with more and more reasons not to give yet another guy in her life a chance. Maggie might've been imagining it, but she was pretty sure it was a pattern that began right after things with Michael had gone south. When Maggie had broken off their engagement and his behavior had first gotten a bit worrisome.

Julie's more fragile nature had been completely consumed with fear for Maggie. It was like she could've never imagined that someone who claimed to love you could turn around and tell you to watch your back or warn you not to date anyone else. It had changed her little sister, and for this more than anything, Maggie could never forgive herself—for ever bringing Michael into their lives. She should've seen the signs of who he really was earlier, but something had blinded her to them.

And now, illogical as it may have seemed, Julie was even more wary of strangers who approached her, which was just sad. Maggie had accepted the fact that *she* would never love anybody, ever again, so she'd transferred all her hopes of true happiness, of finding someone special, of starting a family with them and growing old together, to her little sister.

"Hey?" Julie's voice prodded.

Maggie yawned. "Yeah?"

"Do you remember that time we snuck a bottle of wine out of the house and drank it behind the garage?"

53

"Ha!" Maggie laughed, amazed that she was still capable of doing so after the events of today. "Yes. But it wasn't a whole bottle of wine."

"Whatevs. Half, then. Remember how we came back into the house so giddy and goofy that Mom did that thing with the dish towel?"

"Yes! Oh my God. She threw it, right?"

"Yeah. Across the kitchen—"

"Like it was a paper airplane or something, and it curved off and—"

"Knocked over the salt and pepper shakers, the big wooden ones—"

"Which then fell over onto her recipe book, which bounced into—"

"The jar of cooking utensils, that spilled everywhere, and she got so mad she couldn't speak!"

"Then Dad was like, 'Dammit, Amy!'"

Julie dropped her voice to mimic their father lovingly. "What the hell's going on in there?"

Maggie did the same. "I'm trying to grade paaaaapppp-peeerrs!"

They laughed together, full and warm, as if they were both still up in the tree house on the edge of the property of their childhood home. It didn't matter that it wasn't a string and two cans that separated them, as it had back then, one up in the tree and the other down below, but three thousand miles.

"Okay, ya nut. It's been fun but I gotta get some sleep. Remember. I'm on east coast time. Congrats on the new job."

"Fine. And as for that three-hour time difference . . . it's all on you, ya know?"

"Julie.'

"Cya. Bye." And the phone clicked before Maggie could give her any grief.

Maggie rubbed her fingers through the fur on Zossima's chest. "She's such a brat, Zoss."

Then Maggie forced herself not to think of anything else, but to go to bed with the happy memories Julie had just given her instead. If she did that, then maybe, just maybe, she could get a little sleep.

Once in the bedroom she closed the door, tossed Zossima on the bed and pulled her desk chair from its place, jamming it methodically up against the bottom of the door-knob. Above the door she placed the metal pin into her door alarm, which was little more than a black box that was fastened with two screws over the doorway ledge. This was her final entry defense. The tip of the pin hung a half inch over the top of the door. If the door opened it would dislodge the pin and trigger the alarm, which was piercingly loud and could distract someone entering the split second she might need to rise to her own defense.

She left the bedroom light on, just as she had left on the lights in the apartment, and crawled into bed, the gun still in her hand. Lying there with her eyes turned to the ceiling, she realized sadly that she would find no sleep tonight after all. Her lip quivered, sending a shock wave up her face that tumbled loose the tears that had been fastened in the breaches of her eyes. They were tears of guilt as much as they were tears of fear, bad feelings from lying to her sister encapsulated in salty secretions that burned as they criss-crossed down her cheeks.

A voice in her head, as clear as fired glass, asked the same old question: *Where to now, Maggie? Where do we run now?*

Then suddenly, as if it were pried apart by some unseen ghost, her mouth fell open and she spoke words that split the silence of the room and gave a volume to her fate: "No-where," she heard herself say. "I'm not running anymore. Ever again."

She listened to the words bounce around the room like pinballs, and she was immediately struck with that odd sensation.

"Fuck it," she said. And then smiled. She was beginning to like that word. More and more.

CHAPTER TWELVE

AT 6:00 A.M. her alarm went off, just as it always did, except this time it did not awaken her because she'd been watching it blink its way dutifully to the appointed hour all the way from 3:06 a.m., one minute at a time, zoning in and out, the seconds that made the minutes as long as the hours that followed them. It was as if the day did not want to be born.

Or as if the person trying to live it is already dead.

She reached over and turned off the alarm. Julie had helped chase away the wolf of fear the night before, but now it had returned with the entire pack. It looked cold outside, and gray. She wanted nothing to do with any of it. Not the day, not her job, not the people at her job, or the waiting for his call that may or may not come. All day; waiting. There was no point to any of it anymore.

She called in sick to work. Today was Thursday. It would be busy. Oh well, they'd live. As if to prove this point, she left the message for her boss in her sickliest voice, which she realized was not a hard voice to fake under the current circumstances, and added that she would probably not be in tomorrow either.

Or ever, for that matter, sir, and would you mind telling me now, before I get into this thing with my ex-fiancé, who has been stalking me for five years by the way, why in the hell I haven't gotten a raise yet? I would really like to know what it was on my last review that just didn't meet the grade. Me, with my MBA, who could probably do your job with a little training, having to dumb down lower than I ever dreamed of, all because of . . .

"Love."

The word stuck to her tongue like a bitter candy.

She had loved Michael once, and made love to him, and that only made it all the worse. A one night stand could be imagined away, banished behind a cloud of alcohol-induced excuses or temporary lapses of judgment. Everyone experienced those. One moment your head is in some selfish pig's lap, their feigned concern for you gone so they can focus on their own needs, and the next moment your head is in the toilet, puking up too many shots of vodka. She remembered her freshman year of college. Vance Walters. She had gotten the routine out of order somehow, puking before she was done instead of after. Vance Walters had been a jerk, and an arrogant one at that. She'd puked all over his lap. Maggie smiled at the memory.

But it had been different with Michael, and even now, under the covers, she shifted her body under the weight of his name. How much different? So different that she had let him have her. All of her. In any way he wanted her. All the other times, with other men, had mostly been horrible. Her first time she'd gotten so drunk and high that she blacked out while it was happening, and all the times since then seemed like splintered moments from that same blackout, spread out over the years, moments of trying to please or be pleased, empty moments of inexplicable self-loathing.

But Michael had been different. She wanted more than anything else to give herself to him. His gentleness with her had aided and abetted all the ghosts within her that had been dying to be set free, wraiths and spirits that swept her up and helped her overcome her initial displeasures and vulnerabilities. He made love to her with care and yet with an assertive firmness that made her actually desire her own surrender, his cold blue eyes glancing into her confidently and rooting out her defenses, one by one, until she had no choice but to let him in.

How he was then she could never forget. The way he would smile at her over his morning cup of coffee, or would walk by and playfully tousle her hair for no reason, like a kindergartner. The way he bought her a dozen different flowers for every bouquet, so that no two looked alike. The way he had studied her sifting through a box of See's Candies her mother had sent her one day, watching her pick out the bad ones each with a single bite-and-toss, and laughed, all the while taking note of the ones she did like—Boudreaux, Mocha and Brittles—and never failing thereafter to buy her a box of candy that was custom built of only these three types of chocolates.

Michael had been so sweet and soft spoken and attentive that she failed to notice things that perhaps another girl, more experienced in that harder space between falling in love and staying in love, might've seen immediately. For instance, the way he needed to see the card that came with that box of candy from her mother that day, explaining it away to an obsession with the artwork. Or the way he had insisted that the bouquets he bought her were always to go in her bedroom, nowhere else in her apartment, as if they were sentinels, placed there to watch over her sheets while he was away.

Progressively, each step of their relationship brought more bad signs out into the open, some that she either did not catch or—at times—chose to ignore. Every boy she'd ever dated had kept a jealous watch over her, so Michael's behavior in restaurants or the market—the glares at other men who looked at her at all, much less for a second too long—did not really bother her.

But then there were the times she found him shifting his six foot four frame menacingly in their direction, bobbing his neck to one side and the other, like a boxer getting ready to fight. She had seen how they had looked at him, the other men, even the ones who were equal to his size, as if they'd seen something in his eyes that had made them retreat. Those blue eyes, hanging softly below those firm eyebrows, could darken in an instant and become like the eyes of a crow.

Hindsight was hindsight, but Maggie could not let herself off that easily because, as always, she could not shake the feeling that this whole thing was partly her fault too. Had she been able to see things more clearly, early on, maybe she would've been able to break things off sooner, which might have averted this entire mess.

He'd dated other women before her and, as far as she knew, had never been inclined to do this to them. She remembered what her therapist had said, that men like Michael were lifelong time bombs, waiting to go off, accumulating insecurities from one relationship to the next, until finally, it happened. Boom.

In the random order of the universe, Maggie had been fated to be his trigger, it seemed, or so the theory went. But Maggie was never fully convinced of this. Her therapist had been on a mission to prevent Maggie from blaming herself for simply backing out of an engagement with someone who she realized she could never marry. It happened all the time in places all over the world, between all sorts of people.

But what if Michael would have never have gone off, never snapped, as it were, if she hadn't hurt him so badly? The humiliation of telling friends and family to ignore the invitations they had received six months prior to the wedding and the embarrassment of having to explain it all. Worse still, Maggie knew she had been a cold bitch about it all. Harsh. Abrupt.

He'd begged and begged for an explanation, and it had been so foolish when she finally relented and confided in Michael the real reason why she'd broken everything off.

He hadn't understood at all, and really, how could he have?

How do you tell a man that you are leaving him because of your dreams?

How could that ever have been an acceptable excuse?

CHAPTER THIRTEEN

THE DREAMS STARTED just after she'd accepted his proposal for marriage, and they continued all the way up until she left him. Her. There in the boat, floating. Drifting closer and closer to that isle of heaven, just like in her dream the previous night before the sudden appearance of the Walrus Lady—except it was usually her grandmother standing there, watching the violet tide roll forwards to embrace her feet and ankles, crying, her face carved in dismay.

In her hand she held a small gold ring.

It struck Maggie how the world of dreams was so different. How it spread like plastic wrap over the conscious mind and clung so tightly, obscuring both reason and logic. A half-mile from shore, it stood to reason that Maggie couldn't really "see" a ring in her hand. In the real world, the distance would be too far to see anything that small so clearly.

But in heaven, Maggie came to realize, your five senses were outdated ideas. It was possible to see and feel and hear, touch and taste, in many different ways, as if your whole body had become some fleshy antennae, reaching out, perceiving and receiving signals and input meant more for the soul than the mind.

So it was that Maggie did not have to guess what was in her grandmother's hand; she just knew. It was a ring. A shiny thing that glistened as her grandmother's metallic voice echoed through the fog like a vocal wind chime, words as melody, sound as silence.

Memento mori.

Her grandmother had been a Latin teacher at the local high school when Maggie was growing up, and she'd taught her some words from time to time. But in her dreams Maggie could not understand her. She heard the words, but could not plug in their meanings, so in awe as she was at the sight of her.

The dream always ended when Maggie realized that the ring in her grandmother's hand was not just any ring. It was an engagement ring.

Maggie's engagement ring.

The one that Michael had given her one night, during dinner at a French restaurant, after a few glasses of wine had calmed his nerves and left her a bit dizzy.

When he'd gone down on one knee, at the edge of the table, almost blurry in the soft yellow light of the restaurant, she had to fight an overwhelming urge to cry. Because he didn't know what he was asking, or what he was getting, and if he did then he might not have ever asked. It was then that she realized that sometimes "yes" is a word better left unspoken, if for no other reason than it's simply a denial of a different kind.

She let him slide his claim on her, to place the ring on

her finger, in front of politely applauding patrons as the violinist who was playing softly in the corner came over to play a song just for them. But she had accepted, against that silent scream within her, and then a month or so later she dreamed of her grandmother for the first time, her precious face so confused, looking out at her from the shore, holding the shiny band in her hand as if it were a razor.

Memento mori.

She'd awoken the very first night of that dream and gone to her computer as Michael snored nearby. After typing in a search for Latin terms, she scanned the results until she found the phrase, a dread coming over her as she read the definition.

Memento mori.

"Remember that you must die."

CHAPTER FOURTEEN

SHE MADE IT all the way to Saturday morning before the phone rang again. She answered it on the second ring. Silence.

She sighed, but then the words came easy. "It's over, Michael. I'm not going to run again."

The phone clicked and then soft music began to play, a prerecorded female's voice spilling into Maggie's ear. It was an offer for a four-day Caribbean cruise at half price. But of course.

An hour later, Maggie found herself at the Starbucks on 145th Street, drinking a cup of coffee and eating a maple scone as she scanned the street outside the window in front of her.

She loved the fact that she'd made the walk without a single glance over her shoulder, though she'd been a little nervous as she descended the stairs from her apartment down to the main lobby, the stairways cast in shadows by the small windows at each switchback that let in dampened light from the gray morning sky.

But once outside, and with the Honda nowhere in sight, something in her head had twirled again, an insistence of sorts that things had to come to a head, for better or worse. She was tired of her life being something paralyzed. She wanted to love again, more than anything. To feel and exist beyond the confines of an anxious dread. She remembered one of her favorite lines from *A Wrinkle in Time*, the best Madeleine L'Engle story ever, "A life lived in chaos is an impossibility."

Yes. It was. And Maggie wanted to know again what it felt like to wake up to the possibilities of each day, instead of the impossibilities.

He'd be coming soon. She could feel it. All she needed to do then was provoke him into making a move, in public like this, then wound him until help arrived. With this in mind, it only stood to reason that the gun in her jacket pocket was not only loaded, but cocked, the risk of accidental discharge be damned.

Fuck it.

It dawned on her now that this word had become a talisman, and that gave her a brief moment of self-doubt, because everyone knew that talismans and superstitions were the last stop on a bad trip. She heard her psychiatrist's voice in her head, clear as day: "Well Maggie, it would seem to me that you are so desiring a different 'you' these days, a 'polar opposite' you as it were, that you have begun an artificial attempt to manifest this false self by the adoption of foul language you would never otherwise use."

Brilliant, my dear doctor! Oh, and by the way? Fuck you too.

She bit into her scone and waited for him to appear, the

fragments of conversation taking place between all the people around her mingling in her ears and forming a cylinder of sound for her to dwell in.

He hadn't called all day Thursday or Friday, like she expected him to. There was the off chance that he didn't know where she worked yet, had somehow only tracked down her home residence, but that was unlikely, based on past experience. When Michael scouted, he did his homework. But she knew with today being a Saturday he would have to try her at home one way or the other, and if she did not answer the phone then he would feel compelled to visit, to make sure she hadn't bolted again. Then he would start looking for her. By now, he would know that she liked this Starbucks.

"Excuse me, do you mind if I sit with you?"

She looked up, startled to see a middle-aged man, who was quite handsome with slightly graying temples, looking down at her with a smile. It was obvious by the look in his eyes, not to mention the various empty chairs and tables around them, that he was hitting on her.

Her fingers instantly tightened on the gun, even though he looked nothing like Michael, her anger bubbling just below the surface. *How odd,* she thought.

Maggie shot him her bitchiest look and said nothing, the force of her dismissal conveyed in the turn of her cheek and the roll of her eyes.

He made a sound through his nose, a dismissive gesture of his own, an exhalation of pride that came too late and could not reverse the flush of red in his cheeks. Then he scampered off to a corner table with a glance over each shoulder, looking like a person who'd just tripped in the street and hoped that no one had noticed.

Returning her gaze to the street, she watched the bodies

passing by in their heavy jackets and wool overcoats. A girl in a white Nike jogging suit ran by, the nylon clinging to her toned body, her eyes transfixed on the miles ahead.

Maggie looked back and forth across the sidewalk nearest her, then to the sidewalk on the other side of the street. Men were everywhere, some on morning walks with their dogs or wives, a FedEx delivery man unloading his truck, another pulling his hot dog cart up the sidewalk to prepare for the day's failed dieters. But no Michael.

She sipped her coffee and wondered what she would do if he appeared, and it was while she was locked in these thoughts for a moment, the scenarios playing themselves out to each of their own ends, that she nearly missed sight of him when he stepped around the corner like a man without a care in the world, on her side of the street, wearing blue jeans and a green New York Jets jacket, his hair longer now, pulled back into a pony tail. At first she wasn't sure it was him. The morning sunlight was bright, partially obscuring the clarity of her vision. A part of her was angry that the blinds were up, and she was beginning to question this man's identity until he looked directly at her and smiled. She knew that smile inside and out.

She gripped the gun as her mouth went dry.

I can go out there, shoot him in the leg or something, wound him and then call the police . . .

. . . and they'll drive right out here, arrest him . . .

. . . then tell you that just because he violated his restraining order doesn't give you the right to run up and shoot him, then they'll arrest you too.

But Michael had other plans. His arrival at the window coincided with a woman leaving the Starbucks with a boy of no more than three years old.

Michael approached the woman and started talking

about something, making sure to put her and the child between himself and the window, all in an effort to keep Maggie in his line of sight. As he talked to the woman—*Are you kidding me? He's asking for directions!*—he glanced repeatedly over the woman's shoulder, locking eyes briefly with Maggie and then cutting away. He patted the boy's head. The woman seemed charmed, more than willing to help this tall, strikingly handsome man who had approached her for help.

Maggie's body flushed with anger. She stood up quickly, knocking her chair backwards, her scone tumbling from her hand, her right knee knocking against the table slightly, causing her coffee to spill.

He looked at Maggie, and ever so slightly, as the woman looked down to her purse to extract a pen and piece of paper, he shook his head. It was a secret gesture, meant to fly under the radar of everyone except him and Maggie. But the little boy saw it immediately, and he looked back and forth between the two of them.

So it was that Maggie stood at the window, pinned down by two sets of eyes, one from a man whose face barely disguised his malice towards her, and the other by a three-year-old child with eyes full of innocence. She was paralyzed. Across that glass, not ten feet away, was quite possibly the end of the game, and she couldn't play it out.

She looked to Michael's hands. They were both in his pockets. If she were holding a gun that *he* did not know about, what was there in his pockets that *she* did not know about? And what would he do with what he had? The risks were too high, all the way around. And despite all this, she decided to ignore them anyway. She began to swiftly move towards the door.

His head pivoted in surprise but all the while he played

it out, pacing his goodbye to the woman with a smile. A big smile.

You cocky son of a bitch.

She was ten feet from the door.

She saw him say thanks to the woman and then he turned and hurried back up the sidewalk.

She grabbed the door handle, bumping the man who had tried to hit on her in a strange twist of irony, causing him to stumble into a rack of *New York Times* papers.

"What the hell!?" he shouted, but Maggie was already out the door and on the sidewalk, turning to follow Michael, who was a good forty feet away now.

He was not far from the corner.

"Michael!" she screamed, causing heads all over the street to turn her way, including the woman who had just given him directions and the FedEx man across the street, who was so startled he caught the edge of his dolly on the rear tire of his truck, causing boxes to tumble everywhere.

Michael didn't turn his head. He was pushing on towards the corner, where he waved his arm at a passing cab.

Shit! Don't stop for him. Don't you dare.

As if to mock her and any of the preconceived notions she had about New York cabbies, the cab braked and whipped over to the sidewalk, cutting across a lane and pulling up to the corner at an awkward angle.

People were passing in front of her, first on the left, then on the right, obscuring her vision.

When she managed to fix on him again he was flashing money at the driver.

Dammit!

She began to run. "Michael!" she screamed again.

And this time, after he climbed into the cab, he turned his head to look at her.

Maggie slowed to a jog.

He rolled down his window as the driver pulled off into traffic again.

"I'm not running anymore, you bastard!" she screamed, and the words echoed through the cool air.

Their eyes locked. He was not smiling. Instead he looked perplexed. And angry.

"I'm never running again, do you hear me! This is my last address. Ever." Maggie felt a profound freedom in saying the words, in screaming them, actually, and hearing them said made her want to punch something. Upon reaching the corner, she stepped out into the street defiantly, watching the cab disappear into the distance. She was out of breath, her heart beating too fast. She tried to swallow, but her throat felt as if it were full of rocks.

She turned to walk home, passing all the people on the street who had just witnessed her tirade. She noticed that each one of them was looking at her as they would look at a sick person, someone who was either crazy or—in the only sympathetic eyes that looked her way, in the eyes of a woman carrying a bag from the bagel shop, for instance, or the eyes of the meter maid who had stopped writing tickets—as someone simply in need of a shoulder to cry on.

You have no idea, she thought. *No idea at all. None of you.*

"No turning back now," she muttered. Over and over again. She realized with apprehension that she couldn't stop saying it, and that's when she wondered if maybe they were right, the majority of those eyes.

Maybe she was crazy.

Or on her way there.

CHAPTER FIFTEEN

THAT NIGHT, after she ordered Chinese food in and caught the last half of *The Green Mile* on AMC, her cell chimed. She glanced down and saw the text.

"A STITCH IN TIME . . ."

Maggie smiled and typed her reply. "SAVES EIGHT."

A minute or two passed before another text came from Julie. This one was a photo of her and two girlfriends at a restaurant, each with apple martinis and big smiles, with Julie flashing her trademark "heart hands." With it was a message: "AN APPLE A DAY :)"

"Aw," Maggie whispered. At least one of them was having a blast. "HAVE FUN. BE SAFE."

"OKAY BESTEST."

Zossima sat on the windowsill, looking out at the night sky as he licked at his right paw and then rubbed it over his ear. Maggie stared at this last text and smiled at the nickname they had used for each other since they were little.

Over the next two months, Maggie Kincaid began to

create for herself an entirely new world. One that was free from fear and paranoia, dread and anguish. Slowly, she allowed herself to do something she hadn't done for five, long years: she began to think of a future.

She began to wear heels again, and shorter skirts, when it didn't snow—something she hadn't done in a long time. She wasn't reckless; when she went somewhere she always carried her gun, just in case. But she was done with her circumstances dictating the entirety of her life, of her existence being a thing endured instead of lived.

Three times she accepted invitations from the girls at work to go clubbing, and though she steered clear of the dance floor most of the time—too many bodies from too many angles, just like in the subway station—after a few martinis she usually loosened up enough to try to dance, mostly only with the girls around her. Twice she even danced with some men, always with her purse at her side, odd as it may have seemed to them, the gun in its folds.

When they questioned her attachment to her purse, she blamed it on a fear of having it stolen once, and with it her identity, something she told them happened to her in the past, which was true. Michael had once got into her personal records and had cast a net of trouble over everything, from her credit history to her driving record.

Her acquaintances accepted this as a reasonable excuse, and as she made friends at work it became easier to take the calls that came, here or there, from him. At home. On her cell. At work. Always silence. Sometimes with that stupid hissing sound, sometimes not. It didn't matter. As she began to feel less and less like a loner, she began to become more and more comfortable in speaking to him, in challenging the silence on the other end of the line.

"You're not scaring me," she would tell him, quietly so

no one would hear her. "It's over. I told you: no more running."

Then the line would disconnect. The calls came and went for a little over three weeks after she'd confronted him on the street. Then? They stopped. Incredibly, the Honda disappeared entirely too. After a month of no contact she allowed herself to think that maybe, just maybe, this was what she was supposed to have done all along: confront him. A part of her believed it to the core. When yet another month passed, it became easier to allow herself to agree with this notion

Eventually, she marched through January and into February, one step and one day at a time, a methodology to her stubbornness that allowed her to remove the bars of her self-imposed prison one at a time. She discovered that not looking behind her or around her all the time gave her more time to just look forwards, literally and figuratively. She ate out more often, no more bag lunches in the break room at work and no more Top Ramen at home.

Only poor Zossima seemed to mind, his role as the center of her social life now diminished. Now that he had to spend some weekend nights alone, he would reject his cat box at times, leaving his droppings on her reading chair or in her bed.

Maybe I should buy him a little friend, she thought. *A Siamese would be nice.*

She remembered the first day she saw Zossima, as a kitten in a pet adoption display at the local PetCo in Virginia during a visit to her parents' house on semester break from college. He was the smallest kitten in the pen, and yet the bravest when she reached in to pet the litter, charging to her and knocking his siblings out of the way to claim sole attention from her fingers.

"Somebody likes you," the pimply-faced attendant had said, standing near the pen in her red vest.

"Somebody's sold!" Maggie had said gleefully.

Zossima had been the best impulse buy of her life, far better than a pair of shoes or a new outfit. As a kitten, he had shown a penchant for fetching and retrieving, like a dog almost. Back in her dorm, where pets were not allowed, he had been so loving and gentle with her roommates that he had become a secret mascot, never showing any ill will to anyone. Except Michael.

The first night she'd brought him home to her dorm room, Zossima had simply perched himself on the coffee table opposite them and stared intently at Michael as he sat on the couch. Like a cop on stakeout. Maggie had chalked it off to a fur ball, but by the time they began to make out on the living room floor Michael had become so uncomfortable at Zossima's presence that he had angered Maggie by tossing a pillow at him, forcing the cat to flee for cover under Maggie's reading chair. As their relationship grew, Zossima's dislike for Michael was dismissed as feline jealousy, and it became a running joke between the two of them as to who she loved the most.

She decided that she *would* buy Zossima a little friend. And she would also apply for a job more deserving of her education. Maggie knew this would make her mother and father even happier than they already were. She'd told them and Julie what had happened with Michael, how maybe it was a combination of her making a stand and him finally wearing out, after so many years and so many cities. Everyone had been cautiously optimistic at first, but with each passing month that optimism grew.

After polishing it up to allow for the short work times at each job, she posted her full resume on a few Internet sites.

In truth, she embellished things for any future employer, explaining all the receptionist work as a necessary evil in realizing her post college dream of traveling the major cities of the United States and now, the dream fulfilled, she was ready to settle in New York and start a career. She wrote the cover letter smoothly, though with just enough naïveté to be charming. It would work, she was sure it would.

Then Valentine's day came, that dreaded day. It had to come. It did every year.

But this year it brought nothing.

Not a box of rotting beef, as it did the first year she had ran. Not a life insurance packet filled out in her name as it did the next, the words "Think about it and then call me" written in his block letter style on the front. She had no car now so he could not write the words "Roses are red, I want you dead" on the hood, as he did last year. This time the day came and went, with no gifts, no surprises and no calls. She was elated. And as February drew to a close, Maggie began to sleep longer.

Everything was almost perfect, except for the dreams.

It seemed that even now her grandmother was still not done talking.

CHAPTER SIXTEEN

IN THE DEEP SEAS of her sleep, Maggie's boat was drifting further and further away from the island's shore, and most startling of all, she was no longer alone on the boat. There was now another presence, sitting behind her, steering. In her dream she kept trying to look back, but it was as if there were two invisible hands that kept her from doing so, buffering her at the ears, locking her neck in place. Her sense of peace and calm dissipated. The strange carvings in the boat began to fade, and it seemed to grow rickety.

It occurred to her that between the heaven in her dreams and the world that awaited her when she woke up, there was a dark space that took its cue from a person's REM and pulled back a veil to an uncharted sea that pulsed with currents that seemed to move in every direction at once, a soft ripple of water here, a building whitecap there, all made by the weather patterns in one's mind, high pressures of the past, low pressures of the present. Sleep was less the world you entered than it was the sail you cast, and the sea you crossed was not a body of water but something far more treacherous.

It was a body of memories.

Maggie dreamed of her grandmother almost every night, seeing her there on the shore, the ring in her hand, the tears on her cheeks, and she waited for her to speak again, begged her in her mind to talk to her while telling her that she was safe now, that Michael was gone.

Maggie noticed that her grandmother seemed to be listening, and Maggie was struck with a sense of eeriness as she watched her grandmother's head tilt to the side, like the head of a puppy to a high-pitched tone, every time she said Michael's name.

After a week the dream jumped a step, and she could clearly see her grandmother shaking her head. The suspense caused Maggie to start going to bed early and try to will the dream on, but this seemed to only stifle the moments, dilute them, or throw them backwards into a sort of "repeat" loop.

Finally, one night, when her sleep came naturally on the couch as she tried to stay awake and watch a documentary on Hemingway, her grandmother spoke.

Tabula rasa.

The words were uttered with a tone of grief and tipped with sorrow.

When Maggie awoke the next morning she didn't need to look the term up. She knew it well. It had been a term her grandmother had used when teasing her about forgetting something, like her school book or a chore she had been asked to do. "Sometimes your mind is like a *blank tablet,* young lady!" she would say with a smile. Then, tapping the side of her head with her index finger, she would say it for added effect, "*Tabula rasa!*"

Maggie had told this story to her shrink in Virginia

once, when he had finally pigeonholed her into a discussion on her childhood, and he had smiled when he heard the words. "That's cute," he said.

"Yeah, it is. She was like a best friend growing up. I loved her a lot. So. You've heard that term?"

He nodded. "Yes, but in a different way. 'Blank tablet' is the literal translation, yes, but it is also a term used to describe the mind."

"Really?" Maggie had said, genuinely interested in what he had to say for a change.

"Yes," he said, looking at her over folded hands, his fingers interlaced. "The mind in a hypothetical state, a primarily blank or empty state, before it receives outside impressions."

"You mean like the mind of a child or something?" Maggie ventured.

He jutted his chin out as he thought for a moment and then nodded. "For the most part, yes."

Their conversation had gone on from there to where she steered them, namely to a whole host of dead ends.

Tabula rasa.

Maggie realized that in the dream her grandmother was not saying the words in jest, as she once had; she had been saying them to convey something. Maggie wasn't sure what, but she felt the answer was right there, on the inside, balanced on the tip of some mental tongue, a bilingual thing that had partly to do with who she was and partly to do with whoever was on her boat with her, rowing her—she was sure of it now—away from heaven.

CHAPTER SEVENTEEN

THE FIRST DAY of March was a Friday. It was a surprisingly sunny day, with highs in the sixties, a spring day that had crept in a month early. Maggie decided to skip her morning cereal and instead grab some madeleine cookies from the pastry shop on her way in to work to celebrate the beauty of the sunshine and the end to another week.

The night before, her resume had gotten two replies and one of them sounded interesting: a job at The Metropolitan Museum of Art in the Development Office.

The workday passed quickly, and afterwards she joined the girls and a few guys from accounting for happy hour at Gilligan's, where she had a few beers, flirted with the bartender and then, against her better judgment, agreed to go out for even more drinks after one of the girls convinced her to stop over at her place to borrow an outfit. It was a fun night, with loud music that was still thumping in her eardrums when she finally got back home at just before midnight, still a little buzzed.

She reached her apartment building and swiped her card, noticing the fresh flowers that Mrs. Catherly had put in the lobby next to the mailboxes sometime since that morning, when she'd lectured Maggie on how to properly pluck her eyebrows. She smiled at the memory, wondering now if Monday's lecture might be on bikini waxing. After making her way upstairs, she opened her apartment door and tossed her purse on the desk, clicking her tongue against the roof of her mouth for Zossima to come.

But he didn't. Maggie clicked her tongue again, then looked around.

Oh . . . my . . . God.

She saw a small lump of fur next to the living room wall, in a pool of blood, his broken body cut open, his eyes like those of a plastic doll, his mouth agape in a final, frozen breath.

There was also blood on the wall behind him, no, wait, not only *on* the wall, but going *up* the wall.

He had used her cat like a pen, the letters smeared up and down, back and forth, cat hair matted in places here or there. A sob caught in her throat. Maggie tried to look away, but she couldn't.

Jesus! He killed my Zossima!

The letters that had been written on the wall looked like some ancient, demonic hieroglyphics. Her mind babbled, trying to make sense of the three simple words that were shattering her life.

She brought her hands to her face. They were trembling so badly that she had to still her fingers by balling her hands into tight fists. In her panic, her mind raced to rouse her to the defense, insisting that he was there in the apartment, waiting to pounce. But it was no good. He was not there, she was sure of it. He had done what he had done and—

That's when she saw all the photos, strung up on a clothesline, of all things, that he'd stretched across her living room in staggered rows from end to end; dozens and dozens of photos, all black and white. There were photos of her at a coffee shop with another girl, of her in a sexy lingerie store, of her walking and talking, sitting and—worst of all—sleeping. But Maggie was confused, because she didn't recognize the girl with her in the coffee shop, and it had been years since she had shopped for sexy lingerie. And that's when her mind finally cleared enough to register the true identity of the pretty blond girl that was in all the photos that looked so much like her, so much so that everyone had always teased them for looking like twins when they were little, even though they were three years apart.

All the pictures were of Julie.

It can't be. Please God, no. Don't let it be.

Her mind came full circle, back to where she had started, first to her dead cat, then to those three words that were cast in stark crimson against the white wall.

SHE MISSES YOU

Maggie crumpled to the floor. The world was swiftly painting black.

He had Julie.

Then she was falling over, fainting, going . . .

CHAPTER EIGHTEEN

HER CELL PHONE chime awoke her.

Maggie's eyelids fluttered open. She felt her cheek pressed against the cool of the hardwood floor. Directly in her line of sight was her reading chair, and beyond that, the window, which showed the dark night sky.

Slowly, like a computer being turned on, the transistors sparking sluggishly, she rebooted her mind, the hardware giving birth to the DOS realizations of where she was, which then allowed for the command strings of more advanced applications to unfold: her subconscious, the base awareness of self and the self's condition, her sense of sight followed by the sound of water pipes running beneath the floor, then the smell of something foul, followed by the sandpapery taste of her dry tongue, and finally the sensation of the bones in her right hand coming alive with pain, trapped as it was beneath her body, this sensation leading to the final inclusion of the operating software that was her consciousness, which took command of all her thoughts and tried to make sense of them.

Maggie thought of four things in quick succession.

Why am I on the floor?

He has Julie.

That smell is Zossima.

Call the police.

From there, adrenaline roused her left arm to prop up her body. Her confusion dissipated like a receding fog.

Shit. I fainted. Oh no.

Her stomach churned with the realization that where she was and what was happening had not "gone away" but was real and true.

As if to prove this to herself, she looked to the base of the living room wall to find Zossima's dead eyes looking right back at her, accusingly. *You never should have left me alone. We were always friends, weren't we? I always took care of YOU, didn't I? How many nights did you cry into my fur? How many times did I rub my head against your chin, loving you? And when he came, where were you then? Drinking. Flirting.*

"Zossima. I'm so sorry," she squeaked.

She squeezed her right hand closed a few times, sparks of pain shooting up her forearm. Nothing seemed broken or sprained. A sickening wave of sorrow and desperation washed over her as she wiped her hair out of her face.

When he cut into me, you were nowhere to be found.

No. Stop it. Now Maggie. You'll lose it again. Stop it. Shit. What time is it? How long have I been lying here?

She looked at the clock on the wall: 11:58 p.m.

Dammit. You stupid piece of shit, he has Julie and you fainted?

She got up off the floor and realized she was still very

much in shock, very much in denial, despite Zossima, despite everything she was thinking.

This can't be happening. It just can't. HOW?

The wellspring of her anger was all that she needed. She looked at her cell phone, lying feet away, partially spilled from her purse, which she'd dropped when she fainted. Grabbing it, she could see that she had missed four text messages, the first of which had been sent to her at 11:47 p.m., just after she'd gotten home. She punched the button on the phone to view them:

"A STITCH IN TIME . . ."

"A STITCH IN TIME . . ."

"A STITCH IN TIME . . ."

"A STITCH IN TIME . . ."

Oh! Thank God! It's okay. He doesn't have her. Julie's checking in on me as usual. She thumbed the letters of her reply. "SAVES EIGHT."

A call came in immediately from Julie's phone.

"Hello, honey," he said, and his calm voice was like a wrecking ball, smashing into the teetering walls of her hope.

"Michael? What the hell are you doing!?" Maggie yelled.

"My, my. Is that anyway to greet someone?"

"Michael, this isn't funny."

"No. Shit." He spat the words at her like venom.

She could barely choke out a reply. "What have you done?"

The calm voice was instantly gone. "You stupid little whore, you think I *wanted* to do this? Nope. But you wanted to play hardball, didn't you? So don't come crying to me now."

"Michael, I didn't . . . I don't . . ."

"Don't lie to me. You did and you have. This is what you wanted, right? For me to leave. Fine. I have."

Maggie froze. She didn't know what to say, so she began with the obvious. "Where's Julie?"

There was a moment of silence and then she heard Julie's voice, weak and drained, speaking into the phone. "Maggie?"

"Julie!" Maggie spun in circles, not sure what to look for, first wanting a pen, then realizing that it wasn't likely that her sister was going to give her directions to where they were. She thought of trying to record the message on the answering machine, but the machine would beep as it recorded, giving her away, before she ultimately remembered that she was on the damn cell phone anyway, not the landline.

"Don't come here, Maggie, don't . . ."

There was a scuffling sound. Then silence.

Maggie went cold with rage. "Michael, are you there?"

"Of course I am, baby."

"You listen to me, you . . . If you hurt her, I swear . . . Screw this. I'm calling the police!"

His reply was a firm, three-word threat. "Very. Bad. Idea."

"Yeah? Why?"

"Because if you do? You will never see her alive again, plain and simple."

His words pinned her in on all sides. "What?"

"Say you're sorry for threatening me like that. For even bringing up the police."

"Michael . . ."

"Say you're sorry . . . or I will just rape her now and pretend it's you."

Oh my God! She was trembling uncontrollably. *This can't be happening. It can't be. It just can't.*

But it was. She heard herself say the words, in a tiny,

pathetic voice. "I'm sorry."

"From now on you better talk to me with respect. I mean . . . shit! Always threatening me with the damn cops. Even now! I'm tired of it!" He was screaming into the phone. "After you asked me to leave you alone and I do!"

Maggie was speechless.

Then, with a cunning tone. "You didn't say anything about me leaving Julie alone, though, did you, Maggie?"

"Michael. Don't do this . . ."

"I know you still love me, Maggie. You're just confused. And deep down, you know how much I still love you, too."

It had been so long since they'd talked and something was off. He didn't sound right. Almost as if he were manic.

She sniffed against her terror. *He's gotten worse. Much worse.*

Tired of waiting for her reply, he spoke again. "You do love me, don't you, honey?" Again, his voiced had changed. It was boyish now, almost pleading.

"Michael—"

"I know, I know," he said, cutting her off. "You're not ready. You're upset. You need to think. You never did like to say 'I love you' over the phone. Do you remember that?"

She closed her eyes. "Yes."

Laughing softly, he continued. "Do you remember why?"

"Because phones are insincere," she said, biting into her lower lip. Her mind was like a rat on heroin now, going in every direction but the right one, which was a direction it was simply unable to perceive.

"Exactly." He giggled. "But that's all we've had now for a while, Maggie, the phone, and even then you barely talked to me. Instead you just yelled at me. Like you did that day outside the coffee shop." The switch was flipping again, his voice going from sad to angry. "Where's the love, Mags? What happened to you telling me you loved me?"

"Michael this is crazy, why have you done—"

"Crazy?"

That was stupid, Maggie. Why did you say that?

It dawned on her why people in situations like hers were supposed to call the FBI or something, so that someone who knew what the hell they were doing could handle the calls, or at least avoid the obvious mistakes like calling a crazy person "crazy."

"I didn't mean it like that, Michael."

"Oh, I think you did."

"Michael, please . . ." And then, from somewhere, a moment of brilliance: *Make him pity you, Maggie.* "Look at what I came home to, Michael. You killed my damn cat, and now you have my sister? I meant that *I'm* the one who's going crazy here."

Silence.

Maggie pushed on. "I didn't know you were this angry. Why would you do this?"

More silence.

If he wants hope, then give him his damn hope.

She continued, "First I lose you, then all of this? For what? Of course I still love you, Michael. I just needed some time."

Her words hung there for a moment.

"Do you remember our first kiss, Maggie?"

She couldn't imagine how any of this could go anywhere but someplace bad.

"Yes."

"Where was it?"

"Michael."

"Where was it?"

"On the field trip."

"Which field trip?"

"To Philadelphia. Our schools went together. Georgetown and George Washington. We'd been on one date before we went."

"Exactly. Do you remember where we kissed?" he spoke softly.

Maggie realized that it sounded very much like these were still happy memories for him. Cherished, even. She rolled her eyes to the ceiling. "Somewhere near that park, by the floral shop. You had just bought me flowers."

"Twelve different flowers, each a different color. Do you remember?" he said.

This is nuts. "Yes."

"Ya know . . . every day of my life, now, I'm there on that street, on that day. Corny as it was, I can't forget it. I can still feel your lips, Maggie."

Maggie didn't know what to say.

He continued, "Do you know why?"

"Why, Michael?"

"Because back then, you were honest, ya know? That kiss? It was honest, Maggie. Now? You just feed me lines of bullshit like you did a minute ago." The hardness of his voice cut quick and fast across the receiver. "I mean, did you just actually say 'First I *lose* you?'"

"Michael . . ."

"You didn't *lose* me. You *betrayed* me, and then you left me to die."

"That's not—"

"DON'T ARGUE WITH ME!"

His voice pierced her ear so loudly that she almost dropped the phone.

He's totally lost. Oh dear God, please don't let him hurt

Julie.

"I'm going to give you one more chance to prove you love me, Maggie. I've been chasing you for too long now, letting you play this stupid 'hard to get' game. The way I see it, you owe me. I've proven how badly I want you, now it's your turn to do the same."

"Please, Michael, let's—"

"No. No. No. Please *nothing*. One step at a time. I'm tired of this dance, Maggie. For once, I'd like to lead, and there are only going to be two rules to this whole gig. Do you want to know what they are?"

Maggie began to cry in spite of herself, her disbelief now giving way to sick awe at the unfolding nightmare before her.

"What?"

"First. No cops. No calling anyone for help. No one. Don't get cute, Maggie. You tell one, single soul about this and you had better be good and ready to bury your sister. I swear, I'll leave her in such a mess they'll need dental records. Do you understand?"

"Yes."

"Do you *really* understand? Because you better."

"Yes. I do, Michael. I do."

"Second, I want you to come to me. You'll get hints along the way, of how to follow. But if I go more than a day in any place waiting for you? Game over. Julie is still dead, and I still disappear. For a while anyway."

A chill ran through her. *This will never end,* she thought.

Then Michael, like a master chess player who was four moves ahead and on the verge of boredom, now chose to add a devious wrinkle to the game.

"And if you blow it with Julie? There's still your mom and dad, right, Maggie? They live in Napa now, don't they? I've called, pretending to be the utility man. Your dad s-s-s-stutters now, d-d-doesn't he?"

Another swing of the wrecking ball, this time destroying her denial.

No. I thought he meant me, that he would come back for ME.

Maggie leaned against the wall and slid down to the floor.

"In case you were wondering? The game starts now. Cell phones can be tracked. We both know it. Just in case you still decide to get stupid, I will be tossing Julie's now and only using disposable phones from now on, wherever and whenever I want. Goodbye."

"Wait!"

She heard him sigh heavily. "I have to go now—"

Instinctively Maggie remembered something. "Michael. You promised me a hint."

The line was silent for a moment, then he said, "I already gave it to you."

He hung up.

She looked in dismay at the phone and then cradled it to her chest, sobbing gently. The rat on heroin in her mind scurried about all the corners of her brain again, going over the entire length of their conversation, digging and sifting for the clue. Before long, it was found.

He had wanted to reminisce about their first kiss.

Philadelphia.

He was taking Julie to Philadelphia.

CHAPTER NINETEEN

BEING TASK-ORIENTED WAS one of her strengths. Holding her panic in check, Maggie focused on what had to come next. She needed a rental car. She would need the subway to get her to a place she could get one. She made her way through the apartment to collect her items, averting her gaze from the photos, the wall, and Zossima in particular, knowing that any one of these things could dunk her mind into a cup of fear again.

Everything in the apartment was in order but for one thing. He'd found the .38 in the bedroom. Its usual place underneath her pillow had been raided, and its bullets were spilled out across the bedsheets like trinkets. The gun itself was on her pillow, the round cylinder left conspicuously open. She couldn't risk the fact that he'd tampered with it, so it would have to stay behind. This upset her, but she was still relieved that this was all he'd found. She could still bring the .22 and the mace.

She moved at a frantic pace, not wanting to take the

time to change, but at the same time realizing that this might not end soon. She practically tore off her work outfit, ripping the buttons off her blouse in the process. After changing into jeans and a sweatshirt she put on her jogging shoes, tying the laces so violently that she snapped the nail on her left index finger, feeling it tear and snag. She cursed and bit the remnant of it off between her teeth, ignoring the sharp pain and then forcing herself to quickly pack a duffel bag with nothing but t-shirts, a pair of yoga pants, more jeans and a few sweatshirts. New York to Philadelphia. Either there or here it would still be cold, so she also grabbed a black and white parka from the closet, the dull memory that it had once been a gift from Julie stabbing her in the chest.

"I'm coming, Jules. Hang in there. I swear I'll find you," she muttered.

Hopefully alive.

"Shut up. She'll be alive. I'll find her in time."

Or in a shallow grave.

The panic came in another wave.

Callthepolicenowwhocareswhathesays. No no no no no no.

Something was not right in her head. She lifted her hand and bit directly into her palm, screaming in frustration as she did so, using the pain and anguish to grab hold of her sanity. Feeling herself beginning to cry again, she wiped at her eyes and spoke to herself aloud, to drive it all home. "He's lost it completely. He'll kill her for sure. And why would they be any more help to Julie than they've been to you all these damn years?"

The police will come. They'll see Zossima. The wall . . .

"And they'll say, 'This is serious.' Then they'll start talking about proof, like they always do. How can you 'prove' it was him? Do you have security cameras? No? Are there any witnesses? Did anyone see him going into the apartment? Did anyone see him leaving. Blah, blah, blah."

She cursed herself for not getting cameras installed.

There's gotta be a witness. Someone must've let him in, or he snuck in as they were exiting. There. Maybe you could ask around . . .

"It'll be the same old story. Okay. Fine. Let's say they believe it's him. Then what? 'Okay, Ms. Kincaid. Do you know his current whereabouts? A blue Honda, you say? Hmm.' My God. This is New York City, there are probably a million blue Hondas."

Okay. This is a kidnapping. That means the FBI would probably get involved.

"How long will that take? And how far away will Michael get by then?"

But they're the experts. They'll know what to do.

"You heard him. The minute they take over the calls, or if he senses something's off . . . no. If this were just you, then you could take the chance that he's full of shit. But this is Julie in danger now. The police. The FBI. They're human, and if any one of them makes a mistake, of any kind, you get to live forever with Julie's blood on your hands. Right now it's simple. He wants you. Just get to him. That's your best shot at saving Julie. Period."

She thought carefully for a second. "He wants you to follow him, to meet him somewhere."

Okay. Fine.

Here was the plan, then. She just had to get close enough to scare him off with the gun, or wound him somehow, like she'd been trying to do at the Starbucks that day. Then? She could get Julie back and escape. Then she would call the police. With Julie backing up her story, Michael was done for.

She was packed and had everything she needed, except some money. There was the Bank of America on the corner. After that, there was an Enterprise by her office building downtown. But it was the wee hours of the morning. She could maybe get to the subway and take the 19 to get there. Six stops. A twenty-minute ride. But at this hour it might be closed. She wasn't sure and she couldn't waste the time trying to find out. Her best bet to get a rental at this hour was going to be La Guardia Airport. So, once she had her cash, she'd take a cab there.

She exited her apartment and was down into the street in seconds. Turning north to head to the bank, she ran directly into someone, the surprise of the collision forcing a small yelp to escape her lungs.

It was the Walrus Lady.

CHAPTER TWENTY

IN THE DEAD OF NIGHT, it was just the two them. Traffic sounded in the distance, the lingering vibrations of a city that never rested.

Down here at street level, the first thing Maggie noticed was that although the Walrus Lady was large, she was quite short. Maggie was five foot eight and the Walrus Lady seemed to be at least three inches shorter.

"Excuse me, I'm sorry," Maggie stammered, moving immediately to get by her and continue to the subway.

"He's done something horrible, hasn't he?" the Walrus Lady asked.

Maggie froze and turned to look at her. "What did you just say?"

"I've been watching the two of you," the Walrus Lady said, "for quite a while now. He's done something horrible, hasn't he?"

Maggie was stunned. She looked at the old woman. Her black shawl hung over her head and draped past her chubby face; her eyes were like small slits resting on cheeks that maintained their roundness despite being forced to support her thick jowls. She had moles too, with a particularly large one that rested on the crease between the left side of her nose and her upper lip. She wore a gray sweater, her long black skirt stopping just above her flat black shoes, revealing white leg warmers underneath. She appeared disheveled and disoriented.

"What are you talking about?" Maggie pressed, unable to move.

"The man. The one who follows you. The one in the blue car that's gone now."

A chill went down Maggie's back. She thought all along that she was the only "watcher" on the block, but this was proving to be a misguided belief. She hadn't been the only one watching, or the only one seeing. "I don't know what—"

"I feel so horrible. I knew something bad was going to happen. I was trying to wait up for you to get home, but I sleep at the oddest times—you know, when I do sleep that is, which isn't often."

The Walrus Lady fidgeted nervously, her pudgy hands working the ends of her newspaper.

Maggie realized she was shaking.

"It's okay, he's not around now," Maggie said.

The Walrus Lady seemed angry with herself. "I know. But still. You look so frightened, child."

There was no time for this. She had to get to the airport. "I'll be fine. Thank you, but I have to go now," Maggie said, reaching out to touch the Walrus Lady's arm as she stepped past her.

"Camella wanted me to tell you something."

Maggie had taken three steps before the Walrus Lady spoke the words, but at the sound of them she spun around immediately. "What? Camella who?" Maggie asked.

"You know the answer to that, my dear, don't you?" the Walrus Lady said, a worried frown on her face.

The chill that had gone down Maggie's back a moment earlier returned now, moving up her spine and stretching out over her shoulders like a fishing net. Camella was Maggie's grandmother's name.

"This is crazy," Maggie exhaled.

The Walrus Lady looked down at her feet. "I don't sleep very much," she repeated, "but when I do, lately, she visits me. Your grandmother is worried about you."

Maggie began to tremble. *I'm absolutely losing my mind.* She didn't want to hear anymore, so she began to walk off again.

"She wanted me to tell you something," the Walrus Lady called after her.

In spite of herself, Maggie turned around yet again. They stood there, the two of them, for just a moment, staring at one another, until Maggie nodded for the Walrus Lady to continue.

"She wanted me to tell you that what *she* did not know, *you* must know."

"Jesus," Maggie exhaled, bringing her hands up to her temples. Rubbing. Rubbing.

Don't faint again. Don't. And don't have a nervous breakdown either.

Water began to pool in her eyes. She looked up to see the same was true for the Walrus Lady.

"You poor child," the Walrus Lady said, and incredibly, the old woman opened her arms and walked towards her, enveloping Maggie in quick hug.

"I don't," Maggie said, then caught her breath and continued, "I don't know what to do."

"Yes, you do. You are stronger than you think, and stronger than what anyone could ever do to you."

Maggie nodded, confused. Incredulous to it all. She did not know what to say, and then suddenly, she did. Wiping the tears from her eyes she smiled slightly and said, "My name is Maggie."

The Walrus Lady smiled back. "Mine is Madeline." She sounded so shy that it was instantly endearing.

"You better go now," Madeline said. "But Maggie?"

"Yes?"

Her hands were fidgeting as she looked down to her feet again. "Are you are going to try and find this man?"

"Yes, I am," Maggie said. *And I will.*

"Then please, be careful. Camella wanted me to tell you that he's more dangerous now than he's ever been."

Stunned, Maggie could only manage one word. "Okay."

The Walrus Lady nodded one last time, and then turned and shuffled away.

Maggie stood in the cold air for a second longer, watching the old woman leave, noticing that the gait in her steps from down here on the street seemed more steady and sure, less wobbly than they did from the window above, on all those nights when this person who had just proven to be an ally had seemed like nothing but a freak, nothing but an oddity.

CHAPTER TWENTY-ONE

TWO HOURS LATER she was in a 2017 Kia Forte driving in a light rain, headed south, almost halfway to Philadelphia, her duffel bag at her side and the windshield wipers moving across the window in front of her, their scraping sound almost mesmerizing. Back and forth, back and forth. She had the radio on but not too loud, so she could hear her cell if it rang. Bruce Springsteen was carrying on about his glory days, and the irony was not lost on her.

Before long her mind began to wonder at how Michael had pulled this all off.

It had been a week since she'd last talked to Julie. Enough time for him to get to the West Coast and back, but only at a breakneck pace with all that he'd done, and with impeccable planning. Maggie remembered that in the last week she'd tried to call Julie twice. When she didn't answer, Maggie chalked it up to the usual chaos a new job causes. And besides . . . she'd still been getting her nightly texts.

"A STITCH IN TIME."

Every night. Like clockwork. And every night Maggie texted right back. "SAVES EIGHT."

It was a neat trick they had, but it was only meant to trigger alarm on Maggie's end. They never could have imagined that . . .

Her breathing was getting shallow. The last thing she needed was a panic attack. She hadn't had one for a few years, after fighting them most of her childhood, and this was certainly a situation that could trigger one again.

Slow down, Maggie. Breathe. Slowly. Be calm.

Then, sadly, she remembered that on a few nights they'd even chatted a little by text.

"HOW'S THE JOB?"

"GOING GOOD."

"WATCHA UPTO?"

"SUPER SUPER BUSY."

Eerily, she thought, *My God. I was probably trading messages with HIM, then.*

She imagined Michael, driving through Nebraska or something, texting her from the front seat, smiling at Maggie's messages, with Julie stuffed in the back seat, or worse, tied up in the trunk.

Don't. Don't go there.

She was jumping to conclusions. There was no proof that he drove. But Julie was too smart to be held at gun or knifepoint all the way through an airport, train station or bus terminal without saying something. And these days, good luck getting past all the security with an unwilling partner, or a weapon of any kind. It was possible, but highly unlikely.

He might've told her a story, that he was holding Maggie or something, so that she would be more apt to comply, but that didn't seem likely either.

Maggie was awash with guilt. All these weeks, when she'd thought herself free of him, he had simply made his way to another place. He'd not been chased away or scared away, but had simply diverted to some sick Plan B. While she'd been partying and trying to finally have a life, the noose around her sister's neck had been tightening. How many nights had he watched Julie? How many times had Julie thought she'd heard something just outside her window, only to find nothing when she went to check? In the other photos that were hanging in Maggie's living room, Julie had been eating with a friend, shopping, writing in a binder and crossing a street. And how many pictures had he taken before he decided to make his move?

And when he did, how did he do it? Did he hurt her? Had he hidden in her closet and caught her by surprise when she came home? Had he jumped her as she passed an alleyway, or simply walked up to her while she was getting out of her car? *Poor Jules. You weren't on guard. You had no idea. You didn't stand a chance.*

Maggie pulled her hair back hard and held it there, letting the slight pain at the roots at the front of her scalp relieve the pressure that was building in her head. She closed her eyes for a brief second, aware of the light traffic ahead and the headlights of an oncoming car in the opposite lane. *I just need a second. Just to close my eyes and not to think. Just a second.*

Instead that little voice in her head came back with a vengeance.

You've spent your whole life not thinking. About it. About anything, really.

"Shut up," she whispered into the emptiness of the car, opening her eyes again. "Just shut up."

That familiar voice in her head, her own voice, yet from

a different part of herself. It was getting louder by the hour now, and more insistent.

She diverted her attention back to the road, and Philadelphia. It occurred to her that "remembering" a place was more like remembering a moment. Despite herself, she did remember their first kiss, even remembered his fingers tilting her chin up, the smell of his aftershave mixing with the scents of the bouquet he'd just given her. His kiss had made her insides twirl. She remembered bringing her hand up to the side of his neck, simultaneously feeling his jaw and soft, long hair, and then feeling herself sink into him.

They were in a shopping village miles from the Liberty Bell. Their school groups had just finished lunch at Au Bon Pain when she and Michael had split off from the sight-seeing tour that was supposed to resume afterwards. But this was all years ago, with important details like street names impossible to recall because they were never recorded in the first place, which left her struggling to recall landmarks that might narrow the search for that particular floral shop, one of who-knew-how-many in a place as big as Philly. But she remembered a few things about that park. First, it was large, probably a square mile or so.

Looking up she noticed that she was approaching a toll booth on the I-95, which would now take her south to the New Jersey Turnpike. She paid the fee and then accelerated back up to speed as she returned her thoughts to the floral shop. It had been just outside the large park and was painted an odd teal color. Try as she might, she couldn't remember the name. She did remember one thing though: the display in front of the store had been rather large, shaped like a horseshoe that curved out onto the sidewalk.

Meanwhile, the nearby park had a playground themed around some sort of animal or something. Turtles? Yes. That was it. There were turtle sculptures near the playground and at the park entrance. She had noticed them that day as they walked back to rejoin their tour group, seeing all the children playing, running in circles, dressed in reds and yellows and blues and greens, the colors on their clothes swirling like the colors in her head, everything feeling so good and so right as she began the sudden and giddy process of falling in love with a madman. Michael held her hand softly and teased her gently as they passed the fountain, which had a ring of marble turtles in the center, each shooting a water spout into the air from its mouth.

Springsteen was gone now, and the night sky was open and alive, the moon full and large, casting ghostly light over some drifting clouds.

She played with the dial, her hand awash in the glow of the dashboard lights, and reassured herself. When she got to Philly she would Google "local parks with turtle fountain" and start looking. She'd find it, one way or another.

She laughed softly at the thought.

Because even then, when she did find the park? What then?

CHAPTER TWENTY-TWO

SHE HAD BEEN nine the next time she ventured into her grandfather's den. The room always seemed giant to her, with its floor-to-ceiling bookshelves along one wall, just behind the huge desk that her grandfather sat at, smoking his pipe and working patiently on his crossword puzzles, the sweet smell of pipe tobacco drifting over the room in a haze. Along another wall there were framed copies of The Bill of Rights and The Constitution, which hung alongside a portrait of two people Maggie was told were her great grandparents.

Beneath these portraits rested a small table with a detailed map on it, a push pin with the Irish flag stuck in its proper place on "The Isle" as her grandfather would call it, as if no further explanation were needed. Whenever a guest would come to visit, the pin was always the catalyst for one joke or another that her grandfather would have at the ready, able to get anyone to laugh, if not by the quality of the jokes then by the gregarious way in which he told them.

Maggie usually visited her grandparents on Sundays, right after church. Julie often spent the afternoon at their aunt Mini's home, since most of the kids from Julie's church class lived in the same neighborhood as their aunt. This gave Maggie's parents the rest of the day to themselves before the family reunited for dinner. Maggie usually spent the day making and baking that evening's dessert with her grandmother. But on this particular Sunday her grandmother wasn't feeling well, so the dessert, a boysenberry pie, had been provided by a neighbor, Mrs. Finch. Maggie, having nothing to do on a rainy day, had wandered into the den out of boredom.

"To what do I owe this pleasure, *me lady*?" her grandfather had said with an exaggerated Irish accent, smiling around the rim of his pipe, his pen perched in his hand over the paper.

Maggie smiled back. "Nothing. I'm just bored."

"Bored? My goodness! That's not a good thing. Not at all. Your grandmother is still sleeping?"

"Yes. She's pretty sick, huh?"

"Yep," he said, his white hair bouncing slightly as he nodded. "Just started coming down with it yesterday morning."

"Being sick is no fun," Maggie said.

"For *neither* one of you on a day like today, I imagine," her grandfather replied with a chuckle, looking out through the French doors at the falling rain outside.

Maggie simply nodded. "Did you read *all* those books, Pappy?" she asked.

"Oh heavens, no, dear," he replied, this time with full laughter. Reaching up to take the pipe from his mouth he swiveled his chair to have a look at the books himself. "They're mostly for show, hate to admit. Makes the clients

106

think I'm smart for some reason."

Her grandfather, an accountant, had many clients, though only the important ones ever came to the house. The rest went to his office in Scarborough.

"We missed you at church today," Maggie said.

"Well, that's sweet. But someone had to take care of your grandmother this morning. Though I don't think I could ever do as good a job as you're doing."

He had a mustache as white as his hair, and soft blue eyes that looked at her over the rim of his square-framed glasses with a tender love. "I've seen you go back and forth from the kitchen three times now."

"Yeah. First grandma wanted some toast. Then a glass of cold water. Last time I went I brought her some napkins." Maggie shrugged.

"Makes sense to me," he said with a nod.

"Mom and Dad aren't going to be back for a while, I guess, so I don't know what to do next."

"Well, it ain't much, but you could come over here and help me with this crossword puzzle. I'm kinda stuck."

"Really?" Maggie said. She had only tried doing a cross-word puzzle once before, with her mother when they had va-cationed at The Outer Banks the prior year.

"Sure, get on over here and hop up," he replied, motion-ing with his hand as he scooted his chair out from the desk.

Maggie ran over to him, overcome with excitement. Be-cause her grandfather had always been engrossed in one project or another in his den, sometimes working, some-times listening to old records, Maggie never liked bothering him.

Climbing onto his lap, she noticed right away all the neat objects on his desk: a gold pen holder engraved with the word "Kincaid," a desk calendar scribbled all over with notes, a stapler, and an old-style phone, the kind where the receiver rested on what looked like two "ys" and you still had to dial the numbers in a circle. A small statue of St. Jude stood at the right side of the desk, and there were stacks of green notebooks, each with a different name in black print written on the outside.

Directly in front of her was the famous *New York Times* crossword puzzle. She had no idea why it was famous, or what the *New York Times* was, but her grandfather was always boastful about finishing one. He'd usually time himself and announce to the world when he set a new personal record and then, without fail, remind them that this was no small feat—this was no rookie crossword puzzle, but the "famous *New York Times*" crossword puzzle. Maggie had only remembered it happening three times, and in each case everyone would nod, either impressed or pretending to be.

As Maggie studied the squares, she noticed that her grandfather had only written in a few words. The puzzle looked huge, with lots of numbers and questions, all in small print.

"Wow," she said.

"You ready for the big test, young lady?" he asked, putting the pen in her hand.

"Only if you help, Pappy."

"Don't worry. Together we can do anything," he replied, reaching up to turn off the small cooking timer he had positioned just above the paper. "Today we're off the clock, so there's no added pressure!"

"What do I do now?" Maggie asked.

"Pick a question."

"Oooookay . . . how about this one?"

"Eh." He thought for a moment. "That's a tough one for a first timer. Why not try this one over here? Let's see . . .

Hmm, they ask these questions kinda adult style so I'll have to translate it into kid talk, okay?"

She nodded.

"Alright then. It's a five-letter word and the clue is: red and used to make walls."

Maggie thought about it for a few moments, feeling the pleasant surprise in her mind as the answer popped up, seemingly out of nowhere, as if she had dug it up like a sea-shell at the beach. "Brick!"

"Wow! First time outta the gate and you get it right? Impressive."

She was both proud and nervous.

"What's the next question?" she asked, placing her elbows on the desk and her chin in her hands, eager in her excitement.

"Hmm. Let's see ..." He paused, scratching his forehead with his free hand, his face next to Maggie's as they peered over the puzzle. "Okay. Got it. It's the third wife of Henry VIII."

Maggie's eyes grew big.

"Oh. Dang. Sorry. Forgot to translate that one into kid talk." He laughed teasingly.

"You did that on purpose," Maggie said, looking over the side of her hand at him with a smirk.

"Well, maybe I did." He sighed, and then added under his breath, "If only because any word I got for any queen of England most likely ain't gonna be printable."

He sat in silence for a minute, and then said, "Ah. Bingo. Okay. Same name as your grandmother's best friend."

"Hmm ..." Maggie corkscrewed her face, trying to remember. Then it came to her: "Jane!"

"Oh! Two for two. The girl is definitely my granddaughter."

Maggie clapped her hands gleefully.

Outside the rain began to subside, the clouds in the sky shifting in that odd way that rain clouds do, so that the tone of light they cast goes from one shade of gray to the next, lighter and less depressing.

"You keep going at this rate, Maggie, and we'll be done in no time."

"Maybe I'll set a record."

"You think?"

"I think," she said with a confident nod.

"Yep. *Definitely* my granddaughter."

"So then . . . six letter word this time, and this one crisscrosses with the first question, got it?"

"Brick?"

"Yep. That's how these things get tricky. They start throwing letters into your head that maybe wouldn't be there otherwise, so you start thinking from where they want you to, instead of just thinking the obvious."

Maggie grew somber. "Huh?"

"Never mind," he said with a chuckle. "Six-letter word, starts with the letter "C", right there," he said, placing his finger on the next to last letter in "brick."

"Okay."

"It's a word for something you smile at."

Long minutes passed as Maggie struggled to think of what the word could be. Friend. Mirror. Tickle. None of them started with a "C."

Sitting there with her grandfather, the canopy of pipe tobacco filtering out around her, Maggie felt happy, as if she had just found a new friend. She always looked up to her grandfather, always noticed the way her father and Aunt Mini had revered him, and he had always doted over her, at least when she was younger. This was the first time she had spent any time alone with him, finally invited into his personal space, and it was special. She almost did not want to say the word when she guessed it.

"Camera!" she shouted.

They laughed loudly together in her excitement at being right once again. He watched her as she wrote the letters into the blocks, and as she did so Maggie thought to herself that if her Mom and Dad arrived at the house right then, she hoped that they brought their camera, like they sometimes did on the weekends, so they could take a picture of her and her grandfather.

Because she would've had the biggest smile ever.

CHAPTER TWENTY-THREE

THE TURNPIKE OPENED up for miles ahead of her, a dead spot between one place and the next. New York to Philadelphia was probably a nice drive during the day, but as the night wore on there was less and less to see. The radio had given way to a U2 song that went way back. She knew the album, *Boy*, and the song, "The Ocean," with its opening line about Dorian Gray, very well.

Her cell phone had not rung once, and the night had finally caught up to her, the adrenaline of events having now drained away. She was exhausted, and still unable to fully believe that this was happening. Any of it. She tried to reach back, to the apartment, to Zossima's image, to the Walrus Lady and what she said. But Maggie couldn't. It was as if her memory had fogged over, a side effect of something she could not grasp.

Then she thought of Julie.

In a snap, she realized it *was* real. She tried to imagine her sister jammed into the trunk of the blue Honda, or worse, tied up in a hotel room somewhere.

After the toll on the NJ-90 and going over the Betsy Ross Bridge, she saw a sign for the last interchange ahead. Her phone GPS said that beyond this awaited the 676 and then downtown Philadelphia. She reached into her bag and pulled out a hair tie, using it to quickly pull her hair into a ponytail.

Before long the lights of the city ahead began to blink into existence, sparse at first, then more and more of them with each mile she traversed. She reached up and turned off the radio, cutting off the opening riffs of a Van Halen song. She wanted silence now, if only to think. She spent the next few moments alternating between watching the road signs and trying to figure out what she would do once she got downtown. She'd made good time; it was 4:00 a.m. How likely was it that Michael would risk hanging out at the park with Julie at that hour? Doing so was bound to catch the attention of the police, the homeless, or college types leaving the after parties. Michael wasn't likely to take that chance. She didn't know what car he was driving, he'd ditched Julie's phone . . . it was maddening. There was no way to contact him. She had to wait until he contacted her.

Off the road, to the right, was a Frankie's Bagels in a mini-mall, its lights still on and an "Open 24 Hours" sign blinking in the window. She reconsidered her idea to push on. Until he called she was kind of stuck, anyway. She would get a cup of coffee and something to settle her stomach and then use this time on her phone to research parks around the Liberty Bell. There most likely was more than one and she could use the rest of the early morning hours to canvas them.

She pulled the car into the parking lot and eased into a space, feeling bone-weary. Just the act of stopping the car and shifting her focus from the road made her want to re-cline the seat and go to sleep, but what her body was begging for, her mind would not allow. She got out of the car and walked into the bagel shop, the smell of freshly baking bread filling the air, which abruptly took her back for a moment to her grandmother's kitchen ... sprinkling flour across the cutting boards ... kneading dough alongside her ... when they would bake together, before Maggie stopped going over.

An employee walked out with a wet rack that she was drying. Appearing to be in her early forties, with dirty blond hair that hung just to her shoulders and a skinny frame, she looked surprised to see Maggie. "What can I do ya for?" she asked curtly.

"Can I get a cup of coffee and a cinnamon raisin bagel?" Maggie asked politely, rubbing her eyes.

The woman looked around and out into the parking lot, her hazel eyes a bit wary. "24 Hours" sign or not, it was ob-vious that she wasn't used to seeing people at this hour. "Sure. But the stuff on display is a day old now. Still about an hour or so away from any fresh ones."

Maggie shrugged. "That's fine. I'll take what you have. Easy on the spread."

She nodded. "Coffee's fresh, though. I need that myself to make it through the shift."

"Great. Thanks."

Once served and paid up, Maggie took a seat at a tiny table in the corner and got to work. She went straight to Google Maps and looked up Independence Hall. From there she split her fingers across the screen patiently, zooming out a little at a time, until she found patches of green that sug-gested a park area. She poked and zoomed in on each one. Roosevelt Park wasn't the one, nor was Mariposa, which was far too small. Their shuttle van on the day of the field trip had driven for a while, but she couldn't remember in which direction. Too many years had gone by. So she kept at it, moving south of Independence Hall first before deciding she'd gone too far, then north-east next, where she struck gold instantly. She scoffed at the obviousness of it all.

"Turtle Park." I should've known. What else do you name a park with turtles all over the damn place?

From there she zoomed in and worked her way around the circumference of the park. This part was a bit more painstaking. There were a lot of streets and a search for "floral shops near Turtle Park" gave her nothing. Finally, after a good fifteen minutes, she found it, tucked inside a tiny alcove near the back entrance. Astoria's Floral Shop. The name was not familiar, but when she zoomed to street view there was no mistaking the storefront or entrance filled in a semi-circle wall of flowers.

The park name had been easy, the shop name not so much. Because it was hard to find words and names sometimes.

Life could be a lot like a crossword puzzle; the toughest answers were usually the ones that were the most obvious.

But to Maggie this was an odd thought, because she never did crossword puzzles.

She hated them.

CHAPTER TWENTY-FOUR

A HALF HOUR LATER, unable to wait any longer, she arrived at Turtle Park.

She parked at the farthest end of the street, fighting her instincts to stay in the safe confines of the car. Better to approach by foot. Putting on her parka to fend off the bitter cold, she stepped out the car and looked around. There was no one in sight. One hand shot immediately into her pocket, her index finger slipping into the trigger guard of her gun as her thumb switched off the safety.

The corner where they'd once kissed was remarkably unchanged, physically, after all these years, but it was different nonetheless. The floral shop was still there, though closed for the night, like all the businesses on the street. There was not a bar or restaurant in sight, and the horseshoe end of the cul-de-sac was lit only by a half dozen street lamps that left far too many gaps of darkness between them. Beyond the street lamps lay the near pitch black of the park, a set of dim walkway lights leading off into its depths, with trees on all sides that dripped with an eerie silence.

She took a deep breath. *If I have to walk into that park I might just lose it.*

The buildings around her were cast in the dark shadows of night, their brownstone or brick facades muted, tinged only with a disconcerting mix of the white light from the moon and the yellow light from the street lamps, bathing sections in an odd sort of urine color.

Most of the area was commercial, but there were some upper-floor apartments on either side of the street, a few with lights still on in the windows. She noticed that all the curtains were drawn shut, casting a cloth veil between her and any would-be rescuers if things went poorly. Just enough distance to allow them to ignore her screams, she imagined, and to shield their consciences should the police come knocking later.

From somewhere she heard running water, then saw the faint outline of a drainage pipe at the mouth of the alleyway to her right. There were cars on either side of the street, a white Lincoln and a green Pinto nearest her and to the right, and five vehicles, a Mustang, two Hondas, a new Mercedes and an ominous looking late model Chevy van to her left.

I need to advance up the street . . .

Stay to the right, more light on that side . . .

And fewer cars for him to hide between . . .

And stay as far away from that damn van as you can . . .

What if I'm wrong? What if he didn't mean for me to come—

Her cell phone finally rang, causing her to jump. She reached into her pocket with her free hand, pulled it out, then looked at the caller ID.

It was blocked.

She answered.

"Peek-a-boo, I see you."

His voice was like a Q-tip plunged deep into her ear.

Maggie couldn't speak. She looked around, to the end of the street, behind her, then up again at the apartment windows, half expecting to see him looking out from one. He could be anywhere. She'd never left herself exposed from this many angles.

"Cat got your tongue?" He chuckled. "Oh. Sorry. Bad time for a cat joke, huh?"

"Where are you?" she asked.

"Here, or there."

She suspected instantly that he was bluffing. That he was nowhere around.

"Michael, I want Julie back."

"Ah, ah, ah, ah."

"What?"

"No demands. I'm the one that gets to make the demands now. You look so pretty, Mags."

Her heart seized in her chest.

"I always liked your hair in a ponytail."

She exhaled, her heart out of the gate now and on a full trot. He *was* here. He *could* see her.

"It always brought out the kid in you. Though I have to say, that jacket is a bit big on you."

"I'm here, Michael, so now what?" Her mind looped to a lesson from one of her rape prevention classes, and so she moved towards the center of the street.

She heard him sigh.

"You're no fun anymore."

"I want to talk to Julie."

118

"You'll have your chance . . . when I say so."

Her eyes went where her instincts told her to take them: out into the darkness of the park. She squinted to see on either side of the lighted trail. Nothing. But she was still too far away to see clearly into the distance. She began to move rapidly up the street towards the park, advancing to the buffer zone of light between the last licks of asphalt and the first line of grass.

"Michael, Julie had better—"

"What are you afraid of, honey? You afraid I'm gonna slap her around a bit? Like that nosey chink in Miami who lived downstairs from you?"

"Kim." Maggie did not ask it, but rather affirmed it.

"Yeah. Kim. What was her last name? 'Kim,' too? Kim Kim? Or was it Kim Chee?" He laughed.

"That's not funny."

"She was so on your side, huh, Maggie?"

"You shouldn't have done that."

"Oh, do I sense a little anger?"

"She never did anything to you."

"Except get in my way. I warned her a few times, did she tell you?"

Yes, she did, you bastard. You called her one day and told her that you liked her hair, that it would be a shame if someone ever cut it all off.

"She just wouldn't listen."

When that didn't work, Kim washed the soap off her face in the shower one day, only to open her eyes to see you staring at her from the small window above the stall.

"She was worried about me, Michael, that's all."

"She was jealous of us, Maggie. Of what we had."

"You didn't have to hurt her like that."

"She stuck her nose in business that wasn't hers."

Maggie remembered the day, in late August, the last time she would ever speak to Kim, her face peeking out at Maggie from behind the door of her apartment, her security chain still locked, and refusing to let Maggie in. She was crying, her long straight black hair now shorn and choppy, splotches of her scalp red and exposed.

"You practically scalped her, Michael. First you threatened to do it, then you did."

"Is that all you think I did?"

Maggie didn't know what he meant, and a part of her didn't want to know.

He chuckled. "Of course. She was, if nothing else, a smart girl. I told her that if she ever told you I would come back and kill her. I must've been . . . convincing. I scared her so bad I don't think she even dared to call the police. So . . . she never told you that I did her that day?"

Maggie was stunned. "That's a lie."

"Oh, but I did. Towards the end I think she actually started to enjoy it. The anger in her eyes just seemed to melt away."

Oh my God. Poor Kim.

Maggie had begged for Kim to let her in that day. Remembering the moment now, Maggie had to ask herself: hadn't Kim looked much like Zossima had? Her eyes dead and accusing. *Look what he did to me. You told me he was jealous, maybe a little crazy. You never told me he was psychotic.*

The worst part of it was that it was true. Maggie *had* watered down the truth about Michael, just a bit, just enough to make a new friend, because that was back when she decided that her best protection would be just that: friends. A circle of them, who could act as sentries, as a sort of early warning defense system. Back then the math of having a half dozen set of eyes looking for him seemed to make more sense than having just her own. But that math had proven faulty. Kim had told Maggie to go away, that she never wanted to see or talk to her again, before slamming the door in Maggie's face.

"Psst! You still there?" he said with a chuckle.

"You sick bastard. She never did anything to hurt you."

"Oh, you mean like telling you not to talk to me those nights I called, then hanging up on me when she would answer your phone for you? And what about the self-defense classes, Maggie? Did she take you to those to help you learn to do anything *but* hurt me?"

"Michael . . ."

"Maggie?" It was Julie's voice now.

"Julie!"

"Oh, Maggie . . ." Julie was sobbing hysterically into the phone. "Please help me, Maggie, please."

Maggie closed her eyes, the tears inside her springing out against her will. There was no holding them back. No holding any of it back. This nightmare was real, come full force into the waking world.

"Now, we've got to get going. It's been a nice chat though," Michael said.

"Michael, please, just stop this. You can have me back, okay? Just don't hurt her anymore."

He was chuckling again. "Poor, Maggie. You have it all wrong . . ."

He's in the park somewhere. He has to be.

"You seem to be assuming . . ."

Surrendering all caution, Maggie ran into the park—

"That if I have you . . ."

The phone pressed to her ear—

"I won't hurt her . . ."

Her eyes scanning in every direction—

"When actually, hurting her is becoming almost as fun . . ."

She plunged into the dark of the park, leaving the sanctuary of the streetlights behind her, the smell of dew-covered grass and wet bark flaring into her nostrils.

"As hurting you."

Maggie pulled out her gun and slowed to a jog, bringing it up in front of her, close to her body. There was sweat on her ear, which was still pressed hard against the phone. Despite the cold she was sweating all over, as if she had a fever.

"Look, we can talk, Michael. Just stop this."

"What will you tell your parents, Mags?"

She stopped cold in her tracks, a good fifty feet inside the park now, her eyes struggling to acclimatize to the darkness. To her right she could see the monkey bars and the sandpit of the play area, the cast iron turtles scattered like stone golems between the slides and the jungle gym. There were no children with their parents here to see anything now, no laughter to caress the air and make it a safe place. It was night. Everyone knew it wasn't a good idea to come to the park at night.

"What are you talking about, Michael?"

He'd struck a nerve in her, and brutally so. Hadn't this been the exact thing weighing on her mind, almost the entire drive down here? *What do I tell Mom and Dad?*

"How will you tell them that you came *so* close to saving her?"

Maggie's eyes began to water again. She wiped at them furiously. There were trees scattered everywhere, their thick trunks barely outlined by the small lights along the cement path. Was he behind one of them?

"I'm close, aren't I? Where are you?"

"Poor Maggie. You've been running *from* me for so long, you just can't help doing it even now."

She heard a car engine start up.

From behind her.

From the cul-de-sac.

She spun around to face the street just as his headlights came on, blinding her. Stunned, she brought both arms up to shield her eyes.

The car whipped away from the sidewalk, making a U-turn as Maggie screamed "No!" and broke into a full run after it.

CHAPTER TWENTY-FIVE

As THE HEADLIGHTS turned away and strafed the walls of the buildings, she made out the car. It was the white Lincoln. The one she'd been no more than twenty feet away from when she'd answered his call.

I walked right past him!

The Lincoln began to speed off down the street as Maggie broke into the light of the street lamps, breathing heavy, almost tripping on the sidewalk as she brought the phone back up to her ear.

"Michael. Stop! Don't leave!"

A full block away, the Lincoln's brake lights flashed on. It slowed to a stop, puffs of hot air billowing from the exhaust. Finally, he spoke. "You were *so* close, Maggie. But it's time to get back to memory lane now, okay? So far it's been pretty fun, don't ya think? Ready for your clue?"

"Don't do this, Michael. Please stop."

"I'm hungry for a sky-high burger, baby."

"No. Just let this end here. I'll see it your way now, Michael. I'll see it any way you want me to see it, just leave Julie out of it."

The car continued to idle for a long while.

Sensing hope, Maggie walked slowly up the street towards it. "This isn't Julie's fault. Any of it."

"Hmm."

"Please don't run from me anymore, Michael."

"Ah." And suddenly his voice was pained. "How many nights . . . have I asked the same thing of you?"

"Listen, I will—"

"And what did you do, Maggie?"

"I'm sorry. I just—"

"*What* did you *do!*"

"Michael . . ."

"Just answer the question, Maggie. All those nights I told you how much I missed you and begged you to just love me again, to give us another chance, and what did you do?"

She closed her eyes, hot tears scattering down her face, tracing lines into the snot that poured from her nose.

"I . . . I . . . kept . . ." Her voice was catching now between sobs, but she forced herself to finish. "I kept running."

"Exactly." Then he hung up.

The red of the brake lights evaporated into the cool night air as the rear tires of the Lincoln peeled into the street.

"Stop!" she screamed after him, after the car, and after her sister inside it.

Dammit. I can't let him get away.

She bolted to her car, jamming the phone into her pants pocket as she fumbled for her keys.

Michael made a left at the corner just as Maggie pulled open her car door.

You're not getting away from me. You're not!

She started the car, accelerated to the same corner and saw him up ahead, just making another left. Slamming her foot onto the gas pedal, forcing herself into a reckless turn, the Forte's wheels squealed but held.

He made a quick right down an alley.

Maggie followed. She held her breath and jerked the wheel, swinging the front end of her car into the alley and plunging into an obstacle course of trash cans and boxes. She noticed a few loading docks and surmised that they were driving behind a grocery store of some sort. Ahead of her, Michael accelerated through the alley and out the other side, sliding his car carefully into another intersection.

Shit!

He'd made the turn easily into the sparse, early morning traffic. Blind luck. A luck that Maggie couldn't manage. Braking a tad too late, she slid partly into the nearest lane of traffic, forcing an approaching Explorer to slam on the brakes, its headlights stopping only feet from Maggie's front end. She forced herself into the lane, all the while keeping an eye on the Lincoln. Michael had just cut over into the fast lane and was now speeding away.

She was on a four-lane road and amazed at how many people were driving this early on a Saturday morning. Early morning shift workers, delivery drivers and probably more than a few people making the "drive of shame" home. Whatever. They were out and about, making this harder than it had to be. She looked forwards just in time to see Michael pull a swift left at the next boulevard.

She slammed on the gas. Eying a gap barely wide enough for her car between a Mercedes and a pickup truck, she shot through it and was showered with honks. She had twenty feet to make her turn and stay on Michael's tail, but it was too late. Ahead of her the approaching traffic was already closing in, creating a wall of white light and steel across the other side of the intersection that would force her to brake and await another opening before she could follow.

Screw it.

She turned the wheel a full thirty feet short of the intersection, taking a crude, diagonal turn. More horns blared. Michael was ahead of her now by two blocks. The Forte's engine roared loudly beneath the hood as Maggie glanced into the rearview mirror quickly, expecting to see police lights, partly fearing and partly hoping that she would.

I'm still not gaining. My God, how fast is he going?

She pushed the pedal to the floor, her car spurting up to forty, then fifty miles an hour.

Michael now seemed to hesitate, as if he were checking to see if he had shaken her. Apparently seeing that he hadn't, he sped up again, Maggie having now closed to within less than a block of him. She braced for another quick left, expecting the cat and mouse game to continue across more oncoming traffic. Instead he pulled into the slow lane. Maggie followed, coming up hard behind him.

At the last second he did the unthinkable.

He braked.

Hard.

For one split second Maggie froze, before her mind fired off its own directive to her foot to slam on her brakes too. She imagined crashing into the rear of his car. If Julie was in the trunk, Maggie would crush her to death.

Yet, as her body went into its own set of movements, she second guessed the idea to stop so suddenly, knowing what would happen if she did so. Hard braking on a wet road could only mean one thing and—

It was too late.

127

She went into a free-for-all spin, the red and white car lights forming a pattern broken momentarily by the lighted windows of the shops that had been to her right and the golden arches of the McDonald's that had been to her left. There were so many lights spinning around her it was as if she were stuck inside a Christmas tree.

She braced for the collision that had to come, the car spinning endlessly until at last it came to a stop. When it did, her body was coiled so tight it was all she could do to exhale. Miraculously, no one had hit her.

The last thing she had seen was Michael's car making a right down a street up ahead.

She drove to that street and peered around. It was the only way he could've gone. Squinting, she saw that a half block ahead of her was another cross street, which was a two way. He could have gone either direction. Or he could have gone straight ahead. Or worse. Far worse. He could've taken a freeway on-ramp that lay just beyond the intersection to the left.

She drove forwards and stopped at the intersection, a wave of anxiety convulsing her, the adrenaline of the chase colliding now with the decision that lay in front of her, forcing her to take shallow breaths.

No! God, what if I pick the wrong one?

She screamed in frustration and banged both her hands on the steering wheel.

Think, Maggie. Just stop a second and THINK!

She took the Rubric's cube in her mind and began rapidly turning the colors, backwards and forwards, coloring one side at a time.

He had told her to go home. No. No, he hadn't. She'd asked him where *he* was going and he had said something. What was it?

128

I'm hungry for a sky-high burger, baby!

She looked at the interstate sign in front of her. It was the I-95. South.

It had been a long time since she'd been south of Philly on the 95, so long that she was not sure she was correct in her original assumption. Then all the colors to all the blocks fell magically into place. There was a "side of the road" commuter diner from the fifties, south of here, famous for their big burgers. They used to stop by when going up the coast on weekend trips when they were in school. She couldn't recall the name, exactly, but that must've been what he was referring to. He was headed south.

Time began to warp back and forth, from now to then, and in a very sad way Maggie remembered herself, years before, a college girl in love and crazy with life, stopping in this town or the other, still alive with the buzz of the prior night's partying or the excitement of a new adventure. Michael wanted to take—drag her, really—down memory lane. But that was a problem. They'd had so many adventures, up and down the East Coast—camping in Shenandoah National Park, driving to Virginia University for a weekender, to Labor Day weekend in Ocean City, Maryland . . . dozens and dozens of moments—that it was hard to tell which memory was the one that mattered most right now.

She had to be right about this.

Finally feeling that she was, she sped to the on-ramp.

CHAPTER TWENTY-SIX

AN HOUR INTO THE drive her mind had exhausted itself with the possibilities of how this would all play out. Slowly, the reality of the situation began to mount. She tried desperately to get around his threats, and to find a way that would allow her to turn this game over to the proper authorities.

But, again, she knew better. The authorities had failed her every step of the way, for the last five years, and this was the dominant truth that kept coming back at her. She remembered the very first time that she'd ever turned to them, those magic knights in uniforms and badges, who she had been raised to respect and admire, when Michael had threatened to kill her.

Maggie had come home one day and found him sitting in the living room of her apartment, calm as could be, as if he had been invited over to "Netflix and chill" or something. After they'd argued for the fiftieth time over why it had to end, over why things wouldn't work out, he had taken a book—*Leaves of Grass* by Walt Whitman, she recalled—and smashed it directly through the center of her glass coffee table.

"If I ever see you with another man, I swear to God I will kill you," he said.

It was at that exact moment Maggie realized what an "object" she'd become in his eyes. Indignant that he would ever say such a thing to her, as if he had any right over her body or her life, she still bit her tongue as he turned and walked out the front door. There was something in his eyes. Something menacing and final.

She watched him pull away from the curb and wondered how this had happened, all this craziness that was supposed to have been a love story of some sort. They'd met, fallen in love, and things had just accelerated from there. Too quickly. Before long, she became the marble in a Chinese puzzle board, bouncing through the maze of their relationship uncontrollably, one dead end to the next, until she struck a corner and fell into a hole at the other end. At first she told herself that this happened to lots of women, that they found themselves in exactly the same situation after a series of small, incremental surrenders—letting slide the first time their lover doubted their fidelity or questioned a number on their cell phone, or after they outright accused them . . . or hit them.

Maggie looked over the remains of the shattered coffee table. It was only getting worse, so she did what most anyone would do. She turned to the police for help. And right from the start things were not as she imagined they would be.

She called 911 only to be told by the operator that if Michael was not present in her home or preventing her from leaving her home, she would have to go down to the nearest police station to file a police report. So she had done so, making the ten minute drive, a bit annoyed but angry enough to insist that "something" had to be done.

At the station she was forced to wait almost two hours while the desk officer made his way through the six people who had arrived there ahead of her, one to report a stolen radio, another filing a complaint about a neighbor's vicious dog, the third and fourth arguing about one another parking too near to the other's driveway, the fifth to give a long winded explanation for why she believed the two women who had recently moved in across the street from her were actually prostitutes running a business out of their home, and lastly, an elderly man who had come in to report his own mugging.

When Maggie's turn finally came, she was greeted with raised eyebrows when she began her story, the officer's face a pasty white, a pimple on his chin.

"What does your boyfriend look like?"

"Ex-boyfriend."

He shrugged, as if all the lovers who quarreled their way to the police said that.

"Okaaaay. What does your *ex*-boyfriend look like?"

"He's about six foot four, two hundred and twenty pounds. He has long hair—"

Officer Pasty Face cut her off. "What was he wearing today?"

"A black t-shirt and a pair of blue Abercrombie and Fitch shorts, with gray Toms."

"Were there any witnesses?"

"Excuse me?"

"Was anyone with you when he said this to you?"

"No."

He nodded and kept on scribbling. "Has he ever threatened you like this before?"

"No."

"Were either of you drinking at the time?"

Maggie was immediately put off by the "either of you" part of the question. She didn't know it then, but it would be the first time, of many times to come, when she would find her own integrity questioned in the midst of the situation. As if she were fifty percent to blame for being a victim.

"No. I wasn't."

"Was he?"

"How the hell should I know?"

"Ma'am, I'm just trying to get your statement."

"And maybe I'm just a dumbass, but I thought I *already* gave it: my ex-boyfriend just threatened to kill me!"

"Yeah. I got that. But my job here is to find out, at least up front, in the statement, what the actual risk is here. If he was drunk and talking nonsense, or irrational and flying off the handle, or if he is the type of character who would really follow up on it."

"Well, can't you go arrest him or have some officers talk to him or something?"

"No, ma'am. I can't."

"Why the hell not?"

"Because no actual physical assault took place and—"

"What? He has to *hit* me first?"

"—and because there were no witnesses to what you claim he said."

"Wait. 'Claim?' Are you kidding me?"

"Ma'am, you say the two of you have been having issues now for a few months, right? Fine. I understand. I do. Now he has said something that has crossed the line, but the fact of the matter is—"

She was beyond stunned, over the hill of shock and now deep in the valley of incredulous. "The fact of the matter is he threatened to *kill* me."

"Yes. I know that. As a matter of law, he has made a threat against you, and that is equivalent to an assault without battery, but without witnesses I can bet you dollars to donuts he will deny he ever said it, and at the end of the day, as a matter of law, it's his word against yours."

"So what're you saying?"

"I'm saying that I will file your report, so that it is a matter of public record. But at this point there isn't much more I can do."

"You can't be serious!"

He sighed then, this desk officer who was all of thirty years old, and stuck out his chin, rotating it side to side, as if this were some sort of stress relief exercise he'd learned.

"Ma'am." He glanced down at the sheet. "Ms. Kincaid, look, I can send a cruiser by his home if you would like me to. Maybe it'll throw a scare into him. But we get complaints like this all the time, and usually they don't amount to much."

Maggie shook her head in disbelief. "Usually?"

"My guess is he had a few drinks before he came over and shot his mouth off. Does he work?"

"Yes."

"Where?"

"Giles and Succermore."

He pinched up his face. "Is that a law firm?"

"Yes."

"So he's a lawyer?" he asked with a small sense of dread in his voice, as if now he regretted the offer to send the cruiser by Michael's house.

"No. He's a law student. He's interning there."

"Ah-ha. Okay. So he's in law school, interning at a firm, hoping to have a great career?"

"What difference does that make?"

"Hey. Anybody is capable of anything, ma'am. But he sounds to me like a guy who has a lot to lose if he does something stupid. My guess is he goes home, sobers up, and in the morning calls you to apologize."

"And if he doesn't?"

"I'm going to give you a copy of the report. Keep it. If he makes any sort of statement that is similar in any way to the one he said today, call us immediately and we will make sure he gets a visit, okay?"

Maggie exhaled in disbelief that this was all that could be done when someone threatened your life.

The officer had signed his name at the bottom of the report and Maggie looked at his name badge: Endem.

It was a name she would never forget.

Because in the years of terror that would follow, his name would always come to mind as the first person that was given the opportunity to stop what would become the nightmare that overtook her life. She always imagined that Officer Endem had simply played the odds. He'd said as much to her face that day. There simply wasn't enough for anyone to go on, from the reporting officer to the detective that would be asked to follow up on it, to the DA that would be asked to file charges or the judge who would be asked to sign either the restraining order or the arrest warrant. It was all a process. And maybe Officer Endem was right, maybe most of the time the situation just fizzled out.

But he wasn't.

CHAPTER TWENTY-SEVEN

IT WAS JUST MAGGIE'S luck that her case would prove to be that one case in a thousand that had spiraled completely out of control. From DC to Virginia, to Miami and then Chicago, and from there to New York and now, to a lonely stretch of highway leading her back to Virginia, it had become like a runaway train. In between, she filed five separate restraining orders before five separate judges. All to no avail.

Michael simply did what he always did: he adapted. He knew with his law experience that restraining orders only covered the individual named and cited.

So he simply kept changing his name.

Never legally, mind you. Oh no, that would create a trail of aliases. But if immigrants from China and Mexico with no clue as to how to get a fake ID in this country could still manage to do so within days after arriving by land or sea, how much easier was it for a well-to-do Virginia boy with more than enough money in the bank? Birth certificates and passports could be falsified just well enough to get you the driver's license or Social Security card that you needed that would tie out to someone who was dead or an unwitting victim of identity theft.

Maggie remembered a night in Chicago, when he'd followed her home from a club. She flagged down a police cruiser that was coming down the street, and the officer had stopped Michael to answer some questions. Seeing the terror in Maggie's eyes as she stood just fifteen feet away, he hadn't bought Michael's story. At all. He put Michael in cuffs and leaned him against the back of his car while he checked on his ID and info. The end result was to be expected. The officer—once again, as a *matter of law*—had been forced to release him after everything came back over the radio in confirmation of the fact that Michael's new name was Philip Dourmand. The officer's only available action was a meager gesture to let Maggie walk away first, while he held "Philip" for a while longer.

Then there was the detective in Miami who had "played it all out" for her one day, his yellow shirt sweaty at the armpits and his chin covered with a thick goatee that made him look older than he was, his bronze face handsome and yet frustrated.

"Ms. Kincaid," he had said, "we understand your frustration. This guy, as you say, has been bothering you a long time. He calls you and follows you and scares you, but he's smart."

Maggie had been stunned by the statement, and almost hurt by it. "What do you mean?"

"He's yet to lay a hand on you, and that's when we have a chance to get a little more serious about stuff like this. There's a law against making terrorist threats against someone, and according to you, he makes them. But each time there's no witness. That's intentional. He calls, says it, and in a few instances here you have it on tape," he had said, waving his hand over a few message machine tapes Maggie had brought in with her, "but, even then, he's jacking up his voice so we could never prove it was him from the damn 7-Eleven clerk. We haven't checked, but I'm guessing he's calling you from a pay phone, and probably never the same damn one."

"But you could check?"

"Yes, we could." He sighed, running his hand through his thick black hair, his other hand resting on the humidity-ruined crease in his brown cotton pants. "But let's say we nab his ass. He's still only making threats. He has yet to follow up on them."

"So he has to actually hurt me before you can stop him?"

The detective blinked sadly at her, and nodded slightly.

"The truth is, we can toss him in jail for only so long for making threats against you. Recordings like yours are hard to get admitted in court, and even if you got them in and could prove it was his voice, even then he is making very ambiguous threats, at best."

Maggie put her head in her hands. "But he *is* threatening me."

"When he says stuff like 'It would make me very angry' or 'I am running out of patience' the threat is implied, not stated openly. You said he went to law school?"

"Yes."

"Then it's no wonder. He's avoiding the things that would 'stick,' as it were."

"What the hell are you telling me? That you have to wait for him to kill me before something will 'stick!'"

"No. Not quite. We need him to slip up in public, when you have a witness present to hear the threat or . . ." He paused, shifted uncomfortably in his chair and glanced out the window.

"Or what?" Maggie asked.

"Or the assault, the actual physical assault," he answered, before attempting to reassure her by quickly adding, "if one were to ever take place."

"This is crazy."

He responded with silence.

"Okay then, let's say someone sees him beat me up or hears him threaten me, what then?"

"Ms. Kincaid, I don't know—"

"*What* then?"

He picked up a pen on his desk and twirled it between his fingers. "Does he have a criminal record?"

"I sincerely doubt it."

"Me too." The pen came to a stop in his palm. "With no priors, the threat, taken in light of the restraining orders you've filed, would probably get him from probation to six months. The battery, depending on the severity, six months to three years."

"Shit! That's *it*?"

"Ms. Kincaid, I'm sorry to be the one to have to tell you all this."

"And what if he actually does what he says he will do?"

"Ms. Kincaid, please, don't . . ."

"What if he actually kills me, Detective?" she asked, her throat tight with anger and frustration.

The detective pinched up his mouth and shook his head slightly, a look coming over his face that conveyed what Maggie imagined to be a wish that someone else had offered to help her when she'd first walked in.

"Twenty years to life," he said, before deciding to add, "Florida has the death sentence but it's rarely applied."

Maggie nodded in disbelief, and then stood up quickly

to leave.

"Ms. Kincaid?"

Her emotions were rising like a tsunami. "No. Just forget it!"

"Ms. Kincaid, please. Can I offer you some advice?"

Maggie stopped and wiped a hand across her eyes. A few other detectives in the room glanced over at her and then continued about their work.

"Yes?" she said, and it was the last time she would ever allow herself to hope for an easy answer to any of it, ever again.

"Do what you say *he* is doing."

"What?"

The detective stood up, sidled around the edge of his desk and placed his hand her gently on her arm. "Look. It may sound crazy, but just change your name. You have the restraining orders and everything to get the record sealed. You could simply move somewhere and he wouldn't be able to track you by your name, social, credit cards or anything. Not even a private investigator could access a sealed record of name change."

Maggie smiled weakly, stunned.

Of course.

All she had to give up was her name.

Like a bride.

To a man who didn't deserve the privilege in love, much less now in hate.

"I will never give him my name, in any way," she replied, reaching up to take the detective's hand from her arm. "I would rather die first."

She turned and walked out his office and into the humid Miami air beyond the front door of the station house, utterly crushed by the picture that had just been painted for her, and by the pathetic solution she'd been offered in the end.

Maggie blinked, back now in the Forte on the highway to Virginia, her memories retreating back toward the cunning embrace of her mind.

She glanced at the clock. It was 6:00 a.m.

Her pride that day in Miami had given birth to a monstrosity now, a thing that would've been better served had it been aborted.

"I should've just changed my name," she said into the empty space of the car.

And he would have taken Julie anyway. Or your mom. Or your dad. When he couldn't find you. Hasn't he just proven how far he will go to get to you?

Yes. Yes, he had.

And through all her memories, of Officer Endem on "Day One" and all the days and courtrooms that had followed, to the good-hearted cop in Chicago who tried to get it right, to all the cops and detectives afterwards, their faces and names blending together, to that detective in Miami who had tried to "play it all out" for her, she had arrived at a critical conclusion: as a matter of law, the law could not help her.

She tried to tell herself that maybe, just maybe, it'd be different with the FBI. It was a kidnapping case, like she'd thought about before, and now an interstate one at that. But they had rules to play by too. Too many rules.

Even if she called for help and those G-men got their man, what then? What did kidnapping get you? Ten years, or twenty? How many of those ten or twenty years would she *really* have *any* peace, knowing that someday he would get out? How many nights would she have to pray for the merciful news that some other inmate had stabbed him to death? How many times would she hear on TV of a jailbreak and have to brace herself to hear if it was from whatever jail they had holed him up in?

She couldn't do it.

The only law Maggie was willing to rely on now was her own.

If this made her as crazy as Michael, so be it.

CHAPTER TWENTY-EIGHT

WHEN SHE SAW Piccolo Pete's Diner in the distance she pulled off the road so quickly that she almost lost control of the car and plunged headlong into a field of brush and weeds.

She'd nearly forgotten about this place. In college, when they would have a semester break or make long weekend plans to party with friends in Philadelphia, ski in Rochester or, as was the case one year, go to Niagara Falls, Maggie and Michael always stopped for food at Piccolo Pete's. It was a tradition. Sure enough, there on the sign, just beneath the picture of exploding fireworks, were the words "Home of the Sky-High Burger."

Again, she heard his voice echo in her head: *"I'm hungry for a sky-high burger, baby!"*

Maggie eased the Forte forwards and was stunned to see the white Lincoln he was driving parked directly in front of the diner, sandwiched on the left by a Suburban and on the right by a trailer truck. Besides two big rigs parked towards the back of the small parking lot, there were no other vehicles. She'd been right about taking the highway and right about where he was headed, but she couldn't believe that he'd actually stopped for a bite to eat.

This has to be a trap.

She realized her headlights were still on. She killed them. The sun was beginning to claw its way over the horizon anyway, its rays like fingers reaching for a handhold on the day.

The car and diner were a few hundred feet away. She coasted to a stop on the side of the road and rummaged through the options in her head. She could walk up to the car, slowly, from behind. There was a chance that he'd gotten cocky and thought he'd lost her. You never knew. He might be asleep inside. Or he could be in the diner, eating. But if so, where did he have Julie?

In the trunk. He'd have to have her in the trunk.

The thought that Julie could be right there, within reach, forced her to act. She spun the wheel and pulled back out onto the road, her foot pushing hard against the gas pedal as she sped into the open parking area.

Block his ass in.

She pulled the Forte up quickly behind his car, parking it at an angle, and jumped out.

This close to the diner she could make out a few people inside. One of them, a man in his late forties with a baseball cap on, stared out at her through the nearest window, a coffee cup in one hand, his face twisted with a quizzical look. A heavyset waitress with red hair glanced up briefly from her spot at the register before returning to whatever it was she was reading at the counter.

She scanned the inside of the diner for anyone who

looked like Michael. There were two other patrons, an elderly couple sitting near the door and talking, but no one else.

He's asleep in the car.

She approached the car warily, checking both the side nearest the Suburban and the side nearest the trailer truck first, and then made her way to the trunk. Taking a cautious glance inside the back window she looked for any sign of him. He wasn't in the back seat, and the front seat was clear too.

She tapped lightly on the trunk with her free hand while her other clenched her gun tightly, just inside her jacket pocket

"Julie!" she whispered. "Julie, are you in there?"

There was no answer.

She tapped again, harder.

Still nothing.

If they weren't in the car they had to be in the diner.

She went around the driver side of the car, uncertain what to think. What if this wasn't his car? What if this was just a similar looking Lincoln?

That's when she noticed a white envelope on the top of the driver's seat. Written in block letters, his standard "you'll never trace it to me" writing, was one word: MEOW.

Maggie looked to see if the door to the Lincoln was locked. The handle button was high out of the door panel, meaning it wasn't. Fear overtook her. The idea of taking her eyes off her surroundings to reach inside the car seemed like madness. But she had no choice. The envelope was obviously for her.

She opened the door and ducked into the car in such a rush that she banged her head against the top of the door jamb while reaching for the envelope. This sensation of pain, at a moment when she feared nothing more, caused her to clutch the envelope tightly and jerk backwards against the side of the Suburban as she whipped her head side to side, seeing his outline just at the front of the car before realizing it was only her reflection in the window of the diner. There was something hard in the envelope.

She looked around again, glancing cautiously to see if anyone was watching her. The old man was now turned away from her, facing a television on the counter that was showing sports highlights, and the old couple were still engrossed in their conversation while the waitress was busy refilling their coffee cups.

She had just turned to make her way hurriedly back towards her car when a deep male voice came from behind the Suburban.

"Hey."

Maggie spun around, backed up and nearly yanked her gun out of her pocket before she saw that it was just an old man wearing a Nebraska Cornhuskers cap, both his hands stuffed into his jeans pockets.

"Oh, Jeez. I'm sorry, miss, I didn't mean to startle you," he said.

Maggie quickly gathered herself together. "That's okay. I'm fine."

The man chuckled. "You looking for your husband or something?"

"My what?"

"The guy that was driving this car?" he said, pointing at the Lincoln.

Squinting in surprise, Maggie decided to play along. "Yes, yes I was. Did you see him?"

"Yeah. I imagine that he's gonna be mad he missed you."

"Why's that?"

"Well, he pulled in here about a half hour ago. I was just waking up from my nap in my cab," he said, pulling his hand from his pocket and pointing at one of the large trucks across the lot, "when he rolled in all quiet, lights off and all. I guess his car had broken down or something."

"Really. What did he look like?"

The man looked at her curiously for a second.

Dumb, Maggie. You should know what your husband looks like.

"Oh, I dunno. Tall I guess, had one of them beanie hats on his head. Kinda a big dude."

"Yep. That's him. Did you see where he went?"

"Well, he went into the diner for a quick second."

Maggie couldn't believe what she was hearing. "He ate?"

"I don't think so. He wasn't here very long. I got washed up and dressed and all, by then I was up front in my cab to radio in my schedule when he came back out and started walking down the road."

"He walked?"

"Yeah. I mean, it's twenty-five miles to Bonner from here. I figured the car broke down or something, but I never got the chance to ask."

"Was he alone?"

The old man seemed surprised by the question. "Well, yeah. Sure he was."

He glanced at the envelope in Maggie's left hand, which had no ring.

Maggie read his eyes and thoughts. "He called my cell phone and the message was a mess, all I could make out was the diner name."

The man shrugged, the look on his face much like that

of a person who feels that maybe they've stepped into the middle of something. "None of my never mind, anyway," he added.

"So that's it, he just walked off down the road?"

"Yep."

"Thanks."

"Anytime," he replied with a quick nod before hurriedly walking back to his truck.

She was momentarily stumped. Where had Michael walked off to? And where was Julie? How did any of this make sense?

The envelope. Perhaps it would help explain things.

She looked around, checking her surroundings once again, as she tore it open. Inside was a cassette tape and a set of keys. She squinted down at them in disbelief, her mind frozen. Where the hell was she supposed to find something that could play a cassette tape? And the keys were to what? She studied them. They were car keys.

For the Lincoln.

She began to tremble again, but this time it was almost uncontrollable. She didn't know why. She'd already checked out the inside of the car, both the front and back seats, and they were clear so—

Didn't you think that Julie might be in the trunk?

"Oh . . . please no," she squeaked.

Square key, round key. She guessed the round one was for the trunk.

She made her way to the back of the car again, hands shaking, and fumbled until she got the trunk key into the lock.

It was an old car and the key had barely turned when the trunk sprang open.

CHAPTER TWENTY-NINE

THERE WAS NO ONE in the trunk. But that didn't mean it was empty.

A single piece of white paper was folded on the floor of the otherwise perfectly clean and clear trunk space.

In the distance she heard the sound of an approaching semi. A string of crows had gathered across the road on top of an old a shack and were fighting loudly over a piece of bread. A momentary breeze swept over the road and across Maggie's face as she stared at the paper.

It's a note.

She reached in, grabbed it and opened it, letting the heavy trunk lid fall and shut on its own.

In his usual small block letters, he'd written:

DO YOU REMEMBER OUR FIRST TIME?

LISTEN TO TAPE FIRST.

THEN GO THERE.

She looked around cautiously. The sun was rising higher, and with it more cars and trucks were rolling in for breakfast. He wasn't here, that much was for sure, but even if he was, there were enough people around her now to make her feel fairly safe. She knew how to follow his next clue immediately, but there was the additional issue now of the cassette tape. This wasn't the 1980s. Where in the hell was she going to find a cassette player in this godforsaken town? It wasn't like—

The Lincoln.

She looked again at the old car in front of her. Could it be . . . ?

After walking back to the driver's door, she opened it and peered in. Sure enough, there in the dash, pinched between the knobs of the radio, was a tape player.

She jumped in and closed the door behind her, then put the key in the ignition and turned it to accessory. The dash lights came on, as did the radio. Now she just had to hope that it still worked. She inserted the tape, took a deep breath and pressed play.

After about five seconds of silence, she heard what sounded like someone's hand running over a microphone, then, at last, Julie's voice broke through, loud and clear.

"Maggie? . . . Don't come here, Maggie, don't."

The recording stopped. Then it began again. Maggie heard screaming and shuffling, then Julie's voice again. "Oh, Maggie . . . Please help me, Maggie, please." She was sobbing, almost hysterically.

Hearing her sister's voice so fractured with terror tore at Maggie's insides.

Then? Julie's voice was cut off, and the customary hissing sound of blank tape filled her ears.

Maggie squinted at the dashboard in surprise and frustration.

That's IT?! That can't be it. There has to be more.

But there wasn't. There was no more Julie, no Michael with another hint, no anything.

How can that be? What's the point?

Maggie flipped the tape over and listened to the other side. Nothing. He'd only recorded on one side.

She listened to the other side again, and as she did so a dull sense of déjà vu overtook her.

I've heard this all before.

Of course you have, you stupid idiot! Just now, before you rewound the tape.

No. No. I mean I've heard this all BEFORE.

And her mind took things from there, with brief flashbacks to match the recordings.

"Maggie? ... Don't come here, Maggie, don't." *In the apartment, when all this began.*

"Oh, Maggie ... Please help me, Maggie, please." *Those were the words that panicked you, just before you dashed into the park in Philly!*

It came upon her like a large wave at the beach, crashing down and dragging her under.

He doesn't have Julie with him. He never did.

All this time she'd thought he was putting Julie on the phone and she was hearing her live and in person, he was actually just playing this tape to her. One section at a time.

You miserable ...

That's why he'd never let Maggie actually converse to her.

Good ol' Michael. He was covering all his bases. Right from the get-go. When he had abducted Julie, he'd taken her someplace. Someplace safe. Someplace she could never be found, and this was his insurance policy against a Maggie who maybe wouldn't follow orders, who would maybe freak out and call the authorities for help anyway, regardless of all his threats. And she had come close to doing exactly that, hadn't she?

Zossima. The blood writing on the wall. The photos. It would have at least gotten the ball rolling against him. Michael knew that, and wanted to make sure that even then, he would still win.

It was completely obvious to her now, beyond a shadow of any possible doubt, that she'd made the right decision to come after him alone.

She took a deep breath. He'd last been seen walking up the road, away from the diner. The old man said there was a town nearby. Bonner. About twenty-five miles away. But she wouldn't find him along the road. Maggie was sure of it. Maybe he'd stashed an extra car near here, a few weeks ago, maybe a few months ago, whenever this sick plot had begun to form in his head. There were fields of shrub and forest all around her. He could have parked it anywhere. Then he would be on his way.

But where to? That was the question and it was a crucial one.

She looked down at the note again.

DO YOU REMEMBER OUR FIRST TIME?

Of course she did.

They'd had lunch here at Piccolo Pete's, their flirting growing more playful, more suggestive. And then they'd hit the road and continued their drive up the highway a bit until they came across a beautiful meadow filled with warm summer grass off to their left. It was nearly dusk and a few deer retreated from the meadow and disappeared into the woods at the sound of their car as Michael swerved into the turn-off and told her—point blank—that he couldn't wait anymore. Not one second longer.

Neither could she.

So, grabbing a blanket from the back seat, they'd charged like kids across the meadow and found a spot away from the road, pulled off each other's clothes and made love.

She remembered two more things more vividly than anything else: the warmth of the tall grass on her face, as if the earth had stored up the sun all day in preparation for the dusk.

And that, for the first time in her life, it didn't hurt.

CHAPTER THIRTY

SHE WAS A FEW miles into the drive when the smell of cinnamon and lavender filled the car, beginning to take her back to that place she imagined was just this side of heaven.

She was blacking out again, but this time she was aware it was happening. Fighting the fog that was enveloping her mind, she eased the car to the side of the road and barely managed to put it in park when . . .

The sea was calm.

Her boat seemed to be at a standstill, rocking back and forth with the gentle tide beneath it.

Maggie was lying down, her face pressed against the cool, damp wood of the bow. There was a heavy fog all around her, so thick that the moisture from it made her hair cling to her scalp and face. Her eyes were heavy and she fought to keep them open, something inside her not wanting to fall asleep. Not here. Not now. But it was hard. She was so tired, so spent and exhausted, all cried out and bled dry by despair. She tried to lift her head to see over the bow of the boat, to try to see the island and get her bearings, but she could not.

This time there was no one with her, either rowing towards or away from anything. She was in what sailors called a "dead float," completely at the mercy of what was to come.

She tried to speak but couldn't. Instead something told her to look at the engravings on the inside of the boat, along the hull and floorboards, and before long her eyes focused on a string of symbols and markings that made no sense. Then, to her amazement, as if someone had slipped onto her eyes a pair of contact lenses made of light, her vision burned into the markings and she watched as they slowly rearranged themselves.

Cochella in E-Flat Major.

A piece of music of some sort, classical she guessed. But she had never heard of it.

She looked again. It remained unchanged.

Cochella in E-Flat Major.

A loud horn sounded, and panic gripped her as she realized that her boat must've floated into the path of a much larger ship, one that could crush it. She begged her body and mind to awaken, to break away from the words inside the boat and summon the courage to at least lift her head. The fog began to blow apart with the light from the approaching boat. She screamed in terror as she—

—woke up in the car ... startled by an RV that had honked for some reason, maybe a raccoon in the road or something, on its way by.

When she came to, the first thing she noticed was that the car was still running. The sound of passing traffic helped remind her where she was. She looked around with sleep in her eyes, then grabbed her phone. Two hours. She'd been out for two hours. She rolled down the window for some fresh air, feeling the warmth of the morning sun on her face, put the car in drive and pulled back out onto the road.

She sat up tall in the driver's seat. Her head hurt, and she wished she had brought some Tylenol or something. She rarely got headaches, but this one was especially bad, so she passed on the idea of turning the radio up full blast to help wake herself up.

She couldn't see a mile marker, but she guessed that the stupid meadow should be coming up soon.

All he has to keep him from hurting her is this game, this sick little game he wants to play. But to what end?

She marveled at all that he must've done to assemble this nightmare. Then told herself not to go searching for logic.

He's entirely insane. There may be no reason, for any of it.

The car began to fill with an orange glow as the sun continued its ascent, spilling color across the treetops on either side of the road as white clouds, full and tall, drifted in random sections of the sky.

She changed her mind about the radio and decided to turn it on anyway, not realizing that as she did so her hand began to spin the station dial, past Springsteen and Aretha Franklin, past a weatherman and a station playing jazz, until she found a station playing classical music.

This reminded her of the dream again, and the odd words: Cochella in E-Flat Major.

She couldn't understand what it meant. She never listened to classical music. It always made her sad for some reason.

Then she remembered that there was someone who had loved it, once. Very much. Someone who had played it softly during the middle of the day while he sat and read or worked.

Her grandfather.

CHAPTER THIRTY-ONE

THE MEADOW HAD KEPT them captive that day. After making love they laid side by side, staring up into the sky, watching the clouds drift by the sun, and talked about their lives. And somewhere between telling him about her first soccer goal and listening to him tell her about his first broken bone, Maggie decided that Michael was special. It wasn't the hair or handsomeness, but the way he would chuckle like a school boy and had big gentle hands with a deceptively light touch, which he was using to slowly walk his fingers, back and forth, over her knee as he listened to her.

The irony was maddening. Michael? Special? Gentle? But Maggie wondered how life could be such a spinning thing, like an old LP. You could move the needle as you pleased, between the grooves, backwards or forwards, to skip some things you didn't like, or jump forwards to those you did. Still. What would the Maggie of then had done if she'd known that some five years later she would be chasing the same man who then, on that warm day, had seemed like a dream come true.

She drove down the highway and focused on each open spot she saw, pulling over now and then to look more closely at a few before deciding they weren't the one. The right meadow had been surrounded by towering pines that had rustled with a light breeze as they were getting dressed. She remembered that. And how the trees had cast sideways shadows across some large boulders on the left edge.

Just get there. Fast. If you've kept him waiting this whole time he's gonna be pissed and want to know where you've been. You're wasting time. And if he doesn't have Julie with him, you've gotta find out where he's hidden her.

Then, a horrible thought struck her, like a coiled snake. *You don't even know if she's still alive.*

She is. I know she is.

Just like you were so damn sure she was with him all this time.

Shut up!

He might have taped these words from her and then killed her.

Shut . . . up!

She had no more tears to give, but Maggie could feel that glue in her head slipping again as a collage of thoughts and memories began shifting in her mind. It was all she could do to pull off to the side of the road again, her tires digging into the dirt and gravel of a small turnoff near a patch of tall weeds, before they began to spill out...

Cochella in E-Flat.

Cinnamon.

Love.

Jealousy.

Lap dances.

Mikie Gruner's garlic breath on homecoming night, kissing at her neck and ears, the urge to pee forcing her out of the limo to go to the bathroom on a nearby hillside.

Squatting.

Working out and feeling sick on the thigh machine for no reason.

Bad chicken.

Her grandmother smelling like fresh perfume.

In the coffin.

In the coffin.

Dead now.

Gone now.

You reached out, didn't you, Maggie?

Shut up, shut up, shut, shut up, shut up.

You touched her dead hand.

No.

Yes.

"Grandma, please don't be gone," she said in a soft voice, a little girl's voice, in the silence of the car.

She tried to speak next to the coffin.

Her mother.

Not a good listener.

Too lost in the *Reader's Digest* forever after that. Distant and resigned. As she had been for years.

It'll be okay. Dad still loves me.

Julie on the bouncer at her birthday party, launching off and banging her head on the sprinkler.

Crying.

Lonely.

Better to forget about it.

Easy to forget about things.

Like doing a crossword puzzle.

Easy to forget.

Just concentrate on the words.
Think of all the pretty words.
Letters can spell you out, if you'll let them.
They'll all fit together somehow.
Like magic.
Concentrate.
Pretend.
It isn't happening.
Evening service.
Vespers.
And Psalm 104.
Feeling unworthy.
Sinful.
Stop it.
This can't be happening.
You
Don't
Even
Know
Your
Self
Any
More
"STOP IT! STOP IT, PLEASE!"

She was bouncing up and down in the car, her legs flexing against the floor, her hands cupping her ears, her fingers clawing at her eyes and temples, trying to reach in and turn it off. Turn it all off. Everything. Every damn thought. She screamed gibberish and then the tears came, mercifully so, their wetness and existence a simple distraction, but enough of one to allow her to jerk herself away from the inner series of pulleys and levers that had just spun wildly out of control.

She collapsed sideways across the seat, convinced that she was losing her mind, asking herself if this was what a nervous breakdown felt like, if you could know you were having one when you were having one.

But she knew the answer to that. Her mother had been through one, right after that huge fight with Aunt Mini a few months before Maggie and her family had moved away. After that she had pretty much been okay.

But never the same.

Never willing to answer Maggie's questions about what that fight was all about.

"No!" Her little girl's voice again, escaping her, a feeble and miserable little voice.

Think about Michael.

Get it together, dammit!

The meadow. Get to the meadow.

Julie. Think of Julie. C'mon now, Maggie. Pull out of it, pull out!

Slowly, she forced her hands beneath her and lifted herself back into a sitting position behind the wheel. The gray, sun-starched asphalt of the road before her stretched out to a flat point on the horizon.

Calm down. Focus. Focus.

Her head was throbbing again.

She could kill for some Tylenol.

But no pill could ever take away the pain of seeing her grandmother, there in that coffin, on that desolate day. No more love and no more Latin.

The language of God, wasn't it?

What had God ever done for her, except take away the one person in this life who truly understood her, who loved Maggie to the bone, who chided her in church for talking too much, then bought her ice cream on the way home? A secret

162

breakfast, between two friends, the years between them nothing more than a series of days and breaths, not a separation of souls.

She had read a book in high school one day and it had been the first time she'd heard of the phrase "kindred spirits." She'd rushed home after school to call her grandmother and to tell her how much this notion applied to the two of them.

"Of course we are, dear," her grandmother replied, her pleasure in what Maggie said clearly evident in her sweet laugh.

If only her grandmother were still here. Teaching her and helping her grow. She wished it so much that she even had what she was sure her grandmother would've called a "blasphemous idea." What if she could find someone, a medium or a witch, who could call on the dead, who could bring her grandmother back to her, to help Maggie answer the only question that mattered now: *Where was Julie?*

A wish given sound, she uttered the words aloud.

"Grandmother, where is she? Where did he take her?"

The words jangled like loose keys in the stillness of the inside of the car. Maggie focused on the sound of her own deep breaths as she tried to keep herself from hyperventilating.

Please, Grandma. Please talk to me.

Silence.

She looked up again at the road.

There was no time for this shit.

She started the car and pushed on.

CHAPTER THIRTY-TWO

THREE MILES LATER and the peaks of a section of pine trees, staggered and uneven, with one sole giant in their center, seemed to jog her memory. Next the meadow came into view, still vast but further below the road than she remembered. Green and yellow grasses, life and death, stretched out in a semi-oval shape, with islands of buttercups and dandelions in their midst standing high and tall, light yellow and white, offering color in muted tones against the deep green of the forest all around. She pulled over and hopped out of the car. It was warm, so she took off her parka. The woods held the silence of the morning as a hawk made lazy circles in the distance, a dark "w" against a towering white cloud that divided the blue sky almost neatly in half.

There was no traffic coming from either direction, and a sudden sense of solitude came over her. But she knew better; that didn't mean he wasn't out there somewhere, peering at her from behind a tree. She pocketed her cell phone, pulled the gun out of the parka and palmed it, then locked the car door and began to walk across the meadow. If he was around, then that was fine. There was no way he could approach her, from any direction, without her seeing him coming.

But . . . well . . . now what? It was impossible for her to remember exactly where they'd laid down their blanket that day. He had to know that. And yet, he had made her go to nearly the exact spot they'd first kissed. She sighed with frustration. It had been somewhere on the left side of the meadow, so she worked her way in that direction, methodically scanning around her as she did. Nothing. After ten minutes or so she was ready to give up when she saw it: a path of grass pressed flat, as if something had been dragged across it.

No.

Weaving lazily to an area near the edge of the forest.

Please no.

She saw a clip of white close to the edge of the woods at the end of the trail.

Her stomach lurched. She pushed on towards it, her pace quickening. Both wanting and not wanting to get there. Her dread mounting with each step. As she grew closer the clip of white became a swath of white, and before long it became apparent that it was a sheet. A white cotton sheet.

Covering something that formed a body-shaped lump beneath it.

A hand peeking out at one corner.

"Julie? No, no, no, no, no . . ." she murmured, remorse and sorrow attacking her like wolves.

She ran to the sheet at full speed, still scanning left to right and behind her, just in case he was lying in a patch of tall grass somewhere.

When she was within fifteen feet, she saw a tuft of blond hair at the top of the sheet—and a large splotch of red.

"Oh my God . . . Jules!"

No movement. No response.

She slid on her knees the final five feet to her sister's side. It would be okay. Julie was just knocked out. Maggie would stop the bleeding and call an ambulance. The police too. It would be all be fine. There was no way it was going to end like this, there was no way—

She grabbed at the sheet and immediately felt that the body beneath it was stiff and hard. Terrified of what she was about to see, she rolled it over, yelped and fell backwards.

Before her lie a store mannequin, the legs and arms broken off and strategically placed to create a more realistic illusion of a slumped body. The torso and head were rotated towards Maggie, its painted blue eyes staring at her coldly. The hair? A blond wig. The red? She could smell it: watery ketchup.

There was another note, folded in half and taped to the mannequin's lips.

Gingerly, she reached out to grab it, hearing the paper partially tear against the tape. She looked around again, in case it was a trap. There was no one. After a few seconds, the forest erupted with a brief cascade of bird song. The air was barely moving, but beneath the sun she could see bits of pollen and seedlings being carried across the meadow. She opened the note and read the words:

I'LL CALL YOU SOON.

"Shit. No," Maggie mumbled as she sat back and buried her face in her hands. She was relieved not to have found Julie, for sure. But defeated by her return to more torment. "What the hell? What the hell is happening!" she screamed into the quietness of the meadow, forcing something nearby, a squirrel no doubt, to scatter out of the grass and into the woods.

Feeling overwhelmed, she struggled to her feet and looked down again at the mannequin in disgust.

This time, when her ruminations began to fire, she shut them down. Hard. She was done with questions, guesses, assumptions and deductions. He'd just proven their worth.

After stomping back to the car, she reached for the door handle when her cell phone rang, causing her to jump and curse again.

He was calling already? She answered immediately.

"Hello?"

"H-hello? Is this Maggie Kincaid I'm calling?" A woman's voice, weary and drawn, came over the line.

Maggie was baffled. "Who is this?"

"Is this Maggie!" the woman demanded.

"Yes! Yes, it is."

"Oh, thank goodness. It's me, Madeline."

The name didn't register at first. Maggie was annoyed, thinking maybe it was someone from work who'd gotten her cell phone number or something.

"Who?"

"Madeline. Your neighbor from across the street."

The Walrus Lady.

"Oh! Yes. Hi, Madeline." She was curious about the call and yet still a bit irritated. The timing couldn't have been worse.

"I got your number from your landlady."

"Mrs. Catherly?"

"Yes. At first she didn't want to give it to me, but she seemed a little worried about you too, so she finally did."

Not worried enough to call herself, though.

"Madeline, I'm sorry. I can't talk right now."

"Have you found him yet?"

"Not yet. But I may be getting closer." *Wishful thinking.*

"Stop. Don't do it. Don't do anything, okay?" She sounded frightened.

Maggie was stunned and alarmed. "Why?"

"I can't sleep anymore, I just can't sleep . . . at all . . ." And Madeline's voice began to fade for a second. The Walrus Lady was crying.

"Madeline. Please calm down."

She sounded agitated. "You mustn't go near him now, Maggie. Please promise me."

"Why?"

"I had another dream. I don't know. Nothing makes sense anymore. I've been trying to reach you since last night."

"What dream?"

"It's going to sound crazy. But I'm not crazy. I'm not!"

"Okay, Madeline. It's okay. Take it easy. Tell me about it. I promise I won't think you're crazy."

Because you're not. Because whatever is going on with you, is also going on with me, and if you're crazy then that means . . .

"I was in a boat. There was an old woman. On a shore . . ."

Maggie froze.

"It was Camella again. She asked me to tell you something." The old woman coughed a bit, cleared her throat and then continued. "She kept calling out to me . . . the same thing, over and over."

Maggie forced the words out her mouth. "W-what? What was it?"

"I remember what she said, but I'm sorry, child, I don't know what it means."

"What did she say?"

"Let me think for a moment, I want to get it right. She kept saying *obscurum . . . per obscurius*. Yes! That's it."

Latin. Knocked speechless, Maggie leaned weakly against the car. How was this possible? What was happening?

"Do you know what it means, dear?" Madeline asked after waiting a few seconds in silence.

"I-it's a Latin phrase. I-it means 'the obscure by means of the more obscure.'"

"What?"

Maggie felt a distinct shortness of breath.

"Maggie? Are you still there?"

"Y-yes. Yes I am, Madeline."

"Was that really your grandmother?"

"Yes, Madeline. I think so. But she died a long time ago."

"What does it all mean?"

The less she knows about all this, the better.

"Nothing. I mean, I think she's just telling me to be careful."

There was an odd silence, then the Walrus Lady sighed. "I want you to have my phone number." Her voice was trembling as she said it. "And I want you to stay in touch with me."

"Madeline, I—"

"Please, don't argue with me, just take the number." Her voice was curt now, almost demanding.

Maggie got in the car, her knees weak, and grabbed the complimentary pen from the rental car company from its place in the center console. "Alright. Go ahead." She scribbled the number the Walrus Lady gave her on the ATM receipt she fished from the pocket of her parka.

"I got it, Madeline."

"I'm not having these dreams for no reason, Maggie, and neither are you," the Walrus Lady said, her voice faint now and broken by sniffles. The words hit Maggie with full force.

How did the Walrus Lady know that Maggie was having dreams too? But maybe the answer to that was clear as day. What had she been wishing for, just a little while ago?

For a medium or a witch. For someone who could call on the dead.

But Maggie realized something: Madeline was neither of these things. It wouldn't matter if she was.

Because it doesn't work that way.

She shuddered . . . *We don't call on the dead.*

The dead call on us.

CHAPTER THIRTY-THREE

AFTER HANGING UP, Maggie got back in the car.

But now she had a problem; she was stuck. He could've gone back north from here, continued south or, for all she knew, walked off into the woods nearby. There was no telling until he called, and for the first time she felt a frustration so vast and wide that she screamed, as loud and full as she could, in rage. The sound carried out of the car and startled some brown birds perched on a crooked branch of a nearby pine tree into panicked flight. Feeling vulnerable, she put the windows up, hit the door lock button, turned the A/C on low and caged herself in.

She had to calm down, but that was easier said than done. Her stomach churned with hunger but she felt sick with weariness.

Be smart, Maggie. Turn the phone up. He'll call when he calls. In the meantime, get some rest.

She chuckled at the idea.

You'll need it, Maggie. You know that. You can't go up against him exhausted, and right now . . . so much has happened . . . you're beyond that point. Way, way beyond.

She shook the idea off, not wanting to admit her weakness, wondering how she could be so tired after she'd just freaking passed out for two hours. But. Something wasn't right. Something in her brain was running full speed in an attempt to drag her out of this world and to that place of sleep. It was as if, after years of insomnia, her body was trying to catch up on all those lost hours of rest all at once.

She leaned her head back in the seat and was just beginning to contemplate heading off to find some food when . . .

The sea she was on was slowly turning purple.

The air smelled of burning leaves. Like in the fall, when the trees have been stripped bare and the raking is done. She realized that the feelings she was experiencing were uniquely her own, as if this were Autumn According to Maggie Kincaid, born August 3, in the year 1988.

Her grandmother's voice whispered in her ear.

"We are all what we are, what we feel and what we know."

And then another voice.

"We can be nothing else."

The Walrus Lady's voice.

Maggie couldn't see her across the vast expanse of water, but she could feel her, and she knew with a certainty that at this exact moment the Walrus Lady was asleep back in the real world, whatever that was, in her apartment, all alone and too tired these days to walk at night anymore.

There was a cool breeze sliding over the sea, and the island was still in its place, though her grandmother was no longer on its shore.

Overhead, the sky was a dim gray, pinpricked by specks of pure black. It was nighttime in heaven. She didn't know how she knew that, but she did.

On the shore now was a series of small flags, all different colors, each on a thin stick and blowing in one direction, off to the right, which Maggie knew was not east or west, north or south, but some other direction, not yet definable in human terms. Simply arriving here muted all meaning of direction.

She felt the damp wood of the boat beneath her hands. She was wearing a white cotton robe, the feel of it soft and warm against her skin. Strands of her hair were tickling her face.

Then, through the air, from the heart of the island, she heard a woman singing.

It sounded like her mother. But how could that be? Her mother was not dead.

As it grew louder though, Maggie was sure of it. It was her mother's voice, singing Maggie's favorite lullaby. From when she was little . . .

"Too-ra-loo-ra-loo-ral, too-ra-loo-ra-li . . ."

The words filtered in and out, as if Maggie were listening to them through the horn on an old record player. The words were soft, full of simpler days and quieter times. Times of just her and her mom.

"Too-ra-loo-ra-loo-ral, hush now, don't you cry."

But why was her mother in heaven?

Maggie squinted at the island, searching up and down the shoreline, trying to catch a glimpse of her on the sandy beach. Nothing. No one.

She jumped as the air filled with a second sound, one she knew almost immediately: the piercing squawk of a raven. Echoing.

It came from off to the right, a black flicker out of no-where that descended and landed on the bow of the boat, its talons click-clacking on the hard wood as it advanced a little, back and forth, before it stopped and craned its neck to look at her. Maggie glanced beneath it and noticed that the engravings, which before had seemed to be numberless and deep, were now sparse and shallow.

She scooted forwards for a closer look, startling the raven. It took flight again, flying up and away from the island to somewhere behind her.

Maggie looked down at her hands and gasped. They were not her hands. But they were. There was the familiar mole on her thumb and the half-inch scar across the top of her middle finger that had been carved into her flesh by a fence she had once tried to climb. They *were* her hands . . . but as they had once been, when she was a child.

She looked down at her body. Same thing. She was her nine or ten-year-old self again.

None of this made any sense.

She looked to the island, afraid, seeking her mother's help, her comfort, her healing.

But no more singing came from the island.

It was all still and quiet and lonely.

CHAPTER THIRTY-FOUR

WHEN SHE AWOKE, she was stunned to see that the sun was on the wane. She immediately looked to her phone: no calls.

Her throat was dry. She felt rested . . . for about two seconds. Then agitated.

How could he not have called by now? He's taking such a huge chance that I won't just say "screw it" to this whole game. What the hell is he doing?

If that weren't enough, a new thought occurred to her: how long before that phone rang and it was someone that she didn't want to talk to? Because at some point her mother or father would call. They would call Maggie to see if she'd heard from Julie, and vice versa. When they could not reach either of them, at some point she knew; her father would call the police. Especially when he couldn't reach Maggie.

Then she had a horrible thought.

What do I say if they call me? Jesus, I couldn't lie to them. Not now. Not on this scale.

She shook her head, turned the radio back on and spun

the dial to a local talk radio station, where the debate was over the benefit of a new Walmart opening in some town called Arlandria. Checking her phone, she saw there was a Burger King about five miles south. That wasn't too far, even if she were forced to double back when he called. If he called. But she knew he would. He was having too much fun not to. Regardless, she was starving and desperately needed some coffee to shake off the cobwebs.

Ten minutes later, safely at the Burger King, Maggie used the restroom and splashed water over her face. She was famished, so she got a Double Whopper Combo with a Dr Pepper and a large coffee, then polished them off in minutes. Food, caffeine and more caffeine. But it was okay. For the first time in what felt like forever, she felt rested and energized.

As she sat at a small corner table and watched the traffic passing back and forth on the highway outside, she started to think. She needed to get an edge somehow. Some way.

It dawned on her that Michael had made a huge mistake. Two of them, actually. First, with the tape and then with that sadistic stunt with the mannequin. In his zest to torment her, he'd now made Maggie wonder if Julie was still alive, and this was making it very hard to go on. Without Julie as bait, there was no point to any of this. He needed her alive. It appeared that he'd been lying this whole time. Maybe he didn't even have Julie with him. She could be alive or dead, anywhere out there. That was it. Just like in the movies: she would demand proof of life. Period.

It didn't matter how much he raved or ranted, she would demand it. Because she realized that he was doing it again now: taking control of her life. Before, he was forcing her to flee. Now, he was forcing her to chase. She was sick of it. For Julie's sake? She'd do whatever it took. But if he'd killed her? There was no point in not going to the authorities.

No. Now she was the one lying. To herself this time. Hadn't he threatened to go after her parents too, now? Yes. He had. There would still be one reason left to settle this one-on-one. *To get close enough to him to put a bullet in his head.*

It was then that she had the idea of a lifetime and smiled. Maybe. Maybe it would work. It would be risky, and he might catch on, but it could very well be worth the risk.

As if he sensed she was thinking about him, her cell phone finally rang.

The caller ID read UNKNOWN. She got up and walked out to her car, leaving her trash on the table in the Burger King.

"Hello."

"Hello to you, fair lady."

She exhaled and said nothing.

"Did you find our plastic friend?"

Yes, asshole, I did. "Yeah."

"I thought we needed a little joke to lighten things up."

It was all she could do to keep her bitterness in check. "Sure. Real funny."

"Are you still there, at our spot?" he asked.

"Yes, Michael. I'm here."

"It's dusk, you know."

Of course. I should've guessed. He wanted to talk to me at the same time of day as when we were last here.

"Are you alone?"

"Yes."

"No police?"

"No police."

"Good girl."

"How long is this going to go on, Michael?" she asked, getting into the car for privacy.

"As long as it needs to. There's so much to do, babe. So much to say."

Babe. Terms of endearment now. She was going to rip her hair out.

"Why did you have to bring Julie into this? What did she ever do to you?"

"Nothing, really. Nothing that I could prove anyways. I'm sure she did all she could to get you to leave me, though, to quit talking to me."

"Michael . . . friends and family are always going to try and protect you."

"And a lot of good that's done her, huh?"

"Michael . . ."

"I want you to realize what you've done to me, to us."

"I already know, Michael. Isn't it obvious?"

Patronize him, but gently this time, lightly.

"You don't know anything." He sighed into her ear, sounding sad and tired again.

It was all she could do to maintain her composure. This was her chance. "You're right, Michael. I don't. And I can't go on with this. Not without proof that she's still alive."

A brief silence. Then, "Listen to me—"

A slice of cold ripped through her chest. "No. You listen to *me*. You wanna play this fucked up game? Fine. But I don't know that she's alive anymore. I really don't. So unless you can send me a picture of her, right this second? I'm out."

"Oh, really?"

"The tape. The trick in the meadow. How do I know she's not already dead, Michael?"

"Fine. I'll put her on the phone then."

This was it. She had to sell it. "No. We've been down

that path. You taped her! You play games. For all I know, you're with another girl who's in on this with you somehow and you'll put *her* on the damn line."

"You're crazy."

"No. I'm just tired. Sick and tired."

"I'm hanging up, Maggie."

Control. Control. Control. Here he goes again.

She couldn't buckle. "Fine. You killed her anyway, I know it." *Sell it, Maggie.* She began to fake cry, throwing in a dash of hysteria for good measure. "Screw this!"

She heard him chuckle hesitantly. "Okay. Chill out. You want a damned picture? I'll send you one."

"I need to know it was taken now, at this very second."

"What?"

Her mind scrambled. She hadn't thought this far yet. In the movies it was always a picture with a copy of the day's newspaper or something. But the who the hell read the papers anymore. How could she make sure that . . . a pose. She went with the first thing that popped into her mind: the thing Julie always did in the text pictures she would send Maggie when she was out with her friends.

"I want a picture of her with heart hands."

"What?"

"You send me that, and I'll know it was taken now and isn't some old photo you took days ago. Then? I'll keep playing your game. Otherwise? Forget it."

Again. Silence. But longer this time. She was vibrating out of her skin before he finally spoke. "Fine!" he screamed. "But this is gonna cost you both."

What? What the hell does that mean?

He was walking . . . down a hallway maybe, or across a room . . . walking across wood floors . . . then a door creaked open. There was garbled talk. She made out a few things, "your sister" and "sit up." Then there was a scuffle. Then screaming. More words—"bitch." Then . . . stabbing Maggie right through the heart . . . Julie's voice, weak and pleading, "stop."

There was smacking and dull, thumping noises.

He was beating her.

Oh my God.

No fake tears this time. No fake hysteria. Maggie came apart. "Michael! Stop it! Stop!"

The picture seemed like such a smart idea, didn't it? Now look what you've done.

Julie was crying. More garbled talk, but two words came out clear as day: "heart hands."

When her phone dinged a moment later with an incoming text notification, Maggie couldn't believe it. Had he really done it?

It was a text pic.

She opened it, happy for a split second that her plan had worked, and then horrified by what she saw. Her baby sister, her lips down-turned in sorrow, crying, red faced, one eye swollen shut and her nose bleeding, looking into the camera with so much terror that it didn't seem humanly possible.

Nauseous, Maggie put a hand over her mouth. She wanted to look away, but she couldn't. Her eyes were fixed on Julie's hands, some fingers cut and bleeding, that were feebly shaped into a heart.

His voice came over the line like death itself. "You happy now?"

"Michael, this has to —"

"No. You got what you wanted, big shot. Now you do as *I* say, Maggie. That or suffer the consequences."

"Okay. Okay. Just don't hurt her anymore. Please"

"Go to Virginia. The Iwo Jima Memorial. You've got two hours."

"Fine. I will."

"And if you ever try to tell me what to do again, I want you to remember something, Maggie. You listening to me?"

"Yes."

"Remember that when I hang up this phone, I'm gonna beat up that pretty face a little while longer."

Click.

Maggie Kincaid screamed from a place of rage inside her that had just cracked wide open.

CHAPTER THIRTY-FIVE

AN HOUR AND A HALF LATER, driving at a breakneck pace, she was finally nearing the Iwo Jima Memorial in Alexandria, Virginia. She took the 395 across the 14th Street Bridge and then took exit 8B to the VA-110 into Arlington, letting her GPS guide the way until she was driving down the US Marine Corps War Memorial access road.

When she finally pulled up and parked in front of the up-lit memorial, she breathed a huge sigh of relief. She was fifteen minutes early, which was perfect, as this would finally give her some time with the text pic. She'd been dying to work on it the whole way here, but there was no way on earth she was going to risk being late—due to traffic or an accident—and setting him off again.

She looked around. Seeing no one, she swiftly got to work. He would call when he would call. In the meantime, for once, she was going to be productive.

She had heard about Geotagging about a year after Michael started coming after her. A friend had warned her to close all her social media accounts and to be careful about who she texted photos to, as they could post/share them on their accounts with the same possible risk. She had told Maggie that, essentially, every photo taken on your smartphone was "tagged" by default with the exact GPS coordinates of where the photo was taken. It was a favorite way of child molesters to target children. With just a simple photo they could find out the address of the house, school, park or library where a picture was taken and then track them down from there, which was chilling.

In Maggie's case, though, this would immediately give away where she was and what city she had moved to. This function could be turned off, and with her friend's help she had done exactly that, but by then she was so spooked that she still deleted her Instagram, Facebook, LinkedIn and Twitter accounts, essentially going entirely "off the grid" to protect herself.

But now this little trick might work to her benefit, because it might help her track down Julie. After a few moments watching YouTube videos, she understood the general concept and how to proceed. First, she opened Michael's text photo of Julie, forcing herself not to look at her sister's face again, and clicked the download icon in the upper right-hand corner. It was saved to her phone's "Downloads" file. Then, she went to the Android app store and searched for an EXIF viewer that would help her find the desired information. There were so many to choose from that it was frightening. She ended up going with something called the "3WiseMen GPS Logger." Once it was done loading, she opened the app, clicked the "Load Pictures" tab and . . . amazingly, the latitude and longitude coordinates of where the photo was taken appeared beneath the JPG file on the next menu.

She clicked it and up came three options: "Copy the Location," "Paste the Location" and "Map."

It can't be this easy. She clicked "Map."

It was.

Immediately, Google Maps opened and showed her that the photo was taken on Dumbarton Street somewhere between Thirtieth and Thirty-First Street NW in Georgetown. To her stunned amazement, there was even a push pin on the map. If she zoomed in she could probably—

The phone went off in her hands, temporarily pushing the image to the background as the "Incoming Call" menu popped up.

It was okay. She could pull the map back up when she was done. She had him now. She just had to agree to whatever he said, to buy time, then drive to that location, catch him off guard, shoot out his damn kneecap, and get Julie.

"Hello?"

His voice was like a long fingernail across a pair of new jeans. "I see you've learned to play by the rules again."

"Yes. I have," Maggie said, smiling for the first time in a long time.

"Good."

To keep it real she added, "I can't believe you hurt her, you bastard."

"She's fine now. A little roughed up, sure, but sound asleep."

"This has gotten completely out of hand."

"And the best part is? I'm not finished yet."

"Michael . . ."

"Don't beg. Don't plead. Just listen to me."

The phone beeped in her ear, but there was no way she was clicking over now. Whoever it was could wait.

"Okay. Fine."

He laughed. "You're learning."

You have no idea.

He continued. "I knew this was one order you'd follow. And maybe the one time you might just crack, you know, seeing your sister that way and all. So I didn't wanna take the risk of you bringing Johnny Law."

Again, her phone beeped. Probably the Walrus Lady, calling again. She'd call her back.

"As for me, not that you ever ask, I'm tired as shit and ready for a pitcher of beer. So I'll keep this short."

"Yeah. That's great. Go have some drinks in the middle of all this chaos. Why not?" Maggie said, her voice dripping with sarcasm. She couldn't help it.

"So this is how it's gonna play out tomorrow. You're going to—"

Then his voice, the connection, dropped.

Bewildered, she glanced away from the traffic out on the beltway to check the cell phone display.

Her heart sank, and she realized that the luck that she thought was finally going her way, was doing anything but. Actually, it had completely vaporized.

She'd told herself back in New York, when she was on her way out of the apartment, not to forget it. But she had. With everything that had transpired, it had completely slipped her mind.

It was obvious now that the beeps in her ear had not been a call waiting.

They'd been warning beeps.

Her cell phone battery had just died.

Cutting off Michael. And cutting off her access to the text picture.

She sat in the car as the sky around her seeped over the stars like black ink, the traffic on the beltway in the distance

185

now a blur in the face of her shock.

He must think I hung up on him.

Because . . . and oh how ironic was this . . . how many times had she actually done just that? How many nights had he called up insisting this or demanding that, screaming one thing or begging for another try, until she couldn't take it anymore and had just hung up on him? How many times had she done that, and now, when she wanted nothing but the opposite? It happened anyway.

Her college roommate used to have a term for moments like this: "The fickle finger of fate."

In her mind's eye, she could see him doing what he used to do in the past: hitting redial over and over again, letting it ring and ring, unaware that this time she couldn't answer, even if she wanted to, because that was what he was conditioned to believe.

His rage would just build and build, each time his calls rolled over to voice mail.

Except now, he'll have Julie to take it out on!

She bit her lip. Without the phone she'd lost her GPS too. Cluster bombs of panic began to detonate inside her.

No. This can't be happening!

She could remember Dumbarton Street . . . and Thirty-First, but that wasn't going to get her to Julie. Georgetown was a compact, upper-class neighborhood with lots of very expensive homes. She couldn't just go knocking door to door like some aged-out Girl Scout selling Thin Mints. She'd completely lose the element of surprise even if she got it right.

Think, Maggie, think!

But he had given her something, hadn't he? Yes. Yes, he had.

And she didn't think it was intentional this time, because he had no idea that she was zeroing in on his location when he said it.

"I'm tired as shit and ready for a pitcher of beer." That's what he'd said.

In four years of going to college at GW University, there was one place that Michael favored over all others for a pitcher of beer. On weekends or after finals, to party or to celebrate something. And it wasn't that far at all from Dumbarton Street, was it?

"You son of a bitch," she whispered, with bitter hope, into the suffocating stillness of the car. "You're going to The Tombs."

CHAPTER THIRTY-SIX

HE WAS ON A TRIP down memory lane, while at the same time on a bit of a drinking binge now. Why then would he not combine the two, and end up at the one bar that could give him both?

Maggie remembered The Tombs in all its glory. It was a small pub, over eighty years old, built primarily for the rowing community that used the Potomac back in the early days, and it had never surrendered its history. Over the entryway were two crisscrossed oars, and if the place was still the same now, hung over the entire circumference of the main bar there would be rows and rows of beer pitchers.

The place was built solid, with a black metal stairway that went down below street level. Once inside you were enveloped in the warmth of the architecture, the walls all made of brick a Cherrywood, the bar carved from solid oak.

It had a small dance floor, which like the bar was built for intimacy. On any given night, it would be packed with college students and twenty-somethings, the DJ hidden in the far back corner, in Maggie's day spinning Rihanna and Plain White-T's songs. She had spent many a night there, hanging with friends, tempting the boys with what they couldn't have, and socializing until the traditional closing song hummed into the air.

She could remember that song to this day: "Brown Eyed Girl" by Van Morrison.

She never knew the meaning of the ritual, but it was always the last song played for the night, no matter what night you went. She thought it must have a special meaning to someone, most likely the owner. Whatever the case, it was a signature moment to hear the opening strings and watch the crowded bar erupt in cheers. It was a brotherhood and a sisterhood borne of youth, beer and tequila.

Now it was something new, a place from the past haunted by a ghost who had just descended into its midst for a drink to accompany his murderous thoughts.

Once she made her way to the Key Bridge it was easy. She could get the rest of the way there with her eyes closed. Because she had once loved it there, too.

He's ruining everything, she thought, *even my memories*.

It was as if his level of crime and the degree of his trespasses were only getting worse, more invasive and more personal.

She made a hard left at the end of the off ramp, heading off along the road that ran adjacent to the Potomac shoreline, into the neighborhood beyond, rolling through the intersections with stop signs after only the briefest touch of the brake pedal. She made a right onto a small side street, and then accelerated to the next corner of Thirty-Sixth Street, where she saw the familiar blue and white Tombs sign hanging on the building up ahead. Finding a space on the street, she squeezed into it.

Across the street was a parking lot, the attendant standing by a booth next to the driveway, his white shirt and black vest fitting tight against his body.

As she turned the off the ignition she saw it and almost yelped with joy; pulled into a space at the front of the lot was the blue Honda, the Greenpeace bumper sticker clear as day.

He *was* here.

The neighborhood itself was remarkably unchanged: colonial and federal style homes, muted street lamps and squeaky clean streets. A few people were out walking their dogs in the dark, completely unconcerned about safety. This was a neighborhood for the wealthy and privileged. Senators and congressmen lived here, as did retired generals and the most successful lobbyists. The Georgetown University campus was only a quarter of a mile away. Then she remembered something else in the area: the Radio Shack, which had been right next to the Speedy Copy where she'd gone many a time to prepare a term paper or two, usually the night before it was due. It was only two blocks up the street, across from the Georgetown campus.

I can't leave. I just got here! What if he bails while I'm gone?

You need a damn cell phone charger. You have to risk it.

NO!

But she knew that without the phone, if she lost him when he came out the bar or at any time in the future, the situation could be beyond repair. With the phone, she—and Julie—still had some semblance of a lifeline.

He will keep trying to call you. You know that. He WILL.

Yes. But then what? I have him in my sights right now. I have SOME sense of control over the situation.

You need the charger.

I'm not leaving. There has to be another option.

What about the valet?

What?

Tip the valet. Have him hold the car.

What if he says something to Michael?

Tip him well. Shut his mouth.

This is crazy.

It's an option. It might work.

She was done thinking about it. She got out the car and walked to the parking booth, noticing that her hands shook as she rifled through her jeans pocket for her cash.

Fifty should be enough.

The parking attendant stood in the doorway of his booth, his back to her as he hung a set of keys on a rack mounted on one of the booth walls. She walked quickly up to him, to force herself into the situation as soon as possible, to prevent her mind from balking at the last minute.

"Excuse me?"

The startled attendant jumped and spun around, a nervous smile coming over his face.

"Yes?"

He was a short, balding Hispanic man with, she noticed almost immediately, rings on all the fingers of his left hand, which he currently had squeezed around a short stack of tickets and a pen. In his other hand he held a padlock, probably for one of the booth doors.

"I'm sorry to bother you, but I need your help."

You have completely lost it, Maggie.

"Sure-ting. Whatchup?" he replied in a heavily accented voice. He put the padlock down on a shelf and ran his hand through what was left of his hair, combing it backwards.

"I'm a private investigator . . ."

Sweet mother of God, you've got to be kidding me.

The attendant raised his eyebrows in surprise.

She exhaled nervously but noticed that now, the lie already begun, it was much easier to spin.

"What's your name?" she asked.

"Refugio," the attendant replied, now looking somewhat nervous, as if maybe he was looking down the barrel of some unexpected child support or something.

"My name is Kathy." She extended her hand. "Do you see that blue Honda over there?"

She pointed.

He nodded.

"I'm following him."

A sharp frown developed under Refugio's raised eyebrows. He shrugged and nodded.

"But I'm having a little problem . . ." She paused, gauging Refugio's facial expressions and body language. They said one thing: "I'm listening."

"I need to leave for about fifteen or twenty minutes and I need you to make sure he doesn't go anywhere."

The attendant looked at her a bit confused, even surprised. "He no to leave?"

"Yes."

"How I suppos' do that?"

Maggie let her frustration with Michael come out a little bit on Refugio.

"How the hell should I know? Temporarily lose his keys, block him in . . . Shit, you're the parking professional, right?" She stepped up close and extended her hand to him,

192

the twenties and the ten folded neatly between her thumb and forefinger.

Refugio looked down at her hand. There were a few seconds of debate on his face. To Maggie's relief, he smiled. "Fifteen–twenty minute?"

"Yes, Refugio, there's plenty there for that, and to keep your mouth shut if he does come out. You got it?"

He nodded, but he still didn't take the money.

Instead he glanced around nervously.

Great. The guy thinks I'm here to do a parking lot police sting or something.

"You say you got a 'mergency?" he asked with a quizzical look.

Think fast, Maggie. Think really damn fast.

"Yes." She sighed deeply before she shrugged and shook her head. "It's . . . a . . . ya know . . . *female* emergency. I need to go get some tampons."

Refugio looked away and then nodded awkwardly. "K'lady. But that *cabrone* was mad when he got here, and I don' wan' no problems with him after he drinking, so fifteen or twenty minutes, okay? *No mas.*"

"I promise."

"That fuckin' guy a big guy, lady."

He was thinking too much. Maggie knew she had to leave before he changed his mind.

"I'll be back, probably sooner. Just don't let him leave. Please"

Sugar will always get you further than vinegar.

She smiled at him.

He nodded sternly. Having already appealed to his wallet, Maggie's guess was that being asked for help by a pretty lady was probably more than his machismo could handle declining.

She hurried back to her car and got in, sure that Refugio would keep his pledge, though probably right up to and not one second beyond the agreed time. She turned the ignition and headed to T Street and, as she did, Maggie noticed something odd about herself; she was a good liar.

Now that she thought about it? She always had been.

CHAPTER THIRTY-SEVEN

EXACTLY TEN MINUTES LATER—three of which she had wasted circling the block looking for a parking space—she was heading into the Radio Shack, which had indeed survived the years that had passed, though the Quick Copy nearby was now a FedEx Store and the Yoshinoya across the street had become a Panda Express.

When she was just inside the door, she set off the metal detector. It appeared as if crime in the area wasn't unheard of anymore. There'd never been a metal detector before, and two security guards, who were at the front counter with the cashier, spun around. She wasn't sure if they got a good look at her, but she hoped not.

She instantly thought of one thing. *The gun.*
Dammit!

She retreated swiftly from the doorway and, as she advanced to the corner, she thought of giving up on the idea, but she'd already risked too much simply by driving over here to just go back to the car without the charger. She looked around. There was no one in sight, and noticing some bushes nearby, she pulled the gun from her jacket pocket and ditched it in the bushes, like she'd seen a bad guy do on *Law & Order* once. She then turned around, took a deep breath and walked back to the entrance of the Radio Shack. The security guards met her just as she neared the entrance, putting their hands up and motioning for her to stop.

"Ma'am, wait up," the taller guard said.

"Whoa," the shorter one added.

"Excuse me?" *Play coy.*

But she didn't have time for coy. She could hear Refugio's words in her head: *fifteen or twenty minutes, okay? No Mas!*

"Ma'am, you just set off our metal detector, we saw you," the short one said as he adjusted his black cap. He was blond with blue eyes.

"Excuse me?" Maggie repeated. *Act stunned. Buy time.*

"Please now," the tall one said impatiently. He had dark hair and green eyes, but was younger than his partner.

They were both clean cut. Maggie remembered watching old episodes of *Adam-12* with her dad on Nickelodeon when she was younger. If she didn't know any better, she would have sworn that she was being confronted by Reed and Malloy themselves.

"No. I didn't."

They said nothing. Maggie realized that on any other day she could tell both of these guys to take their wanna-be-policemen attitudes and go straight to hell, but today, now, she needed them. Without them backing down there was no way she would get into the store.

She dropped her eyes to the ground and shook her head slightly.

"Okay guys, I'm sorry. I admit. It was my hash pipe. I

thought you were cops and I panicked."

Reed nodded approvingly, apparently proud of the ease at which they had extracted her confession.

But Malloy, oh that veteran of the Security Guard Association, he wanted more.

"And where is the pipe now?" he asked.

Reed stopped nodding.

But Maggie knew where to take her eyes and her smile. She looked right at him, all of about twenty-two years old as he was.

"I chucked it across the street somewhere." She turned slightly to look behind her. "Into those trees or bushes. Hell, I don't know. I just chucked it in that direction."

Reed smirked.

Malloy stood waiting for more.

She had none to give.

"Look. I'm sorry. I'm just here to buy a charger for my cell phone, that's all."

"Yeah?" Malloy asked.

"Yes. I lost mine and my phone is dead. Please cut me some slack here?"

"Tough night?" Reed asked. His sympathy for her was evident immediately.

"Worse than tough. It's been shit," Maggie said, nodding and widening her eyes slightly, playfully.

"Which bushes did you say you threw the pipe into?" Malloy pushed.

"Jesus, Bob, give it a freakin' break already. The girl needs a charger, that's all."

"Hey man, I'm just doing—"

"Yeah, yeah. You just wanna know so you can smoke what's left in it after your shift, ya jerk off."

Bob laughed. "Screw you, Ty."

They chuckled together before Maggie uneasily joined in with them.

"Go ahead, get what ya gotta get," Ty said, flirting back with her now as he stepped aside to let her pass.

"Thank you so much," Maggie replied, moving instantly past him and walking into the store.

"Man, do you ever give it a break, Ty?" she heard Bob asking.

"Shh, man. Don't," Ty hissed, evidently worried that Bob was messing with his "game."

Bob busted out laughing.

Once inside the store Maggie wasted no time. She showed the clerk the phone and asked *him* to get the proper charger so she wouldn't waste time searching the walls or aisles. As he walked away she remembered to emphasize that she needed a car charger, not an AC charger.

Within a minute or so he was back with it.

She paid, thanked the cashier and hurried out front door to find that Bob and Ty had moved down the sidewalk. They were now perched at the corner.

Her heart sank. There was no way she could get to the gun with them there.

Dammit! What do I do now?

Ty turned to look at her.

"Get your charger?"

Maggie, deep in thought, waved the bag at him. "Yeah. Yeah, I did."

They stood there, the three of them, awkwardly for a moment.

This is the part where I walk to my car, or off down the street, or whatever . . .

"Hey, listen." Ty shrugged slightly, "I don't mean to be quick out the gate here, but it's not like I'm likely to see you around anytime soon, so . . ."

Maggie could see it coming from a mile away.

This can't be happening.

"I thought maybe you'd like to go out sometime?"

Give it the patented answer. You've done this a hundred times before.

"Oh, how sweet. I'm sorry though, I have a boyfriend," Maggie answered, standing still, trying to think her way past the situation, the *real* situation, not lover boy here, but the gun and how to get it back.

"Oh. You do?"

Bob chuckled softly off to the side. Probably had a gentleman's bet on this one, the two of them, and with Maggie's words Bob had just won it.

"Well, hey, you never know. If I can't get your digits, maybe you could take mine and call me sometime, if the urge strikes." Ty laughed, trying to save face.

Time. This is all taking time.

She deliberated over what would get rid of him sooner, taking the number or not. Kicking him to the curb would probably be the best option, but who the hell knew.

"Listen, I'm sorry but I don't think that would be the best idea."

"No?" Ty replied, an animated look of hurt coming over his face.

"In the name of honesty and all, I mean, you know, to my boyfriend."

"Okay. Fair enough. I understand. But at least let me walk you to your car."

Shit, and shit again.

"No, that's not necessary."

Time, Maggie. You are WASTING time here.

"No. I insist. It's getting late. The tweakers get a little

bolder the hungrier they get. I'm sure your boyfriend would appreciate it. Hey Bob, cool by you?"

"No prob. It's your lost cause, man," Bob said, shaking his head as he turned and made his way back to the store.

Maggie sighed as she stole a glance towards the bushes where she'd tossed the gun. It was in there somewhere and they were thick. She was going to have to dig around to get at it. "Listen, Ty, right?"

"Yep. And your name?"

"Alisa."

It was the first name that popped into her head.

"Alisa? Cool. So where's your car?"

You're pushing your luck, Maggie. If Michael just stopped for a quick one to take the edge off, he's probably already getting ready to leave. You're going to have to come back for the gun later.

No! I can't leave it here.

How are you going to get it with these two jerk offs standing around like this, and with one of them escorting you to your damn car?

"I really don't need an escort, Ty, but thanks," she said, throwing it out there in desperation, knowing what it might cause.

And it did.

Almost instantly, a slight look of suspicion came over Ty's face. She couldn't tell if it was over the whole hash pipe story or the boyfriend bit, but his look changed.

He looked to his left, down the street, his eyes scanning around.

Oh, man. I better let him walk me to the car before we end up with another round of Q&A on the whole metal detector bit.

Screw it. Just walk off. Tell him to screw off, and then

200

walk away.

Yeah, right. Perfect. Just walk back to The Tombs, and when Michael comes out and drives off, then what? Call Uber? Not to mention the fact that these guys might decide to be pricks about this and call a real cop.

Dammit. She knew then that the charger had cost her the gun. At least temporarily.

It's well hidden, if nothing else. Unless some homeless guy picks that particular bush to nap in tonight, I can come back later after I've tracked Michael to wherever he goes tonight and after the Radio Shack is closed.

Still, the thought of being left with nothing but her mace made her sick to her stomach.

"Okay, what the hell," she said. "Why not?"

Like most men, his penis being the greater of his two intellects, he dropped his suspicion immediately and gave her a pleased smile. "Cool."

"I'm parked down the street a bit. The Forte over there."

Ty walked her to the car, desperately flirting every step of the way. He cracked a few lame jokes, but for Maggie right now laughter was a thing so impossible to fathom that it was all she could do to offer up a few fake chuckles. Once at her car, and with her mind now calculating that she had been gone close to thirty minutes, he mustered the courage to make one more run for her number.

Fed up, she relented, telling him that she had her old cell phone number from New York still, just in case he noticed the plates on her car.

"1–602–968–9474."

He smiled, proud of himself, the pig that he was, as he wrote her number on his palm.

Typical. Every man wants an honest woman, but they're more than ready to make one dishonest if they get the chance.

She got in her car and drove off. He stood in the street and watched her go. Whatever bet they made, Bob had just lost, as long as Ty never told him later that the number she just gave him was bogus, and she doubted he would.

Maybe it was just being back in her old college town, but those last seven digits had come back to her instantly, the translation playing out in her mind and giving her a small glimmer of satisfaction as she headed for T Street and then back to The Tombs at a breakneck pace.

1–602–968–9474.

1–602–YOU–WISH.

CHAPTER THIRTY-EIGHT

SHE WAS BACK AT The Tombs ten minutes later, sure beyond sure that she had blown everything completely. She could almost feel that Michael had left before she even got there. Having been forced by the one-way side streets to pull back around the block from the opposite direction, she hadn't been able to drive by the parking lot to verify his car was still there, which made the torture of not knowing all that much worse. She'd also lost her prior parking space on the street, and as a result she had to park further down the block than she wanted.

Unable to concentrate on opening the charger packaging and hooking it up to her phone until she had visual confirmation that Michael had not left, she slid out the car and stuck to the shadows on her side of the street, keeping a wary eye on the people coming in and out of the bar as she did so, until she had crept up to the far side of the parking booth. Refugio sat on a stool, smoking a cigarette. When she saw the Honda, still parked where it had been, a sense of relief washed over her that was so great she could hardly stand.

A relief that was immediately replaced by a sense of fear and loss. Just seeing his car reminded her of her proximity to him, which in turn caused her to mourn the loss of her gun. Without it as an equalizer, he could kill her easily.

She retreated back to her car, and moments later, her paranoia running rampant, she worried that with the way her luck was going now, the idiot Radio Shack employee had probably given her the wrong charger. She attached the phone to the plug, and the plug to the car charger, and waited . . .

The green power light came on immediately.

She sighed and swallowed hard, waiting to see if he had left any messages. He hadn't. But she had seventy-four missed calls.

Her heart sank. Here she was, parked, alone and afraid, her sister somewhere probably feeling much the same, while Michael was inside, nice and warm, simply having a drink or two. Her life had become a maze of catch-22s. No option was a real option. She was like one of those toys that roll on the ground and bounce, wall to wall, from object to object, aimlessly, able to sense dead ends but little else.

She had felt this way before, as a child, when her parents had told her that their family would be moving away from their hometown. Maggie could remember that day, her father sitting her and Julie down on the front porch after dinner, her mother hovering nearby, aimlessly watering a few potted plants.

"Daddy has gotten a promotion, girls, but it's going to require a change for all of us."

The words were painted in her mind forever, like emotional graffiti.

Unlike Julie, Maggie had seen this coming, having

picked up fragments of conversation between her mother and father in the preceding weeks. The hushed tones, the quite debates; a bigger house, a shorter drive to the new office, a better school.

She had begun to tear up almost instantly.

"Now, Mags, there's no need to get upset, honey. It's a good thing. You'll see," he had said, his brown hair dancing in the slight wind that had been blowing that day, the fading sun tinting his face orange.

Julie, not understanding yet, listened intently to every word her father had to say, and then promptly threw a fit, angry that she would have to make new friends, not wanting to hear anything about how wonderful the new neighborhood would be.

Through it all, Maggie's mother said nothing, perhaps in a silent protest of her own.

Their father did his best to paint the move in the best possible light, and then, as if that were enough, the logics and logistics of the situation now properly sketched and drafted, he went inside to watch the evening news. Her mother stood, still watering the plants, the stream from the hose just beyond a dribble, buying time it seemed, for some reason.

"I won't go, I swear it, I won't," Julie had screamed after a few moments of pouting. She jumped up and fled down the street to her friend Megan's house to spread the bad news.

Maggie remained on the porch, sniffling, trying to sort out her feelings and thoughts, unable to put a finger on one elusive emotion that dwelt in the core of her stomach.

She thought of her friends and her home and the neighborhood market, where they served the best frozen ice-cream cones on summer days. She thought of the street they lived on, curved like a half moon and ending in a cul-de-sac, where she could ride her bike in circle after circle and dream the day away. She thought of what it would be like to lose all these things, each of them piled high, reason after reason, to keep from thinking of the ultimate loss that this was going to mean.

They were moving far away.

From her grandmother.

After she exhausted all her thoughts but this last one, she broke into tears, burying her head in her lap, her hands folding over her face to cover her shame at being such a baby, at being so weak.

She heard her mother turn off the faucet and approach her, then felt her mother's hand run softly through her hair. Maggie reached up to hold her hand and her mother sat down next to her. She looked into her mother's face and saw a softness there that alarmed her. Then, her mother said the oddest thing to her.

"It's not your fault, honey."

She'd only seen her mother cry a few times before, so she had been caught off guard to see her mother's eyes water. Overwhelmed with emotions she couldn't understand, Maggie buried her face in her mother's chest and cried. For hours it seemed, until her father came back outside to help comfort her.

Now, sitting outside The Tombs, all these years later, waiting for Michael to reappear, she could still feel the cool of the air that night, and she could still smell her mother's perfume as they sat there, just the two of them, on the porch. Maggie again recalled her mother's tears, and in so doing she realized that those tears had been different than she had originally thought as a child. Her mind *then* had registered the difference, but at that young age, it had been unable to understand them properly. But now, those tears came back to Maggie in their proper context. Her mother had been crying that day, but not *with* her. Her mother had been crying *for* her.

Maggie's eyes having remained fixed on the bar entrance this entire time, she was startled from her trance by someone who looked like Michael exiting the bar. After verifying that the gait of his walk was all wrong and that he was much heavier than Michael, Maggie returned her attention to the door.

She turned the radio on again, a ritual now in her stakeout routine, and laughed when she heard the tune: "Could It Be I'm Falling in Love?"

She wondered how long she could leave the car on accessory, charging the phone and playing the radio, before she would kill the battery. She looked to the bold label on the charger package: FULL CHARGE IN ONE HOUR!!!!

She decided she would start the car every fifteen minutes, just to make sure.

Michael had evidently decided to stay, eat dinner and go on an hours-long bender. But he was too old now to stay in there too late. As the hours passed, the crowd grew. She smiled in spite of herself. The Tombs was still the place to go, it seemed. Before long there was a line to get in and two bouncers on the sidewalk. The usual meat market routine began: three to five girls in, for every one guy.

She saw the guys paying the cover. The girls were getting in for free, or so they thought. Some things never changed. Objectified at every turn. It was all fun and games now, and she did not want to rob them of that fun, but what every guy paid in cash, Maggie knew each girl would pay in emotions.

The hair, the makeup, the outfit. The extra quarter inch of fat at the hips that had made them skip dinner tonight, increasing the odds that those drinks they would be getting for "free" soon would be even more intoxicating than usual. The odds of a mistake in judgment only increasing by the moment that, if made, would find them in a strange bed tonight, with a body pounding against them feverishly as their buzz wore off and their regret grew, all of it climaxing a day and a week later, over and over again, when the phone never rang as promised.

They had always been such fun days, hadn't they? At times, yes, and at so many other times, they'd been anything but. Too many of those nights had been like monuments to loneliness, and tombstones to hope.

It was just as the dinner crowd had grown to a full swell, about an hour later, that Michael finally exited.

She shook her head in disbelief as, contrary to what she had expected, he began to *walk* up the street, away from her and away from his car.

He was leaving the area on foot.

And she didn't have her gun.

CHAPTER THIRTY-NINE

SHE HAD JUST OPENED the car door and swung her feet out when her cell phone rang. "Hello?"

"Well, well. You're one stupid bitch. You decide to answer *now*? Huh? Who the hell do you—"

"Michael, my cell phone died. I swear. I didn't have my charger!"

"Bullshit!"

Just talking to him, every time, she would shake. This time it was the worst. "I swear, please, believe me, I'm not playing around here . . ."

No gun. Shit. A half block behind him and I don't have my gun.

It's okay. Calm down. You still have your mace. Settle the hell down.

He crossed the street, heading north, and kept walking.

Doesn't want to drive under the influence, probably. Still playing it safe. But maybe not. Maybe he's walking to where he has Julie.

As she crept past the parking lot she looked to her right. Refugio, standing there solemnly as if he too had been awaiting Michael's exit, nodded his head slightly at her. She reached into her jeans pocket and felt the small round cylinder of pepper spray there. It was a little more comforting, but not much. He was so much bigger than her, and after that long in the bar, it was a safe bet that he was drunk now.

Michael was walking at a fast clip, his head down against the chill of the night, the collar of his jacket pulled up across the back of his neck.

"Maggie, you had better be telling me the truth."

She sighed deeply, relieved that he was beginning to believe her.

"I had to drive and buy a damn charger, $9.89 plus tax. I can show you the receipt. I'm not stupid, Michael. . . ."

"Good. Because Julie pays the price for anything stupid you do. Remember that."

When he hit the corner, Michael stopped to wait for the light. Maggie slowed, ducking behind a utility box by a bus stop. She laid her head against the box and peered around its side to keep an eye on him.

Maggie sighed. "I know that. I do."

"I'm doing all this for a reason. You just . . . you just don't understand it yet."

"What reason?"

"It's not the right time. You wouldn't appreciate it. You wouldn't understand."

The light at the corner going green, Michael stepped off the curb and continued down the street, his pace the same; hurried but not rushed.

"Yes, I would. Please, just tell me," Maggie replied, waiting a second or two before stepping out from behind the box in case he made a sudden left or right on the other side of the street.

"No. It's too soon. But you've pissed me off now, Maggie. You really have. I'm beginning to think I can't trust you anymore."

"Listen to me, I just want this to end. Whatever it takes."

He was continuing directly up the street, so Maggie hustled to get back to within half a block of him, just making it through the intersection before the light turned red again.

"Of course that's what you want. Now. But that didn't seem to matter so much to you when you were the one in control, did it?"

"That's not true—"

"As long as *I* was the one suffering, it was all good, wasn't it?"

"No! No it wasn't."

She'd forgotten how short the blocks in Georgetown were. Already at the next intersection, he made a left this time, disappearing around the corner of an old brownstone complex.

"Yes, it was. Just admit it. You stopped caring about me."

This was what she had feared the most: losing sight of him.

"Michael, what was I—"

What if he's stopped and waiting just on the other side of that wall?

"You didn't care about me, even whether I lived or died," he accused.

Maggie pushed forwards cautiously down the street. "That's not fair."

Nearing the corner she veered hard right, trying to maximize her range of vision around the bend . . .

What if you turn the corner and walk right into him?
"Not fair?!" he almost screamed.

She couldn't see anything except the dirt of the wall and the dark of the street beyond, but she had no choice but to continue. She slowed her pace, almost coming to a complete stop, before catching his jacket in the light of a street lamp, already halfway up the street.

He continued, "Did you just say that? Did you just really use the word 'fair,' Maggie?!"

She hit the corner hard and again sped to close the gap between them.

"Michael, I'm sorry. God! How many times do I have to—"

"Is it fair to leave someone because of some bad *dreams*, Maggie? I mean, are you *kidding* me?!"

They were passing through a residential area, but just up and across the street, at the corner, she could see a small neon sign that read "Budweiser."

Great, another bar.

She realized they'd been making their way east, in the opposite direction of the Radio Shack, and her gun.

"I couldn't help it, I told you—"

"I proposed to you, Maggie. I loved you, so much, and what pathetic excuse did you give me to humiliate me when you left?"

"I didn't—"

"Dreams!" He was laughing now, his voice coated in mocking disgust.

Three-quarters of the way up the block, he caught Maggie off guard and crossed the street.

Need a beer that badly, Michael, and so soon?

She froze. Stuck there on the sidewalk, she had nothing to hide behind. There were cars parked all along her side of the street, but she was afraid that if she moved he would spot her in his peripheral vision.

Making it to the other side of the street, he continued, "Amazing. Ya know. I like this."

"What?"

"This is hands down the longest conversation we've had . . . in years."

Maggie crossed the street cautiously, figuring he would enter the bar when he made it to the end of the street, but again he proved unpredictable. Instead he stopped just short of the entrance as a couple of guys crossed his path and entered ahead of him. He continued on, passing the doors and going to the corner, where he made a right, again disappearing from her sight.

The geotag pushpin on the map was north-east of The Tombs. We're heading in that direction. Maybe. Maybe.

Maggie picked up her speed. "I couldn't help it, Michael. It wasn't you. You know that."

She pulled out her mace and prepared for the worst. As she neared the bar she heard a Pearl Jam song, "Rearview Mirror," blaring from within. A girl with long black hair exited as she walked by, the noise of the crowd inside spilling outside along with her. It sounded as if everyone was having such a good time.

She turned the corner . . .

And Michael was there.

Not forty yards away, and standing still now. "You . . ." He grew quiet.

Maggie stopped and retreated the ten feet back to the corner, having nowhere else to go.

He stood motionless, his back still to her. She saw him lower his head. "You couldn't help it, huh?"

"No, Michael. I've told you a million times. It wasn't you. Please. I've told you that so many times."

He shook his head back and forth, hunched over a bit, seeming older now, perhaps a trick of the dark or the faint moonlight. He ran his hand over his head, as if he were thinking of what to say next, before he began walking down the street again.

"Maggie, Maggie, Maggie . . . you can never help anything, can you?"

What the hell does that mean?

"Michael, will you please just tell me what you want?"

"I told you, all in due time. I'll call you back."

His call disconnected as she watched him angrily push the hang up button on his phone.

He walked another two blocks, his pace slowing. Maggie again took her place right behind him, bobbing and weaving behind posts and trees as she did so, just in case.

Then she saw him dialing his cell phone again.

Shit! He'll hear my phone ring!

Panicking, she ducked behind a minivan and wrapped her cell phone in her jacket, trying to mute it as much as possible.

But it didn't ring.

She peered out from behind the van. He continued walking, the cell phone to his ear.

Who are you calling, Michael?

She began thinking feverishly. Could she have been wrong about him doing this alone? Could he have enlisted an accomplice in this? After a few moments, she stepped hesitantly from behind the van. Michael was now almost a full block away. She had no choice but to continue the chase.

They were in a fully residential part of Georgetown now.

All high-end red brick and brownstone homes with manicured lawns. Pick the driveway of your choice, a Mercedes
or BMW was parked there.

*There's no way you live in this neighborhood. Where
are you going, Michael?*

She saw his hand with the cell phone drop in front of
him.

They walked another two blocks north before he made
another right, his stride now smooth and purposeful. Wherever he was going, it was quite a distance. He walked a block
west, then made another right.

What the hell is he doing? He's walking in circles.

They walked another two blocks west before she saw
him again raise his phone to his ear.

She'd put her phone on vibrate and kept it buried in her
jacket, her left thumb poised to answer, her right hand still
gripping her mace. When her phone began to shake in her
hand she jumped.

"Hello?"

"I still love you, Maggie."

They continued their tango up the street.

"I know, Michael. I'm so sorry I hurt you."

"No, you're not."

"Yes I am."

"I want to believe you. But I don't."

"Please . . . Jesus." The emotions came upon her suddenly, cracking her voice. The entire walk her hand had been
almost steady, but now the shake returned.

She didn't know what to say anymore, or what to do.

CHAPTER FORTY

"JULIE IS FINE. I've kept her safe. You need to know that."

A raspy sigh escaped her. "She has nothing to do with anything that happened between us, Michael." She remembered what she had heard on news shows and in the movies; it was important to humanize the victim, to make them seem more like a person and less like an object. "Before you did this, she was so happy. She'd just gotten a promotion, and made new friends in LA. She was going to visit my parents. She had a new guy she was starting to think seriously about."

He was walking straight ahead, the whole time. In the distance, a few blocks up, Maggie could see the buzz of traffic. A major street was coming up.

"I know all that, Maggie."

She squinted, unsure what he meant.

"She told me all of that," he continued. "She begs a lot. She's afraid. I can understand that. It sucks, 'cause we used to be kinda tight when you and I were together." His voice had gone chillingly robotic, as if he had compartmentalized everything he was saying.

"Please, just let her go."

"I will. I promise you that. All I want is you. That's all I ever wanted. You know that, don't you?"

There was tenderness in his voice now. She remembered that voice. It was the way he used to talk to her when he was opening up to her, confessing something, sharing something. She remembered what a friend had once told her; every boy wants to be mothered, for the rest of his life. This was that Michael. The little boy Michael. The "hold me" Michael.

"Yes. I know that now."

Then his voice went cold. "But I'm tired of your lies, and you need to understand that now, or Julie really is as good as dead."

His words were like thunderclaps.

"I'm not lying about—"

"Where are you?"

Shit.

She stopped walking. "Michael, what does it—"

"No more lies, Maggie."

He stopped at the corner of the busy intersection, despite that the light in front of him was green..

He sighed. Waiting.

"I'm . . . I'm in DC. There. Okay?"

He chuckled. She saw him shake his head.

"From lies to half-truths. I guess that's an improvement." There was a defeated tone to his voice.

"What?"

"You and I . . . we have to make a pact, right now. Because we're running out of time."

"What are you talking about?"

"It won't be long, you know, before you want to give up."

"What—"

"I've been there. I have. Rock bottom. But it's your turn now. It's going to happen sooner than I expected, but what the hell. You were smarter than I thought, that's all."

He remained at the corner, looking from left to right, kicking at the ground.

She began to walk again, nearing him cautiously, nervous that he might move off into the crowds of people that were filling the street around him.

What if he called a cab? Oh, shit.

"Michael, I want to see you."

"You will, Mags, soon enough. But right now, we have a pact to make."

"What pact?"

"I want you. I need you to realize how much you want me. Until you do, I swear that Julie won't be harmed one bit. But I need a show of loyalty from your side, Maggie."

"What is it?"

"When you hit rock bottom? When you're scared and desperate?"

What . . . the . . . hell?

"All you have to remember is that if you don't betray me, she lives. I swear. I will contact you later, and we can meet and end this. But if you betray me? They can come for me all they want, but remember, I will slit her throat the minute they show up."

"What do you—"

"Do you know how long it takes for someone to bleed out after you've cut their jugular? Two minutes. Tops."

Oh my God, he's completely lost it.

A hand, hard and firm, closed around her left bicep.

She screamed and jumped, dropping the phone. Desperately, she spun around, trying to bring her mace up.

Jesus, someone IS helping him in this! Someone—

Two more hands grabbed her right arm, one hand bending her wrist back, forcing her fingers to let go of the mace before she could discharge it.

"No!" she screamed, kicking and struggling. "Somebody help me! Help!"

She was spun around, and then she saw them: badges.

"What are you doing?"

"Calm down, ma'am," one of them said. "Just calm down."

She glimpsed them briefly before she was face down on the grass next to the sidewalk. Police. They were both cops. One of them was black and thin, the other a stocky white guy who evidently spent a lot of time in the gym.

She heard a siren chirp up the street.

A police cruiser pulled up, right next to Michael.

What the hell is going on?

She heard Michael's voice again, loudly, in her head, repeated audio from seconds before: A PACT.

The words bounced between her ears, her confusion at them, at everything that was happening, multiplying by the millisecond.

Another two police officers climbed out the cruiser and approached Michael, who had now turned around and was pointing at her.

He's pointing at me? What? He knows I'm here? He knew I was behind him?

"Don't let him get—" she tried to scream, but it was no good. Between her struggling and the initial scare of the mace she'd tried to use on them, the cops that held her were taking no chances. Her face was shoved into the grass by a big hand, cutting off her sentence.

She jammed her cheek against the wetness of the ground, using it to her advantage to turn her face to the side so she could speak again.

"Please! Just listen to me, I—"

The black cop spoke again as she felt handcuffs being closed around her wrists.

"Ma'am, my name is Officer McQuarter. I'm with DCPD, and I'm telling you, no talking now. You'll have plenty of time to speak in a minute or two, okay?"

"No, listen to me, this isn't—"

"No talking, right now. Do you understand that?"

He half screamed it, his fingers closing the cuff on her right hand with extra force.

The other cop, Gym Boy, was fumbling through her pockets. "Didn't dispatch say she might be armed?" he asked.

Oh my God!

"Yes. That was the call," McQuarter responded. "You find anything?"

"No."

"Ma'am, do you have any weapons hidden on you?"

Maggie's head flashed hot, her body now convulsing with wave after wave of shock. "N-n-no!" she managed to stammer.

Her eyes began to act as camera shutters, quick shots of this or that filling her mind: her cell phone on the sidewalk where she'd dropped it, not ten feet away; Michael in the distance, handing something to the police officers with him; a black shoe next to her ear, belonging to Gym Boy, who was now standing over her.

She heard a car pulling up.

"We cool?" someone said from inside it.

"We got her. No guns or knives, but she tried to mace us."

"No! No, I didn't!" Maggie screamed.

"Ma'am, I'm going to lift you up now," McQuarter said.

She found herself being lifted by her arms before being placed against the car that had just pulled up—another police cruiser, with another cop.

Looking towards the intersection again, she could see a crowd forming.

The two cops with Michael walked towards Maggie and her entourage.

I have to tell them everything now. Right now. Something is screwed all to shit here.

No! You CAN'T. Remember what he just said about Julie.

You can't be serious. I'm in over my head here. He's lost it so bad I can't do anything but tell them everything now.

Again the audio in her mind played his words: WHEN YOU HIT ROCK BOTTOM.

Her chest heaved in sudden sobs.

WHEN YOU'RE SCARED OR DESPERATE.

She dropped her head, her hair draping across her face, sticking against her cheeks with the glue of her tears.

DON'T BETRAY ME.

Oh God, what . . . is . . . going . . . on?

AND SHE LIVES.

Maggie shook her head, not believing this was happening, refusing to believe it. How the hell was it that she was the one being arrested?

"Sarge, she's tripping," the cop who'd just pulled up in the cruiser said.

"Ma'am, you need to just settle down," Gym Boy warned.

221

BETRAY ME.

"This can't be happening, it can't be," Maggie cried out.

"Well, it is. So calm down," McQuarter said firmly.

SHE DIES.

No.

I WILL SLIT HER THROAT.

"Julie, Julie, Julie . . ." she whimpered.

"What the hell is she saying?" Gym Boy asked, a tone of concern now in his voice.

"I dunno," McQuarter replied, irritated.

Michael was standing there, not ten feet away.

One of the cops with him motioned at McQuarter.

"What ya got?" McQuarter asked, stepping towards him.

Maggie came to within a razor's edge of vomiting out everything to them, everything, when the worm finally turned.

"We got restraining orders, Sarge. Shit. Miami, Virginia, Chicago . . ." He took off his cap, revealing black hair cut in a military style, his eyes widening in disbelief as he looked at the papers he was about to hand over to his sergeant before he continued, "Most recently in New York. Looks like she's been after him for quite a while."

A weight of a thousand pounds crushed her instantly. *Restraining orders? On ME?*

Maggie looked Michael dead in the eyes.

Standing between the two officers that had walked him over to her, she noticed his lips were straight and firm, giving the appearance of a very grim man.

But his eyes were smiling.

CHAPTER FORTY-ONE

MAGGIE SAT IN the backseat of the police cruiser, directly behind Gym Boy, her head resting against the window.

"This is bullshit," Maggie said to McQuarter through the protective screen of the cruiser.

"You've already told us that," McQuarter responded.

"A dozen times," Gym Boy added.

"I've never stalked him."

"Really?" McQuarter chucked. "That's not what we saw. We followed you for blocks, and it sure looked like you were stalking him."

"How in the hell . . . ?"

"He said he didn't even know you were behind him until he heard music from a bar he passed a minute earlier in his ear again, this time over the cell phone. That's when he called us."

The bar. Pearl Jam. Those guys opened the door to go in when they passed in front of him. That girl opened the door to come out when you went by. Shit. Shit. Shit.

"I wasn't following him the way you guys think."

"Then, ma'am, in what way, exactly, were you following him?" Gym boy half laughed.

"This isn't funny," Maggie snapped.

"Ms. Kincaid. We read you your Miranda rights, and—"

"And I waived the right to an attorney because I have nothing to hide, Officer."

"Well. That's fine. We will be at the station in a few minutes. You'll go through booking there and they'll give you all the details of what's to come. In the meantime, is there something you want to tell us?"

Yeah. You dipshits just let a kidnapper who has spent the last five years of his life stalking me across the country just walk off, while you arrested me and most likely sentenced my sister to God only knows how many days of torture, if not death. How's that for a news brief?

"No," she replied, because she'd seen the look on all their faces, in McQuarter's and Gym Boy's, in the two cops who had escorted Michael over to her and even in the eyes of the cop who had pulled up after the fact. They'd all already judged her. Now, seated in the back of the cruiser, she could see why. They'd been trailing her, watching her duck behind cars and trees, watching her behavior, and it was obvious that, for Maggie, it didn't look good. It didn't look good at all. Then, when Michael had produced the restraining orders, it simply cemented their opinion of the situation, and subsequently, her fate.

She still couldn't fathom how he'd pulled off this last magic trick. Counterfeit restraining orders? A friend in the legal community? No. To have the balls to hand them over to a police officer? They had to be legit somehow. He had them on him this whole time.

And this whole time she had, indeed, been trying to follow him, all the way from New York. It was brilliant. He'd taken a semantic scalpel and cut her with it, knowing that the difference between following and chasing, like so many other things in life, was all in the eye of the beholder.

She'd confronted Michael, there on the sidewalk, just before having her head pushed down as they seated her in the back of the cruiser.

"Those aren't real, they're fake. They don't mean anything!" she screamed.

"Maggie. Please. Just stop this. Please?" Michael pleaded with her in a sympathetic voice, as if he felt bad that she was being arrested.

"Sir, why don't you just step away now so we can get some notes," one of the officers with Michael cut in, rubbing his mustache.

Maggie almost folded. "Ask him where my—"

But Michael had seen it coming, his eyes going beady as he cut her off completely. "Restraining orders are like *pacts*, Maggie. Remember, they're binding."

Stunned to silence, she simply stared at him.

"C'mon, Maggie, can't we just stop all this?" He smiled, sounding all the more like the perfect boyfriend who just wanted to end things on a good note and is terribly saddened by how things turned out.

"Fuck you!" she spat back.

"Okay, that's enough! Get her in the car," Gym Boy had said, intervening.

Now, trapped in the backseat of the cruiser, staring out at the passing pedestrians and store shops along the way, Maggie imagined how things were wrapping up on his end. She didn't have to imagine very hard, because she'd been that person before, the one consoled by the cops, told that the person after them would be detained for a day or two, that it was safe to go home now, that a detective most likely would be calling to follow up on the police report.

All those times, in the past, it had been *her* doing the reporting of the crime. Only once had they actually nabbed Michael and driven him off, but she remembered the feeling that night. The feeling of freedom. The feeling of walking away when the other party was headed to a jail cell, if only for twenty-four blissful hours.

But this time, it was her heading to jail.

And Michael was the one being left to roam freely, to wherever he was headed, to do whatever he pleased.

Maggie knew beyond a shadow of a doubt where he was headed.

To Julie.

And she couldn't do a damn thing about it.

The rest of the drive she stayed silent.

She knew something was wrong when, after arriving at the station, being booked, photographed and fingerprinted, they escorted her to her own cell. The jail was fairly crowded, with two corridors that split off from the main booking desk: males to the left, females to the right. A female officer with latex gloves and a brown bob haircut frisked her down while another female officer watched. Noticing that she still had some fingerprint ink on her hands, the officer at the door of the cell produced a paper towel from a dispenser just outside the gate and handed it to Maggie.

"Ma'am, do you have anything hidden in any of your body cavities?"

Maggie rolled her eyes.

"I'm a stalker, right? Not a heroin addict," Maggie responded, immediately regretting the words. Everything was being recorded now, she knew that, if not on tape then at least in the written reports.

"Fine. This is your cell for now. The sergeant recommended that you be kept under watch, for your own sake."

"What? Are you kidding me?"

"No. I'm not. My name is Officer Cabrilla. I will be just outside your cell this evening, should you need anything."

"They think I'm suicidal?"

"No one is saying that, ma'am."

"Christ! What is it with the "ma'ams" around here? They train you all the same way? My name is Maggie, okay?"

"Fine. Maggie it is. Do you have any further questions, Maggie?"

"Do I get a phone call?"

"Yes, once your booking is completed and you are entered into the system."

"How long will that take?"

"I don't see it happening for a bit. My advice to you is to get some sleep."

"Yeah. Right. I'll sleep like a baby, I'm sure."

"All you can do is try." Officer Cabrilla stepped out the cell . Her partner closed the door and it clanked into place.

Maggie, free of the handcuffs at last, stood and rubbed her bruised wrists. She noticed that there were no sheets on the double set of bunk beds against the opposite wall. Her tennis shoes were loose. Looking down she saw that Officer Cabrilla had not only dug her fingers in and through them but, while in the process, she had also removed her laces entirely.

They think I'm nuts, that I will hang myself or something. This is crazy.

"Officer Cabrilla?"

"Yes?"

But Maggie could think of nothing else left to say, her

call meant only to stall, like that of a child about to be left alone in a strange room at bedtime.

"Nothing," Maggie finally replied, as her eyes bored a hole in the pale blue tile floor.

Officer Cabrilla stood there for a second before turning and walking down the hall. When she didn't return after ten minutes, Maggie figured that there must have been some sort of mix up. Hadn't she said that Maggie would be "under watch?"

Rolling her eyes up to the ceiling as she sat down on one of the beds, Maggie saw a small black camera mounted in the upper corner of the cell.

But of course. Twenty-first century and all. No more need to post a guard all night at the cell door. Now they just put you in a nice, clean, Orwellian box and watched you. All night long.

Loneliness crept over her, and she wished she had a book. Certainly Dostoevsky would have something to say about this, right?

Maggie shook her head at what was happening. Then, defeated, sure that nothing mattered anymore, that they were right now checking into every little detail about her that they could, realizing that she could be locked up here for quite a while if the DA so chose to keep her, and—worst of all—realizing that in all likelihood she had failed everyone, most of all Julie, Maggie lay down on her bunk and buried her head in a case-less pillow that smelled of nicotine and vomit.

She hadn't cracked though. She hadn't betrayed him. All of these things added up to the most frightening realization of all: she had nothing left to hope for anymore.

Except for Michael's pact.

It was beyond pathetic. But some part of her clung to

the memory that Michael was always big on promises, on not making them lightly and on keeping them at any expense. It was a part of him that had made him so perfect and so special when they had first met, that he was so boyish and so loyal.

At least she wasn't starving somewhere, like her little sister was. The same little sister who always ate like someone twenty pounds heavier. She imagined him spoon feeding her something vile, just enough of it to keep her alive another day or two, for whatever grand finale he had planned.

Maggie Kincaid turned her face into the pillow to muffle her sobs, as she slowly succumbed to her fatigue.

CHAPTER FORTY-TWO

THE WATER WAS COLD and she noticed, for the first time, that it was more gelatinous, like protoplasm inside a cell. She didn't know when she had slipped out of the boat, but she had, one hand still clutching the bow, the other tentatively stroking the water.

She decided to make a swim for it, to that soft golden shore. Being even with the horizon of it, she could see nothing over the cresting waves but the swaying tops of the palms trees.

A part of her was afraid. Partly because she had the feeling that what she was doing was not allowed, and partly because she had no sooner gotten into the water than she saw things begin to move about, just below the surface. She gasped, a small swell catching her lower lip and bathing her tongue with the taste of anisette, which reminded her instantly of the cookies her father used to eat with his coffee on Sunday mornings.

She looked up to the backwards sky, the nighttime colors still in reverse, the stars as black specks against a gray blanket. Day in heaven was like a soft glow that warmed the eyes and never ended.

She let go of the bow and stroked at the water in the smooth stride she'd learned long ago, on the swim team in high school; long, even arcs of her arms counterbalanced against strong kicks from her legs. She lowered her head and focused on her one conscious need: to reach the beach.

But she realized immediately that her movements were causing her pain, not so much in her limbs, but in her mind. Voices, so many voices, all the voices of herself, at all the ages of herself, like sound waves through the water, reverberating into the bones of her arms and legs and up to the hard shell of her skull, squeezing and squeezing at her brain so hard she had to stop immediately for the agony she was in.

Before long she was hit by a flood of memories, from all sides, until a nausea gripped her stomach, her mind overwrought with too many perceptions, conceptions and realizations, piled on one another like so many junkyard relics, the millions upon millions of recorded bits of information, from what was the first smell of a banana to the lingering sight of a seagull on the horizon, to what it was to miss her parents as an infant, or to realize at last the sum equation of recollection.

All around her they swam, the fish of her thoughts in a school of memory, in what Maggie now knew was the very sea of her existence. They crisscrossed between her legs and breached the water's surface as if they were in as much pain as she was, and Maggie knew that her only hope was to get back into the boat immediately, before the sea swell of what she had done grew to a tsunami that would ravage her mind entirely.

My God, my God.

She cried and swam the ten feet or so back to the boat, screaming as she went, forcing herself to make it the distance, despite the pain, until she could barely reach out and clutch the side of the boat again.

Not a hundred feet away, she saw a large black fin pierce the water, closing fast on her legs. But she was too weak.

From the boat the Walrus Lady appeared, her arms outstretched, but she was a much younger Walrus Lady. Maggie didn't know how she knew, how she could possibly know the memories and life of another person so easily, but it was as if in this place, a blended self could lead to blended realities, and knowing another was not all that much different than knowing yourself.

Because souls were not just sent here, but grafted like branches to a tree.

This was the Walrus Lady who had worked the New York brick mills during the Second World War so hard that she came home every night with fingers that were split and bleeding. The Walrus Lady who loved to watch for the sunrise every morning, especially after rainy days, to see if the golden colors could break through the clouds, as if she were playing hide and seek with a secret friend. And this was the Walrus Lady who grew up in a migrant Slavic village just on the outskirts of Bellingham, England. Who was fourteen when she ran into a nice man named Henry next to the Plackard's Brewery one day while walking home from school. A man who told funny jokes and always made her laugh, until the day he raped her as she lay silently next to a bale of hay in a farmhouse two miles up the road from the brewery, where he had convinced her to meet him so he could show her the horses.

This was the Madeline Govenia who loved horses as a child, but who would never be able to look at one the same way again, because of the look in their eyes that day in the barn, as the man forced his thing in her, and hurt her, over and over again.

Maggie felt her body leaving the water as she struggled.

The fin closed in, slicing through the water now in a straight line. Faster. Faster.

Maggie looked at the side of the hull and noticed for the first time that there were carvings on the outside of the boat as well, and one of them was in English: **Me and Julie Running from Thunder.**

And despite the fin, despite the Walrus Lady's tugging, Maggie's mind drew her back to that summer day in the Pennsylvania forest, where she and her family had gone for vacation, when Maggie and Julie had wandered deep into the trees before hearing the first ominous rumblings of thunder in the distance. Knowing that it was dangerous to be caught in the woods during a storm, and knowing that they had marked their trail only with bits of cotton candy that the rain would wash away all too quickly, they had taken off running back to their camp.

And promptly gotten lost.

The storm descended with no sympathy for their plight, adding heavy rain to the hot, humid air. The whole forest became like a sauna. As their path twisted and turned, Maggie in the lead and Julie following, up and down the trails, from one switchback to another, lightning twisted through the sky in violent strips, cutting dangerously close to the treetops.

Before long, what they hoped would be a short storm became a long one, and their panic increased until they stumbled into a clearing, and to, of all places, a farmer's equipment shed, a plow parked beneath the open-faced building. In the distance stood a house, but not interested in anything but getting away from the rain and lightning, they chose to take refuge in the shed. And just like that, perhaps due to the warmth and safety they had so desperately sought now finally being found, relief boiling full in their bellies, they had both been stricken with a severe case of the giggles.

"What do we do now?" said Julie between laughs.

"Wait out the storm, I guess," Maggie replied.

"You got anything to eat?" Julie asked.

"No. You?"

Julie reached into the extra pouch of her overalls and pulled out the leftover cotton candy she had tucked away from earlier in the hike. They sat together, laughing and talking and eating the candy as the rain fell in melon drops, splashing all around, for the next half hour, at peace in a storm that moments earlier had seemed like the end of the world.

The memory of Julie saved her, giving Maggie the strength she needed to scale the side of the boat and climb safely in.

She looked back just in time to see the fin descend below the surface, just as it reached where she had been a moment before.

As it passed she sensed that in it, too, was something of her mind.

Of course, she thought. *Of course.*

It only made sense.

If good memories could save, then the bad ones could almost certainly kill.

THE SNOW GLOBE

CHAPTER FORTY-THREE

"Ms. KINCAID?" a male voice said to her from somewhere far away.

Maggie awoke groggily and looked up.

Standing at the door of her cell was a man in his mid-forties with a receding hairline and a not-so-receding waist-line. He had bushy eyebrows and deep eyes that were boxed by square glasses. There was a small manila folder open in his hands.

"Yes?"

"My name is Detective Meyer. The shift officer is going to be here in a minute to bring you to an office down the hall for an interview. It says here that you've declined counsel. Is that correct?"

I probably shouldn't, but it only adds time to the process, only allows them to keep me here all the longer.

"Yes, it is. I just want out of here."

"I'm sure you do. First things first, though, okay?" he asked, looking at her over the edge of his glasses.

"Fine."

Maggie watched him walk away, and then she stood to stretch off her sleep.

She could remember her dream entirely, but she did not want to think about it.

Instead she made her way to the toilet to pee, noticing thankfully that they had at least left her toilet paper to use. Only one ply. Probably because it was possible to hang yourself with the two ply, she surmised.

Before long another female officer appeared, too pretty to be a cop, short and petite, the high school beauty queen still looking for a validation of some kind. She opened the cell door, and with the help of a male cop who'd accompanied her, they cuffed Maggie and escorted her down two hallways to a beige door.

Inside sat Detective Meyer, and no one else.

"Have her sit down," he said, looking up from his folder only briefly to motion at the chair opposite his own at a small square table.

Maggie looked around the room. Four walls. None made of glass. She expected the old-fashioned interrogator setup you always saw on television, but with only one detective in the room, it appeared that she did not even merit the old "good cop, bad cop" routine. She was slightly disappointed.

"Ms. Kincaid, how are you today?" Meyer asked, still not looking up from the folder.

The two uniformed officers left the room, closing the door behind them.

"You didn't really ask that question, did you?" Maggie said, shaking her head in disgust.

"Yes, I did," Meyer replied blankly, finally looking up with a pinched smile. "And you really didn't answer it, did you?"

"I want out of here."

"Yes, as you've indicated."

"This is crazy."

Meyer briefly bobbed his head from side to side while jutting out his lower jaw, his expression conveying that he thought "crazy" was a subjective term, if nothing else.

"You seem upset to be here."

"Why wouldn't I be."

"Is this the first time—"

"My God! Yes. I've never been in jail a day in my life. Until now."

"Well, you seem like a rational person. Why, then, keep acting so irrationally with regards to Mr. Baines?"

Mr. Baines?

Another fake name, to match the fake ID he probably gave them as well.

"I . . . I can't believe this. I am *not* stalking him."

"Hmm." Meyer separated a series of green and white sheets out on the table in front of him, the green sheets to Maggie's left, the white ones to her right.

"Do you see these?" he said, tapping the green sheets.

"Yes."

"Those are the reports from the two arresting officers last night. They seem to think that stalking Mr. Baines was exactly what you were doing."

"They're wrong."

Meyer calmly placed the sheets in front of him and began to read.

"Suspect was seen crossing Q Street and Thirty-Fifth within three minutes of radio call, walking at an irregular pace and talking on her cell phone. Victim was thirty to thirty-five yards away, directly in front of suspect. Myself and Officer McQuarter then tailed suspect eastbound on Q for two blocks, then southbound on Thirty-Third for another block. Suspect consistently maintained a walking pattern and direction consistent with that of the victim, and used—"

"I've heard enough," Maggie replied, shaking her head.

But Meyer wasn't finished. He glanced up at Maggie with a look of irritation. "*And used* evasive measures in an attempt not to be noticed by suspect, including, but not limited to, using cars, trees, property walls and utility posts to hide behind."

"Look, I'm sorry but I'm not able to—"

"Ms. Kincaid, what I have just described to you is, if nothing else, consistent with just about everyone's definition of stalking."

"Or simply following."

"True enough. Which is where *these* sheets come into play."

He slid the white papers closer to Maggie. She knew the forms immediately. They were court orders. Photocopies. Obviously of the ones that Michael had produced for the police the night before.

She was dumbstruck.

Each one was a different restraining order, filled out and signed, just like the ones she had filed against Michael over the years, except now it was *her* name, not Michael's, in the DEFENDANT's box. She checked for and found the signature of each judge who had issued the individual orders, as well as the standard municipal stamp and seal that made them valid.

My God, how can this be?

"Do you know what these are?"

Play stupid.

"No."

"You've never seen them?"

"No."

"Well, I believe that."

"Look, I don't appreciate the sarcasm."

"No. You misunderstand me completely, Ms. Kincaid. I'm not being a smartass. I actually do believe you."

Maggie's heart jumped with hope.

"Because it appears that in each instance, from Virginia to Miami and so forth, you never bothered to appear in court to defend yourself."

He tapped his finger at the bottom of three of the pages.

IN ABSENTIA.

IN ABSENTIA.

IN ABSENTIA.

He sighed. "The other orders say the same thing."

"And that proves something, I take it?"

"Only that you're good at dodging the court, and ignoring subpoenas."

"That's not true. I've never been served a subpoena for anything in my life."

"So . . . perhaps you could do me a favor and tell me something then."

Maggie sighed. "What?"

"On these orders?" he asked, now sliding all five of them in a neat row in front of her.

"Yes?"

"Are these addresses ones that you've ever resided at?"

She checked each sheet.

Don't answer.

She looked at the floor, trying to buy time.

"C'mon now, Ms. Kincaid. I can run your ID and Social and get the answers if you don't want to cooperate."

You probably already have. Maggie swallowed. Her mouth and tongue were bone dry. *How the hell can this be?*

"Yes, I have lived at those addresses," she finally answered.

"Each one?"

"Yes. Each damn one."

"So?" Meyer asked, leaning back in his chair, his hands in his lap.

"So . . . what?! I lived at those places. That doesn't mean . . ."

She had an idea. Sitting up, she began to inspect the orders more closely. In particular, the dates. The dates on the orders had to be wrong. But they weren't. She had lived in Miami from summer 2014 to spring 2015. If she recalled correctly she had been in Chicago from sometime in fall 2012 to May 2013. The rest of the dates also checked out.

Dammit

But wait a minute. Did they?

CHAPTER FORTY-FOUR

BY YEAR THE restraining orders checked out, but . . .

She'd left Miami in late March, having secured her lease in New York by then. She had chosen to fly home to visit her parents for her mother's birthday, which was the twenty-ninth.

She checked the Miami court order.

The original complaint was filed with the court on April 1.

April Fool's Day. You. Bastard. Ha, ha.

With the subsequent court order issued by the bench on May 20.

Son of a bitch.

She checked the Chicago order.

She had made it to Florida in time for the annual Hemingway Festival in Key West, a lifelong dream come true, a three-day distraction from all her worries about Michael. That had been around the July 11, because there had still been some lingering Fourth of July decorations up in some of the local bars where she'd partied with a bunch of college girls in town from Harvard and ended up at a dive called Pablo's or something, drunk and playing darts, missing the dartboard half the time and plunking the darts into the wall.

He filed the Chicago complaint July 3.

No. No. No. NO.

Her anger began to boil.

"Ms. Kincaid? You still with me here?" Meyer asked, breaking the silence but by no means disturbing her analysis.

She scanned all the remaining documents.

This is why he never followed you immediately, whenever you fled.

"I'm still with you. Please. Just give me a sec," Maggie replied.

She felt him watching her.

Dammit all to hell, he used your own game against you.

He had you served when you moved. Right AFTER you moved. Within days.

Because he knew you never, ever left a forwarding address.

"You rat bastard," she said with a sigh.

You know the routine, Maggie. So the complaint is filed. They make three attempts to serve you. Twice by mail, once in person. Meanwhile, the order marches its way through the system. The court date, your hearing date, everything . . . every-damn-thing . . . comes by mail. Mail that can't be forwarded. At last you fail to show for your hearing. But he does! HE does. He actually walked into a court of law and did all this. Not once. But multiple times. Almost every time you fled.

She did the math. He had three restraining orders

against her.

She had five against him.

Smart legal beagle, Michael. You learned quickly in law school, didn't you? It happened to you once and you somehow got this twisted idea to simply flip the cards on me from then on.

She looked up to see Detective Meyer staring straight at her.

"You want to tell me something?" he asked.

"I thought you already knew everything?" Maggie replied with a flat stare, unsure of what the hell to do next.

"Not everything. Though we do know that you were watching him for quite a while. I mean, you must've been . . . seeing as you're a private detective and all."

He glared at her.

Oh, shit. They backtracked me to the parking lot somehow. Refugio.

"What was it? Your name was Kathy or something, right? Kathy with a menstrual problem?"

"That doesn't prove anything."

"Mr. Hernandez has you down as actually admitting to him that you were following the victim. You lied to *him*, Ms. Kincaid. Why don't you stop lying to *me*?"

Maggie had enough. "Screw you."

"Fine, Ms. Kincaid. It's obvious you don't want to cooperate. It's also fine that you want to deny everything here. That's all your choice."

He retrieved the sheets of paper and stacked them into a neat little pile in front of him.

"Are you aware of VAWA?" he asked.

"Excuse me?"

"The Violence Against Women Act?" he said.

"Yes."

"So you know that federal law requires each law enforcement agency, in each state, to honor restraining orders such as these, particularly with regards to stalking cases, from other states."

"So?"

"This means that even though we have no formal order issued by a DC court, we can treat any one of these other orders as if we did."

"And?"

"It means I can hold you for up to five days, instead of the usual three. It also—"

The words struck her like a hammer.

Julie.

"Am I the only one missing the irony here? That you're using a law to protect women *against* me." Maggie's eyes widened. This couldn't be happening. It just kept getting worse.

"Female stalking is rare, but not unheard of. And the law protects both genders equally. So . . . that means I can recommend that the DA file formal charges against you, and that, with this many violations across this many states, with the most recent violation actually witnessed by two peace officers while during the act . . ."

He placed both hands palm down on the table and leaned forwards.

I've got to tell them everything now. I have to. I have no choice. None.

"Well, let's just say that you are in deep shit, Ms. Kincaid."

He had been quite effective up to that point, scaring Maggie to the core, but there was something about the way he said this last sentence, something reckless and fake, that made Maggie exhale deeply.

She looked him in the eyes and wondered. It couldn't be this easy. It just couldn't. Too many people, even Hollywood stars with bodyguard details, could not reverse the habits of their stalkers, time and time again. She knew herself how nearly impossible it was to stop it. So why was he making it sound so easy?

She decided that she had nothing to lose, and enraged to be yet again faced with an officer of the law who was being anything but helpful, she vented.

"I have a few questions for you, Detective," she said.

"Oh, really?"

"You say tomato, I say tom-*ah*-to. You say stalking, I say following."

"With this kind of history?" he asked with smirk, waiving the papers in the air at her.

"Please let me finish," Maggie said through clenched teeth. "You're accusing me of 'stalking' him, but your own officers told me in the cruiser that they only saw me 'following' him for 'two blocks.' Do we have body camera footage of that conversation to review? How about a vehicle camera? And didn't you say the parking attendant used that word, 'following', too?"

He blinked. "The subpoenas clearly aren't working in your—"

"All filed *in absentia*, Detective Meyer. You can see it as clearly as I can. I had no idea he ever filed them and had no chance to respond. So how about you and I cut the shit?"

"Fine." He put the papers in the folder and closed it, shaking his head.

If Michael could flip the script, so could she. She knew all the questions that had let him walk free, so many times before. Now it was her turn.

"Did I assault this man?"

He smiled, but did not answer.

"I'll take that as a no?"

He shrugged.

"Did I commit a battery against him?"

He squinted his eyes briefly at her, but still did not speak.

"So right now, I'm looking at time for . . . let me get this straight . . . *following* someone. Because you know that is how my attorney will end up arguing it."

"I thought you didn't need an attorney, Ms. Kincaid."

"I'm beginning to rethink that, because, sir, I just wanna know. This 'time' you're talking about me doing? Will it be spent picking up freeway trash or lecturing small children on the hazards of smoking?"

"This interview's over," he said calmly.

"I get a phone call."

"Within twenty-four hours of your arrest," he replied, holding his watch up in front of him in an exaggerated fashion. "Which by my time means you have a good twelve hours to go since, due to your cooperative nature, we will not be able to let you make that call until, oh, sometime in the twenty-third hour."

"Bail?"

"After the hearing."

"Will the hearing be here in DC?"

"Within thirty-six hours."

Maggie shook her head.

"My dad used to have this old saying, Ms. Kincaid."

Maggie returned her eyes to his.

"No one is blinder than he who will not see."

Maggie smiled in spite of herself and nodded. "I understand that you're just trying to do your job, Detective. I hope you understand that I just can't help you do it."

He nodded in return. "Fair enough."

He escorted her back out into the hall, where they waited together in silence until the two officers who had brought her to him returned to take her to her cell, where they removed her cuffs.

As they closed the metal door, she heard the lock engage again.

She leaned against the concrete wall, unable to concentrate on anything now except the two words that swung back and forth, like monkeys, between the prison bars. Mocking her over and over.

In absentia.

CHAPTER FORTY-FIVE

HOURS LATER, as she sat at the foot of her bunk and stared at the specks of black in the concrete floor of the cell, she tried not to think. But truths were beginning to wander the halls of her mind.

You are as much to blame for all of this as he is.

The notion was so insane at first that it merited a complete denial instantly, but her reason took hold of the suspicion like a dog with a towel, to pull and tear at it.

Maybe you allowed Michael to follow you. City to city. Maybe you wanted the game to continue, at every turn.

Why would I do that?

Silence. She waited for it to come back now, an idea made a boomerang, streaking through the clouds of her thoughts, intent on striking something or returning for another toss, until something *was* struck. She didn't have to wait long.

Because that was easier than making it stop.

Isolated. Alone. The coolness of the cell surrounded her. Someone out in the booking room was raising his voice at someone else, but it sounded very far off now.

She leaned her head back and rubbed her fingers into her eyes, trying to stop the blood pulsing heavily in her head from going there. *That isn't true. I made it stop when I refused to keep running.*

No. No. No. You stopped running from Michael, yes, but not from everything.

What?

She heard metal on metal. Startled, she jumped and looked to the cell door.

There was a new female cop on duty now. Heavyset, with bulging eyes and cropped hair. "My shift change notes say you want something from your personal affects?" she barked.

Maggie sat, unable to speak for a moment, unable to stop thinking . . .

What did that mean? Of course, we were talking about Michael. What else could we be talking about? What—

"Hey! You with me here or not?" the cop shouted.

Reluctantly, Maggie came to.

"Yes. I'm sorry. I was just thinking about something."

"That's great that you can think. Like I give a shit. Now, what was it you wanted?"

"In my jacket there's a phone number on an ATM receipt in one of the pockets. The right pocket, I think."

"You need that for your call?"

"Yes, please. I can't remember it offhand."

Maggie noticed her name badge: TOTH.

"I'll check with the equipment desk and get it pulled for you. What color is your jacket, just in case the numb-nuts down there have mixed it up?"

"Black and white. With a North Face label."

The cop looked Maggie up and down and nodded, as if

to silently confirm that Maggie was just the type of girl who would wear North Face on a regular basis. Maggie wondered what Officer Toth would wear, when off duty. The answer came almost immediately: baggy sweats.

"Fine. I'll get it for you."

"Soon?" Maggie asked tentatively.

"You'll have it by the time you get to make your call, if we can find it, how's that?" Officer Toth responded, irritation in her voice.

Maggie nodded, and sat back down on her cot.

She thought momentarily of returning to her inner debate, but she was tired of fighting with her dreams, as she had been since this all began.

She knew before Officer Toth came back later to chaperone her out of her cage and down the hall to the pay phone mounted on the wall who her phone call would go to. It wouldn't be to her mother or father, or anyone else. It would be to the only person in the entire world Maggie felt could truly help her now.

The Walrus Lady.

CHAPTER FORTY-SIX

PRICK THAT HE WAS, Detective Meyer had evidently left word with the desk that the stalking suspect in the back corner cell was not to get her call until the last hour. Maggie assumed as much, but that didn't make the day go by any quicker as she waited. In jail, seconds were like days, hours like years. And the meals were as bad as advertised.

Yet now, standing at the phone, her ten minutes on the clock about to start, she was terrified to dial the number on the small slip of paper that had been handed to her by Officer Toth. If the old lady did not answer the phone, Maggie would have no choice but to call her parents. There was no one else left to call. Then what? She held her breath, and dialed, praying that Madeline would be home and not out walking the neighborhood. In two rings a familiar voice answered.

"Hello?"

"Madeline?"

"Maggie?!"

"Yes!"

"How are you? Are you okay?"

"Well . . . not really."

"Oh dear. What's wrong? Did he hurt you? Are you—"

"No. No, I'm fine. But I'm...I don't know how to say this, Madeline."

"What is it?"

"I'm in jail."

There was an uncomfortable silence on the other end of the phone.

Maggie understood it immediately.

"I didn't do anything, Madeline."

She heard the phone being roughed up by the old lady, as if she were transferring it from one ear to the other.

"What happened?"

Maggie glanced around. She didn't think it was legal to tape phone calls such as this, but she noticed the camera at the end of the hall. It might be legal to film the call and at least record one end of the conversation. She decided to be careful.

"It's a long story, and I don't have much time. But I'm in Washington, DC and I have been falsely accused of stalking him."

"What?" the old lady exclaimed.

"Yes. I know." She glanced up at the camera with an irritated look. Maybe Detective Meyer was watching right now, maybe he would just watch the tape tomorrow, but whichever was the case, she wanted him to know how stupid she thought he was. "The cops here get their training from watching old episodes of *NYPD Blue*, I think."

"Oh, no. What can I do to help?"

Maggie hesitated, but she had to do it.

"At some point, they're going to set bail. I don't suppose you would be willing to—"

"Where do I wire the money? How much?"

Maggie was surprised the old lady was willing to help so easily.

"I'm at the Carter Center Facility, just outside of Foggy Bottom. The number is 909–989–0003, ask for the front desk, they will tell you what to do."

Madeleine sounded genuinely flustered now. "Let me make sure I have a pen, oh dear, give me a moment . . ."

Her voice trailed off as Maggie waited.

"Okay. Got one. What was the number again?"

To be safe, Maggie repeated everything, then had Madeline read the information back to her.

"You don't have a bail amount yet?"

"No, my hearing is in the morning. They said 9:00 a.m. So if you call after that they should be able to tell you, though you might have to keep trying until all the paperwork is processed."

"Okay, I will."

"Thank you so much, Madeline. I promise I'll pay you back."

If I live to get the chance.

"Maggie?"

"Yes?"

"Is everything alright, dear?"

"Well, this place isn't—"

"No. I mean . . . in your dreams?"

She glanced over her shoulder, feeling very much like a crazy person.

No more fighting it, Maggie. "I dreamed about you last night, Madeline. I was in the water . . ."

"By the island?"

"Yes. By the island. And . . ."

"I was in a boat?" Madeline asked, cautiously.

This is insane. How is this happening? And she's just as freaked out now about this as I am. "Yes. You were."

"You saw me, Maggie?"

"Yes. I did. Didn't you see me?"

"No. I had the feeling you were out there somewhere, I kind of saw something, I kept hearing something, and I was reaching out to it but . . ."

"That was me. That was me in the water," Maggie replied.

"Oh."

There was a stilted way in which she spoke the last word that caused Maggie concern. "What's the matter?"

"Nothing. N-nothing at all."

She was lying.

"Madeline?"

"It was just a dream. That's all. Some may be real, and others not, right?"

No. No I don't think you and I are working on that wavelength, Madeline, but if it makes you feel better? Then okay.

"Yes," Maggie lied back.

"I kept looking for you. I knew you were out there. But I kept hearing these words, so loudly, over and over in my head, from behind me it seemed."

"What words?"

"It . . . it was horrible, Maggie. There was blood in the water, so much blood."

Maggie's heart sank.

That couldn't be. I made it back on the boat. I made it in time.

She took a few moments to catch her breath, before asking, "Are you sure?"

"Maggie?"

"Yes, Madeline?"

"Do the words *in absentia* mean anything to you?"

A breath caught in her throat before she was able to force out her answer. "Yes. Yes, they do."

"Those were the words I kept hearing, and it worried me so."

She lowered her voice. "It's fine, Madeline." She decided the old lady deserved to hear the truth this time. "He has filed restraining orders against me, false ones, in different cities, never when I was around. That's what *in absentia* means: 'not present.' That's probably what my grandmother was trying to tell you."

Silence came looming through the receiver.

"Madeline?"

"Oh, my. I, uh . . . I don't know what to say, this is so odd, all of it, and I don't understand how I am . . ."

"Madeline, just spit it out."

"Well." She sighed. "In my dream?"

"Yes?"

"It was a man's voice saying the words, not your grandmother. A . . . strangely familiar voice."

Her disbelief crushed Maggie like a stone.

"And he was talking about your grandmother, not you."

Try as she might, Maggie couldn't speak.

There was blood in the water. Blood.

That couldn't be. I made it back to the boat. I made it in time.

The words ricocheted around in her skull, as she struggled to answer the Walrus Lady, who was shouting in her ear now.

"Maggie! Maggie! Are you still there?"

What if I wasn't the only one in the water?

"Oh God," she said aloud.

"Maggie? I don't know that it means anything, you know that, don't you?"

Maggie rested her arm across the top of the pay phone. Her fingers, which were hanging off the edge, were shaking violently.

Officer Toth stepped up beside her. "Time's up."

"I have to go now, Madeline."

"Maggie, it'll be fine. I'll get the money there tomorrow, I have plenty in savings. Ha, I've been saving all my life, it seems." She laughed uneasily, her voice sounding as if were thick with phlegm. Maggie realized the Walrus Lady was crying.

But she was unable to comfort her, the sensation of shock having spread throughout her body, so she simply repeated herself. "I have to go now, Madeline."

Then she hung up the phone.

"Ready?" Officer Toth asked, grabbing Maggie just above the elbow of her right arm.

"Y-yeah," Maggie replied. As they began to shuffle down the hall together, Maggie could barely manage her balance. She felt the officer's eyes on her, studying her face.

It was a man's voice. Who? What man?

Somehow, some way, she made it back to her cell. When she arrived she simply walked in, her back to the cell door.

"Shit, you're acting like you've seen a ghost," Officer Toth replied.

"Please, leave me alone," Maggie said. As she lay down on the bunk again, she noticed the smell of bleach in the mattress pad.

The cell door closed and Officer Toth walked away.

Over the next several hours the other cells in the jail began to fill. Evidently a fight had broken out at a rally near the Capitol and a number of people were arrested for disturbing the peace. She heard men and women all shouting and screaming about their rights, about being detained illegally, about police brutality and several other issues.

Through it all, Maggie remained the sole occupant in her cell, though twice a flustered officer on shift had tried to put someone in with her by mistake, each time being reprimanded by Officer Toth.

They really think I'm nuts, Maggie thought.

She wondered if maybe they were on to something, then snickered in anguished defeat, remembering a line from one of her favorite poems by Emily Dickenson. "Pain has an element of blank."

That's pretty much what she felt like now: nothing.

As she lay on the bunk the entire time, she kept her eyes forced open, afraid to fall asleep again, afraid of the boat, afraid of the island and, yes, afraid of herself. But she had to sleep, for two reasons: real life was becoming too hard to deal with, and because her dreams might have something more to tell her.

But they did not.

CHAPTER FORTY-SEVEN

THE NEXT MORNING, she was awoken at six o'clock and herded with a dozen of the protesters and a few crack addicts into a small bus parked at the back of the police station. After a fifteen-minute ride they arrived at a small beige courthouse across from the Washington DC Athletic Club.

As they were ushered off in alphabetical order by last name, Maggie glanced up to the sky, noticing the sun had been drowned out by a sea of light gray clouds. The air smelled of cigarette smoke and exhaust fumes, the former from a lit Marlboro in the bus driver's mouth, the latter by the backfiring of a passing VW Beetle that had been leaving the parking lot they had pulled into.

Through it all, encapsulated in a fog of fatigue and resignation, Maggie refused to show any emotion.

When it was her turn to appear before the judge, she listened briefly to the public defender who had been assigned to her case, and at his direction, and after repeated assurances that by doing so she would not delay the setting of her bail and possible release time, she pleaded "Not

Guilty."

The judge, a woman, looked her over calmly before setting her bail at ten thousand dollars. "Is there anything further you would like to say in regards to this complaint, Ms. Kincaid?"

Maggie simply shook her head, stunned. She was surrounded by cops and judges and lawyers. She was the safest she'd ever been in years, and the most grief stricken. If she wasn't determined to save Julie, she likely would have plead guilty, just to end her own misery. After all, in jail Michael could never get to her.

Once all the cases after hers were heard, she and the rest of her group were loaded back onto the bus. She noticed four people were missing. Probably sent off to a more secure prison, she guessed.

It wasn't until seven that evening that her cell door was opened and she was informed that her bail had been posted.

She was escorted to the front desk for what they called "exit processing," and once that was completed, she was handed a brown bag with her clothes in it. Her jacket was given to her also, as was a clear plastic bag that held her keys, cell phone and cash.

Her mace, of course, was missing. They informed her that they would be holding onto that until after her verdict was rendered, and that, if she were found innocent, she could come back to the station house to pick it up with copies of the court documents necessary to do so.

When she stepped out to the street, a free person once more, she knew she was anything but. One set of bars now behind her, the old, familiar set was now back, slamming down all around her again. This was the "Prison of Michael," and she was aware of it immediately.

When she saw him, waiting just across the street, leaning against a mailbox at the corner, she froze.

He pointed at his hand.

In it was his cell phone.

She reached into her bag and pulled out her phone, hopeful that someone had turned if off during her booking. Looking down, she pushed the power button, held her breath and waited for the display to light up. When it did, she exhaled. It was Monday. This nightmare had now gone on for nearly four days. She noticed that she had half a battery charge left, and an open signal.

She looked up to see him again, but he was gone, probably off around the corner and down the street by now.

Her phone rang.

"Yes?" she said, the hostility in her voice apparent even to her.

"How was your stay?"

"I'm tired, Michael, of all of this shit."

"You pled 'Not Guilty.' I'm very impressed. Do you think that is the same as pleading 'Innocent?'"

"Whatever. Whatever you say."

He sighed into the phone before continuing, "You had to go through that. You had to see what that was like for me all those times."

Maggie didn't reply.

"Okay, Mags. I understand. Best to keep this chat short, I guess, so you can get yourself some rest. There's a great hotel up on London Court. You may remember it?"

She did. They had celebrated their one year anniversary there, in the master suite. Another one of his happy memories and one she could've gone without. "Yes, I do."

"You don't have to stay there if you don't want to, but it would be nice if you got yourself some rest somewhere for the big dance tomorrow night."

"The big what?"

"Yeah. Getting arrested, you almost blew it. I was going to post bail myself if I had to, though that surely would've caused a lot of unnecessary questions."

"So what about tomorrow night?"

"It's a dance. Actually, a ball. A formal ball."

"You can't be serious."

"Yes. I am. Serious enough to remember you once told me you always wanted to go to one because they were so romantic. There was the one we had lined up that one year, don't you remember?"

"No, I don't."

"It was going to be a winter formal, with a large dance floor, and all the guests would dance until the morning?" He sounded wistful.

She closed her eyes. *Their wedding. He was talking about the wedding they had planned.*

"Michael . . ."

"My mother was going to be there too. She was going to dance with me, and then you had that flower she was going to take off my lapel and give to you, some sort of Irish tradition or something like that?"

"Yes."

"But that can't happen now because, well, for a lot of reasons I guess . . ."

"Michael, if you want to—"

"One, you aren't sure you love me anymore," he interjected. "And, two . . ."

His voice trailed off for a moment. Then she heard him murmur, "My mother's dead now, Maggie."

She was stunned. "What?"

"No one for me to dance with but *you*, now."

"How did —"

"Lung cancer. She was diagnosed shortly after you called off the wedding. You remember when you first went to Chicago?"

"Yes."

"It took me a while to catch up, no?"

It did. She never knew why. Never even cared at the time. But this explained it. His mother.

He continued, "I was busy with the funeral arrangements and all."

I'm screwed now. Worse than ever.

"Michael, I'm sorry to hear—"

"No. No you're not. She could've died knowing her son was going to be taken care of, Maggie. She loved you to death, don't you remember?"

His mother had been a great person, and a decent human being. Maggie could remember her, very well. "Yes, I do."

"She died worried sick about me, Maggie. Worried sick. She couldn't believe you left me like that. She didn't understand."

Oh man, oh man, oh man.

"Every time I called home . . . through the chemo and the radiation, through the coughing fits that were so bad she could barely finish a sentence . . . all she wanted to know was if I was doing okay, if we had patched things up." His voice was wavering and tight, as if his own words were strangling him. "Can you believe that shit?"

"Michael, I'm sorry to hear all of this." For his mother's sake, she was. For him? Not so much. "I never—"

"Go to Penn Ave and H tomorrow. Playa's is the name of the dress shop. There will be a dress waiting for you. I think it's the right size, but they'll do a final fitting."

263

She rushed to delay him, to get a grip on everything. "Michael, wait, I—"

"Keep your phone with you. I'll call you tomorrow with the place and the time."

"*Michael!*"

For a moment she thought he had hung up, then his voice returned to her ear. "Oh yeah, I almost forgot something. I fed her cream corn and a chicken leg the night before last, macaroni and cheese yesterday for lunch . . . She said you and her used to make that all the time together when you got home from school on rainy days?"

Maggie's heart buckled with his words. They had indeed shared that rainy-day ritual, all the way through high school and up until Maggie moved away for college.

Michael continued, ignoring her silence, "Last night I was out late so, unfortunately she missed dinner, but this morning I made her pancakes with jelly."

Maggie couldn't speak. It was happening again, that feeling in her mind. That ache and slip.

"You there, Mags?" he asked confidently.

He wanted to hear it. He wanted to hear her tears.

She burst out crying. "Why? Why have you done *any* of this?"

"Easy. So you would know how much I love you. I've already told you that, haven't I?"

"I can't take this anymore, Michael. I can't do it . . ." She rubbed her fingers repeatedly against her cheek, the heel of her hand pushing against her chin.

"Oh there, there, honey. It'll be fiiiiine. I promise. I have something else for you, as a reward, you know, for keeping our pact."

"What?"

"I thought for sure you would crack. I did. You and a jail

264

cell? I don't think even Vegas would've taken those odds."

"As if I had a choice."

"Loyalty, Maggie. It's very important."

"What's my reward, Michael," she said sarcastically as she wiped the tears from her eyes.

"You get one listen, no more."

She heard his cell phone knocking up against something hard and then, amazingly, came Julie's voice. "Maggie? Maggie, are you there?"

Her tears dissipated with caution. She'd been down this road before, all for nothing, all for a plastic audio tape.

"Julie?" she asked tentatively.

"Maggie, I'm here. Are you okay?"

Her knees gave way, collapsing her to the sidewalk, her buttocks landing on the back of her shoes.

Am I okay? Unbelievable.

"Yes! I'm fine. Are you? Has he hurt you, is there—"

"My leg's hurt. He keeps taking me to different places— *Ow!* Stop it!"

Maggie jumped to her feet, her adrenaline pumping and her rage swelling at the sound of her sister's scream. She ran to the corner where he'd been standing and looked for him.

Nothing. *Shit, which way did he go?*

"Maggie, are you there?"

"Yes, Jules?"

"He wants me to read you something . . . a poem or something . . ." She was crying now. He'd hurt her.

"What poem?"

Julie cleared her throat and began. "How many loved your moments of glad grace . . . And loved your beauty with love false or true . . . But one man loved the pilgrim soul in you . . . And loved the sorrows of your changing face."

Maggie knew Yeats all too well. *He's making her read*

your favorite poem.

"Maggie? I love you," Julie said feebly.

"Julie! Don't let him—"

She heard the phone being pulled away from Julie.

"Playtime's over, Maggie. You wanted proof? There's some more proof. Don't get cute, and do as you're told. It's almost over. Playa's. Tomorrow! Got it?"

"Yes," Maggie snapped back.

He hung up.

It was all very clear now.

The end game was in play.

CHAPTER FORTY-EIGHT

SHE MADE HER WAY two blocks north, looking for a cab that was nowhere to be found. She glanced east and saw what looked like a fairly busy intersection that way. As she walked, a sudden bite rose in the air, the cold snap that always forewarned of a coming storm.

She zipped up her jacket, mindful now of her vulnerability, all the way around: no gun, no mace, no anything. She fell back to the only defense she had left: her keys. She slid them between her fingers, splayed outwards like claws. If he had been bluffing about the dance and the dress thing, if she found herself instead facing off with him one-on-one here in the street, he would have a distinct advantage, but there was nothing she could do about that. Yet.

Mindful that the street was well lit and currently populated with a sprinkling of people on foot making their way to and from a small market across the street, Maggie put the rest of her attention on getting to the corner. She wanted to thank the police for discharging her from a station located in a seedy part of town, after dark. Just two blocks up the street she noticed a gang of boys, talking and smoking, circled around a small car. They were all looking at her.

Maybe I'll get raped now, too.

Nervously, she crossed the street to the market, finding what she was hoping for, a shelter from the cold.

She opened her Uber app and was surprised to see someone—Benji with a red Prius—pick up her request quickly. Then she stared forlornly at her GeoTag app, remembering what Julie said. "He keeps taking me different places." Her plan was ruined now, for a whole host of reasons. Things were already sketchy before; a push pin that at least narrowed down the street to Dumbarton. Now with the time to zoom in, the app might be able to give her the exact home.

But then what? It wasn't like she could knock on the door. She could break in, but who was she kidding? The home might be alarmed or a neighbor might hear and call 911. Then? Another visit with the police. And no doubt a longer stay in jail.

She'd ruined her chances of going to the police now, too. They'd think she was nuts for sure: out of jail, on bail, accused of stalking, showing up with a GeoTag app and asking for help? Yeah. Right. Sure. But none of it mattered, did it? No. She was wasting time even thinking about it. Not because of what Julie had said, but because of what Michael had said, the night she was arrested.

"I will slit her throat the minute they show up."

She put her head in her hands, already feeling overwhelmed again.

"Do you know how long it takes for someone to bleed out after you've cut their jugular? Two minutes. Tops."

Even if they were still at that house, it didn't matter who tried to get in, Maggie or some cop. Michael had meant what he said.

She thought of Julie bleeding to death, a sick smile carved into her throat from a knife in Michael's hand. No. She couldn't risk that. Especially now that it was likely that he'd moved her to some other place anyway.

Ten minutes later, Benji and the red Prius pulled up.

"Where we headed?" asked the fat bald man inside, an argyle-style golfer's cap on his head, resting just above his eyebrows, which were dark and too skinny for his face. He looked like a "Sal" or a "Bob," not a "Benji."

"I don't know. Kinda need your help for that one," Maggie replied as she climbed into the backseat and closed the door behind her.

"Okaaaaaay. Well. Let's figure it out quick," he prodded, hitting the door lock button and looking around nervously.

"Well, I have two stops. First, I need to go by the Radio Shack on . . . Jefferson, I think?"

"No probs. Be there in a jiffy," he said with a nod, reaching a pudgy hand to tap his cell phone for the pickup confirmation.

Maggie watched the neighborhood around her grow darker and darker as the storm moved in.

Soon they passed a Circle K that jogged her memory; she'd seen that store on the way into the station the night she'd been arrested, and the Foster Freeze a half block later. From what she could make out of the neighborhood, it was the polar opposite of Georgetown. Almost every house had a fenced yard, and most of the cars in the driveways were either late model American made or tricked out imports with rims almost as big as the tires. At times she would catch sight of one person or another, mostly black, some looking as dangerous as the boys that had been staring at Maggie earlier on the corner.

"Quite the neighborhood," Maggie deadpanned.

He chuckled. "You expected something else?"

"I don't even know where we are."

"Fairplex District. Nothing but druggies out this way. I woulda passed on your call if it wasn't such a slow night," he finished with a laugh.

"Fairplex District," Maggie repeated. "Never heard of it."

"How did you get over this way? A friend give you a ride or something?"

"No."

She didn't offer an alternative answer. After a few moments silence the driver said, "My name's Benji." He smiled into the rear-view mirror. "Yours?"

"Maggie."

"Maggie's a cool name."

"Thanks. And I wasn't here buying drugs, if that's what you were wondering."

"Hey, none of my never mind."

"Okay."

A few minutes and a half dozen blocks later, his curiosity got the better of him, as she expected it would.

"So what—"

"I was in jail."

"No!" He snorted, glancing in his rear-view mirror again. "Pretty little thing like you? For what?"

"Stalking my ex-boyfriend," Maggie answered, meeting his eyes in the mirror. "Or something like that."

"Oh," Benji said, sounding stunned.

The rest of the ride to the Radio Shack was made pretty much in silence, with the exception of him asking her permission to roll down the window.

What's the matter, Benji? That make you nervous? I

270

ain't so pretty all of a sudden, am I?

She felt bad for scaring the old guy, but it shut him up. On any other day, a short Q&A to pass the time between destinations might've been a good idea, but not now.

Now she had only one thing on her mind.

Her gun.

CHAPTER FORTY-NINE

NEARING THE RADIO SHACK, she asked Benji to pull over a block shy, noticing immediately that the store lights were on. There was no way she was going to walk in the store and give lover boy a chance to bitch at her about the bogus number she'd given him, if he were on duty, but this presented another problem now. Benji would notice when she didn't go into the store.

"I'm going around the corner real quick to see if my girlfriend is home and to pick something up. Can you wait here?"

"Sure you don't want me to drive you?"

"Nah. I wanna keep it low profile."

"Mm-hmm," Benji replied dryly.

Maggie had a thought. "It's just that . . . her boyfriend doesn't know about us." She smiled.

A look of pleasant surprise came over his face.

Woman on woman. The mere thought of it for most men was like being hit with a stun gun or something. He would probably fantasize about that until she got back.

Whatever. As long as it kept him waiting.

"It's cool," he said, trying to act nonchalant.

Maggie made her way down the sidewalk, her head down as she passed the Radio Shack and quickly glancing into the store. Only one guard on duty tonight, a tall man who hovered near one of the computer displays, checking out some papers. She sighed in relief.

Turning the corner, she used her memory to sift through the landmarks she saw. A pile of old boxes was still where she remembered them, stacked next to a fire hydrant along the street. She'd tossed the gun opposite these boxes, in a row of bushes and heavy grass that ran alongside the building wall.

Please, God. Let it still be there.

Glancing over her shoulder one last time, she dropped to her knees and began fumbling through the bushes, her hands running through the cold grass.

Nothing.

She scooted a few feet down and tried again. Nothing.

Dammit!

She looked around, ducking her head along the row, trying to peer beneath the overgrown branches. Moving down another few feet, she tried over and over, her hands raking through old soda cups and a few beer bottles, her fingers poking and prodding at the soil, all to no avail. Panicking, she backed up to where she had started and began again, this time moving in the other direction, towards the corner, where the bushes tapered off sharply into a patch of dirt.

I didn't throw it this close to where someone could find it. I know I didn't.

Still nothing.

No! This can't—

Her right index finger struck something metal. Her other fingers clutched at it in eager surprise.

Oh, thank God!

She knew it by the feel of it, by the weight of it, so similar to that day her father had given it to her, when she had felt safe all of a sudden, like it was a totem of some sort. She pulled it from the bushes, her eyes verifying what she suspected.

Thank you, God! Thank you, thank you, thank you.

She stuffed it immediately into the waistband of her jeans and covered it with her jacket before heading back to the car.

Hopping in, Benji was alight with hopes and dreams, like he probably was as a kid at Christmas, visions of sugar plums dancing in his head. Except now the tiny glitter of imagination in his eye had nothing to do with sugar plums.

"So? How's your friend?"

Maggie smiled, annoyed. She had what she wanted now. No need to play games. "She has a yeast infection."

Benji grimaced, instantly done with the conversation. "Damn. So, where to now?"

The entire time in jail they'd never gotten into how she'd made it into town. They probably just assumed she was a run-of-the-mill stalker, transient, moving around all the time. That meant that, if she were lucky, her rental car would still be where she left it.

"The Tombs."

He drove her the short distance in silence, and as they turned the final corner she spotted the Forte, still where she'd left it, though now with two days of parking tickets stuck beneath the windshield wiper.

Screw it. I'll take the tickets. Just give me the car, and the charger inside it.

"You can drop me off here, thanks."

He pulled over, cracking his neck as he did so, and punched his cell phone to finalize the ride.

"Do you know where the nearest hotel is from here?" she asked.

He thought about it for a moment. "The Belmont. About eight blocks straight up the road."

"Thanks, Benji," she said, handing him a tip. "Have a good night."

"Much appreciated. You too," he replied.

Getting out of the cab, she noticed the air was going from cold to frigid. Snow was coming. She watched Benji drive off into the distance and had an eerie thought. She wondered if he would remember her name, or this night, come tomorrow or the day after, when maybe he would read the paper over his morning cup of coffee and see her face.

How will he feel about that tip when he realizes it came from a dead person?

CHAPTER FIFTY

MAGGIE PLUGGED IN her cell phone and eased into the familiar comfort of the Forte, feeling like she was on a roll now, at last.

The gun, the car, the charger.

Everything she had needed before her slight detour with the police.

After a few moments, she turned the key in the ignition and drove up the road. Seeing that The Belmont was a small hotel, she decided to park her car on the street at an open meter.

After getting out of the car, she made it to the sidewalk with more effort than she would have liked. It hit her; she was exhausted. Everything that happened to her in the last seventy-two hours had been capped off by a night in which she had refused to sleep. Now, with the night in full bloom, she could barely stand.

Sleep. And the boat.

You don't want to go to sleep tonight either. You know that, don't you?

But she knew she wouldn't be able to stay up, there was no way, and a part of her didn't care anymore.

Walking up the sidewalk she noticed a string of small shops, all closed for the night, leading up to the hotel. There was a tailor and a barbershop, and a collectibles shop that had a lighted display window like ones you would see at a Bombay Company store, with small replicas of civil war soldiers spread out over a mock battlefield surrounded by antique wood figurines and a series of custom smoking pipes in their own individual cases.

Her mind registered the pipes, on some level, long before she reached the next store window. But as she continued down the sidewalk, thoughts of a hot bath and a warm hotel bed for the night beckoning to her aching body, she saw them there, just ten feet in the distance, reflecting through the window of the shop.

She stopped cold, stricken with awe.

Lined up from the top of the window to the bottom, on staggered shelves, faintly back-lit to illuminate them, were dozens and dozens of snow globes.

Some were of elves at play or of fantasy castles, others held picturesque scenes of imaginary ocean bottoms and stellar constellations. There was a dancing moon face in one, a Ferris wheel in another. Some had animals, like a mouse reading a book or a seal balancing a ball on its nose, others held small displays of people, trapped like ghosts beneath glass skies.

She shuffled across the sidewalk, edging closer to the display, drawing so close, at last, that her breath began to fog against the window.

All that sparkling snow, in all those orbs. Fake. She could see it, just as the real snow began to fall now, down

277

from the sky, with short-lived kisses on her cheeks and fore-head, the storm having finally arrived. And that was all it took, really, for the landslide within her to begin.

The snow globes reminded her of that one special snow globe, perched there on the shelf in her grandfather's den.

The bookshelf behind his desk.

Where they had sat together and guessed at words to the crossword puzzles, and talked and . . .

They had been stuck on a three-letter word for "a light meal or social gathering."

They had none of the letters to work with.

He had been busy . . . doing some task or chore.

Starting the record player. Yes, that was it. The violins in Cochella in E-Flat Major breaking out in mid-phrase in a sort of sorrowful glee, something only violins could make possible, before the cellos moaned and the clarinets danced into the piece and filled it up, so much so that it was as if the song were a great cedar chest filled with gifts.

But how could that be?

Putting on a record?

In the middle of the strings?

Who sets down the needle, midway through a piece of music?

No. He had been with her . . . in the chair . . . the piece was *already* playing . . . it had been for some time. Yes. They were both in the chair, stuck on the missing letters. A three-letter word for "a light meal or social gathering." But he wasn't helping her . . .

because . . .

because . . .

He was busy.

Doing other things.

THE SNOW GLOBE

He was . . .

Fondling her chest,

for brief periods of time . . .
                                        She knew it was wrong.
            She knew.

            Her mother had told her . . .
What boys wanted.

            Not what they *really* wanted . . . she would find that
out later.
            When she got older.

            No, her mother had only taught her what boys wanted
without knowing why.

            So she had been taught to cover her chest on cold days.
And how to sit with her legs crossed and with her hands in
her lap . . .
                                        When wearing a dress.

Which she never wore on cold days . . .

                    Or days when she knew . . .

            when she knew . . .

            that she would be seeing her grandfather.

                    Wasn't that something she always avoided?
                                        Why?

She knew why.

It had begun that day . . . when she was . . .

was . . .

stuck on a word.   A . . .
three letter word . . .

that would fit into the puzzle.

And suddenly he was running his hands over her body.
So her confusion was instantly twofold;
Mute . . .

and yet compounded

by her simple inability to understand

what was happening.

This . . .

was not a boy.
This was her grandfather.

This was a grownup that was supposed to
lover her—*NO!*

Love her.

Someone who she looked up to and respected. So . . .

confounded by it . . . too

young . . .

to understand it . . .

she chose to ignore it.
At first.

She attributed a false sense of innocence to his hands.
Denying what was happening.
Until she could deny it no more.

As the incidents and durations would later increase . . .
she would feel sick . . . she would push his hands away,

or try to get off his lap . . .

but
this only seemed
to make him bolder,
her silent protests
leading eventually to her silent sufferings

a misbegotten thing

as his hands began to find her stomach, her legs,
hands, hands everywhere.

Shortly after she began to have nightmares about those
hands, and in her dreams each fingertip had a mouth of
sharp teeth. Those fingers were always . . .

hungry.

But never rough. Strong but never rough.

Never to the point of bruising.

At some point, in the middle of it all, she began to age, her mind lost to older thoughts. She began to realize that he must've done this before, because his timing was always deliberate, his actions succinct. More daring when others were around, but more aggressive when they weren't.

Her forehead was pressed against the window of the store. It was cold. So cold.

She was sliding slowly, ever so slowly, downwards. Her body had abandoned her. She was falling now. Fainting. Falling.

It was a crossword puzzle, like any of the other dozens they had done together, both before and after that day.

But they had none of the letters.

"No. No, no, no, no no," she said softly, then, and now.

Please make it stop. Mom? Dad? Can someone make it stop?

It had been on a Sunday, right after church, when he had first made her touch him. Her parents and grandmother had sent her home with him while they took a detour by the market. Her grandmother needed carrots for the stew, carrots for vitamins, you know, to help you see. But no one had seen the look in her grandfather's face that day. No one but Maggie.

She'd tried to protest, to go to the market with them, but her mother had been worried about Maggie's constant colds, and she didn't want Maggie out in the winter air any longer than necessary. So Maggie had tried a diversion that would haunt her for life, not thinking of what the consequences could be. Julie was so young then. Only four. Maggie had asked if she could come to the house too, but even then Julie was a mama's girl. Julie had said no, sealing Maggie's fate.

Later that night, awake in her bed, unable to sleep

again, her mind replaying the horrible events of the day, she prayed and thanked God for keeping Julie away from him. What a mistake that could have been.

Her grandfather had gotten home as fast as he could drive, and practically yanked her from the car, because she knew it was about to get worse. All of it. She could see by his level of excitement.

No. I don't want to think about this anymore. Please.

The DC sidewalk was brutally cold, the snow beginning to stack, flake by flake, upon it. As her face touched down upon it she was vaguely aware that her head was hurting. She rolled over and looked up at all the snow globes, above her now, like a window to her past, and tried to focus, tried to pull out of it all, but the window, and the brick around it, was beginning to fade, back in time.

He had pulled her into the den and sat her in his lap, as he always did, but this time he had edged his chair close to the entryway, to give him a clear view through the living room window to the driveway beyond, so he would see the instant her parents' car drove up. This made it worse, her fear, because he had never been on the lookout this much before.

That was when she felt it pressing against her wrist, naked and warm, like a thick finger. He had insisted she put her hand around it, digging his fingers into her side for effect when she had initially refused. When she finally complied, he began to breathe heavily, the smell of pipe tobacco fresh on his breath.

She had closed her eyes and pretended that none of it was happening. None of it. Her parents would be home soon.

And her grandmother too.

They would bake cookies together and they would still

love her, even though she was a slut and a whore.

Those were the words her grandfather had told her he would tell them she was, if she ever told on him. He would tell them this was all her fault, for being such a bad girl, for flirting with her own grandfather.

Her eyes blinked back to the present, which was little more now than a veil over the past, and, staring up into the dark night of the sky, she watched the flakes coming down in cascading sprinkles as a soft, begging wail escaped from deep within her.

He'd said they wouldn't love her anymore.

Ever.

That they would *hate* her.

That her mother would never speak to her again.

And her father?

Oh, the shame he would feel. How disgraced he would be of her.

He would never be able to look at her the same way again.

They would be mad at her for seducing him.

For seducing her own grandfather.

For being a little slut.

For being a whore.

So she had closed her eyes and pretended she was somewhere else, until she felt warm liquid all over her hand and arm.

She hadn't looked to see what it was.

And then, it finally dawned on her.

It was tea.

Yes.

That's what it was.

A three-letter word for . . .

"a light meal or social gathering."

Tea.

CHAPTER FIFTY-ONE

HER MIND NOW was a thing she could no longer hold onto or put back together.

It was a jigsaw puzzle, with all the corner pieces missing; with no place to start, there was no way of knowing which way to go.

She awoke herself as one does after a night of heavy drinking: by sheer will alone, against all the body's urgings against it.

She was laying in the snow, in the dead of night, still in front of the store, her back now thankfully to the window and the snow globes within it. She feared what might happen if she looked at them again.

She felt nauseous and filthy, inside and out. Swallowing hard, she forced herself to stand, her bones aching from the cold and her muscles numb. All around her a light snow was falling, and to Maggie it was as if there was no escaping it, any of it. It was as if she had gone from looking at snow globes in the window of the shop, to being inside one.

The street she was on, all the shops and cars on either

side of it, the hotel only a half block away, all were miniature things now, as was she, in a giant globe of glass, the air she was breathing thick, like water. She reached out to touch the snowflakes, convinced they were only little bits of shaved plastic, an odd one here or there incandescent enough to catch the light and dance it through, to the outside world, where the rest of humanity lay in wait, eyes aglow in amazement at this frail little plastic girl who just couldn't stop her dreams.

Desperately, she stumbled up the street to the front entrance of the hotel.

Even if she had arrived fresh and clean, wearing makeup and with her hair properly brushed, she was completely underdressed for The Belmont Hotel. The entrance consisted of thick glass storm doors that slid open automatically. Beyond them was another set of doors, wood framed with etched crystal windows, a giant "B" in old-world type centered within smooth glass ovals that were just offset from the handle on each door.

The lobby was carpeted in deep red with gold trimmed edges. She noticed that the concierge desk was closed for the night, so she followed the carpet until it ended at a large marble floor area, which led straight to the front desk. A small man, who looked to be in his late fifties, stood watching her from the counter.

Maggie walked up to the counter, fishing for her credit card. She didn't know the rates, and she didn't care. All she wanted, in the entire world right now, was a hot bath and a large glass of cold water.

The gentleman's eyes told her that she would have a hard time getting either.

He looked her up and down. "May I help you?"

"Yes. I need a room, please?"

"I'm afraid we're all booked up, madam."

"Oh, God," Maggie exclaimed, leaning on the counter, her forehead in her hands. Her head was killing her. "Please. You've got to have just one room. Please. Just one?"

He looked at her stoically, as if answering the same question twice was not something he liked to do, unless the person asking it was rich and could tip him enough to ask however many times they wanted.

She noticed him looking at her jacket. Looking down, she could see what was bothering him. Her jacket, her jeans, everything was wet. At some point she must have rolled over into a patch of mud, because her left thigh was covered in it.

Dammit. What do I tell him?

The truth.

"Sir?"

"Yes?"

"Look. I know I look bad. I'm sorry. I have a horrible migraine right now. I passed out earlier, just down the street, while on my way here. I have the money to pay," she said, looking into his eyes as she slid her Visa across the counter to him. "And I'm begging you to please just give me a room so I can go to bed and get some rest."

He looked down at the card, his upper lip twitching beneath his tailored mustache as he considered her situation. When he spoke, he kept his lips so firm that they barely showed his teeth. His eyes were a cold brown, and the remainder of his hair only small crops over each ear.

"Madam, I can check for you, but our rates here are over four hundred dollars a night and—"

"I will pay that. Happily. Just a room. Please."

He raised his eyebrows, as if deliberating the situation further, then looked past her and out to the street.

Maggie followed his eyes to see that a limousine was

pulling up.

He doesn't want a scene.

"Look, the sooner I get that room, the sooner I'm out of your way," Maggie said, mustering a weak smile. She needed his pity, but had no energy left to solicit it properly.

He looked disappointed and yet not upset, as if, for whatever reason, he'd felt mildly obligated to be the good gatekeeper and, having done that, the sooner he was finished with her the better.

He nodded slightly. "Very well then."

Maggie said nothing, which made him uncomfortable enough to offer an explanation. "We have a convention this week, and the rooms are sold out starting tomorrow."

Yeah. Sure. I bet they are.

"Great. Thank you."

He nodded, walked a few feet down the counter and, after conferring with his computer monitor and running her credit card, returned with a small plastic key card.

"Your room is on the third floor, number three-ten. I booked you for single occupancy. I trust you won't be having any guests?"

What an asshole. He's afraid I'm a hooker or something.

"No," Maggie said, barely able to hide her contempt. "No guests at all. Just me."

"That's good," he said dryly, sliding the key card and her credit card back to her across the counter. "Have a nice evening."

When she made it to her room she could think of nothing but the bath. She ran the hot water and undressed. Catching sight of herself in the mirror, she gasped.

Her eyes were bloodshot, and black bags had swollen beneath them. Her hair was going in almost every direction, and there was a smudge of mud on her left temple. She looked pale and sick.

No wonder he was so hesitant. It's a miracle he let me in. A miracle.

CHAPTER FIFTY-TWO

SHE QUICKLY DRANK a glass of water. Then another, and another. She was so thirsty she could barely handle it. Unable to wait for the tub to fill up, she sat down in the tub when it was half full and began to dig her fingers into the small parchment wrapper that covered the bar of soap. Both were imprinted with the same formal "B" insignia that was on the front doors of the hotel.

When she was finally able to wash, she began to weep bitterly. "You bastard," she whispered, then she repeated it, louder and louder, until it was almost a shout, her hands pummeling the water in a fit of rage, water splashing everywhere, mixing soap suds into the tears that streamed down her cheeks.

"Oh my God!" she screamed. "How could you? How could you have ever done that to me?"

Her body wracked with grief, she slid slowly down into the tub, feeling the cool porcelain against her neck as she turned sideways and tucked her legs up to her stomach. With one arm pinned to the side of the tub, she used her free hand to rub the soap on her back, neck and face.

It was as if she were a retracted thing now, not borne of light but of darkness. An inner darkness that had always been there, just beneath the surface, bending and reflecting the real person she wanted so desperately to be into the Maggie that could disguise herself, and what had happened to her, so many years before.

How many days and nights did I waste trying to forget you? Until I finally did.

It started when we moved away, at the joy I felt when you were finally too far away to hurt me anymore . . . Yes.

I told myself every night, after my prayers, that it never happened.

That it was all a bad dream.

She moaned and nodded, feeling the bar of soap on her forehead and right temple, rubbing, rubbing, trying to get clean. To be clean.

At first it was hard to believe but then the joy hit . . .

"Oh God," she cried, sitting up again, pulling her knees to her chest.

We moved and I finally had the second chance that I'd longed for and dreamed of for so many days and nights.

She opened her eyes. Through her tears she found a shampoo bottle sitting at the edge of the tub. She grabbed it and squeezed some onto her head before emptying the rest under the running tap, watching as it began to instantly foam with bubbles.

She felt so dirty that she was afraid there wouldn't be enough soap to clean herself with.

I was finally free of him. Mostly. It was hard at first. . .

"Because of the holidays," Maggie said aloud, reaching up to grab a hand towel that was hanging from a brass hoop next to the tub.

Yes. I was spared Thanksgiving, though. It was too soon after the move.

And at Christmas, I got lucky. He was beginning to get sick. He mostly stayed in his room, and when he called for me I made Daddy come in with me, to say . . .

"To say Merry Christmas!" she screamed. "You son of a bitch. I had to say Merry Christmas to you! I had to smile! And pretend! With my, wi-wi-with m-m—"

Her sobs were uncontrollable now, catching in her chest like earthquakes.

With my dad standing right there!

She hurled the shampoo bottle across the bathroom. It ricocheted off the faucet and then the sink before bouncing up against the mirror, over to the toilet seat and down to the floor.

But I made it through that. Even after he smiled at me, lying there, half dead. That look still in his eyes.

Then you worried about your next birthday.

Life went on.

But it always circled around the next time you would have to see him.

My birthday was in May. I made myself sick. With worry.

And you got to stay home. Thanking God with every breath as you heard your mother call your grandparents that day, dialing the phone, canceling with them at the last minute. Oh, the relief. The joy.

Then a miracle happened, didn't it?

Yes. You could think of it that way.

He died. The bastard died.

When he died, it was easier, wasn't it?

Easier to what?

Easier to bury it all. To make yourself forget. It was

easier to pretend.

Yes.

That none of it ever happened.

Why?

Her mind clicked and whirred and spun on edge, the old excuses spitting out like tickets from a game at an old arcade.

Because none of it did happen.

None of it.

It couldn't have.

I would never let myself be hurt that way.

Used that way.

Lied to that way.

I wouldn't. No. I'm smarter than that.

I'm better than that. A better person. A better girl. A better woman.

And my dad . . .

My dad . . .

Your dad what?

Shut up! I don't want to think about this anymore.

No. Say it. Your dad, what?!

"Daddy!" she screamed, pushing her arms through the hot water, flooding it over the sides of the tub. She reached up and turned off the faucet, her teeth grinding away at themselves. The words were there, on the tip of her tongue, but she loved him so . . . how . . . how could she say them aloud?

Say it. Let it go.

"Mom knew, Mom knew. She did. She knew something was wrong."

No. Don't change the subject.

That day on the porch. What she said. How it wasn't my fault that we were moving. How could she?

Don't change the subject.

"She knew!"

Maybe she did. Maybe she suspected. And you made her pay, didn't you?

Yes.

You walled her off. No Hallmark-like mother-daughter relationship here, Ma! No. All your secrets, all your revelations, all your private discussions of fears and dreams...where did they go?

To Daddy.

Yes. So quit changing the subject, because that's what has made this all so much worse ...

Shut up!

You went to the one person who—

"Daddy? How could you not have *known*!?"

—let you down the most.

How many moments had she waited for him to notice that her happiness was fake? How many times had she waited for him to come rushing through the door of that den to see what was happening, and to save her? How many nights had she asked God to tell her father what was happening, so that he could stop it all?

Why did you need God's help to tell him?

Please, leave me alone.

She leaned back in the tub and slid down, holding her breath as she dipped her head beneath the waterline, the hot water spilling into her ears as she hoped it would, in an attempt to drown out the voices within her. She wanted to die now. To let it all go.

It was no use.

Why did you need God's help to tell him?

Because it was ...

She brought her head above the waterline again and exhaled deeply, wiping her hands across her face.

The bathroom was silent.

"Because I was afraid he wouldn't believe me. Because . . ."

Because why?

Because it was HIS father that was doing it to me. Because I knew . . .

"I knew. I just knew," she cried into the empty bathroom, her words bouncing across the tiled walls and right back at her, "that if he loved his dad . . ."

Half as much . . .

"As I loved him?"

She opened her eyes and stopped her crying and the world lurched to a hard stop.

"Maybe he'd never believe me."

These words did not bounce anywhere. They stayed where they were, in the air, just outside the reach of her tongue, where they could still be felt.

It's not your fault.

Yes, it is.

No.

He would have done something. I know it.

There was nothing—

I should have trusted him enough to tell him. And now he's old, and it's too late to tell him. It would break his heart, it would kill him.

You didn't know it then, that he would've believed you.

I was scared to say it.

But you know now, don't you?

And she did.

Because every lie comes hooked, as though with fishing line, to a truth.

She just had to find a way to reel it in.

CHAPTER FIFTY-THREE

AFTER SHE HAD MADE the voices in her head stop talking, she forced herself to get out of the tub, for fear she would pass out in it and drown. For a second she may have wanted to die, but not now.

Her legs were like rubber, and her exhaustion now was beyond extreme. Making her way to the bed, she collapsed, still in the bathrobe she had found wrapped and folded on a stand between the tub and shower.

She was asleep in seconds . . .

Her body was bobbing, up and down. Tonight it was warm in heaven, and peaceful.

She opened her eyes to see the sky had gone from grayish to gold. A gold that bled down the walls of the horizon and into the water, turning it almost pale yellow as it touched and warmed her from her sleep, the sound of the rolling tide spilling into her ears as the waves splashed against the sides of her boat. It reminded her of something she'd read by Nabokov. "The breaking of a wave cannot explain the whole sea."

She sat up and looked around.

She was closer to the island now, much closer than she'd ever been, and yet still she could not help but scan the water for that large black fin.

"*In absentia.*"

The words startled her, but the voice that spoke them brought an instant relief.

She realized that the voice was coming from behind her, and on instinct alone she went to turn her head again, forgetting that this had always been impossible before. But this time there was nothing holding her head in place. Seeing behind her at last, she caught her breath as her eyes took in a sight she hadn't seen for too many years. It was her grandmother.

She was seated on the bench that stretched across the stern of the boat, her hands folded in her lap and a smile on her face, looking like a school child, attentive and yet distracted. Her face was the same as it had been when Maggie was a young, without as many wrinkles as she had in her older years. And her eyes were free of that somber look they had carried, just before she died, when the cancer had shriveled her up inside and the dementia had stolen her mind.

Maggie felt like crying, but the joy inside her blotted out any such idea.

"Grandmother!" she said, spinning around, intent on throwing herself into her grandmother's arms and letting go of that other world, beyond the horizon, her life, forever.

Her grandmother recoiled. "*Noli me tangere.*" Touch me not.

"Where are we?" Maggie asked, looking at the open sea

around them, missing the embrace she wanted to have, yet full of relief to finally be here without being alone or afraid.

"*Locus in quo.*" The place in which something happens.

"What? What happens here?"

"For each one, only what one needs to know."

"Why?"

"Because only by knowing can one understand, and only by understanding can one ever see."

"See what?"

"What one could have been, had one been given the chance."

Her grandmother seemed to sense Maggie's confusion because the small smile that had crept over her lips was now replaced with a slight frown.

"I love you so much, child," she said, holding her hands out to cup Maggie's face but stopping just short of her cheeks.

"I love you too, Gran."

How many times had Maggie prayed to God for the chance to have just one more moment with her grandmother? Given that moment now, she was overcome by a tempest of emotions, from sadness to relief, happiness to disbelief.

Tears formed in the corners of her eyes, but held their positions.

"There is no need for that, Maggie. Not here. Ever."

There was a comfort to her grandmother's gentle chiding that brought the old sassy Maggie back to life for a moment. "If *you* can *frown* in heaven," she said with a smile, "*I* can *cry* in it."

Blinking, the tears fell from her eyes and dissipated almost instantly, the hot-water sting she had been conditioned over her lifetime to expect on her cheeks never arriving.

Her grandmother smiled again, the green of her eyes twinkling against the faint white glow of her skin. It was as if someone had taken an airbrush and sprayed her into form, the paint never drying and the colors still vibrant.

"This is not heaven, child. That much I am allowed to tell you."

Maggie was stunned. "Then where are we?"

"That much I am *not* allowed to tell you," she said, pulling her lips together and raising her eyebrows, anticipating the frustration this would cause Maggie.

But Maggie, looking to the island, simply grew quiet. She was so close to it she could see the sand. It was the color of ripe melons, with small sparkles in it, and it moved slightly, back and forth, in the breeze that was sweeping across it from the sea.

"I never knew," her grandmother said.

"You never knew wha—" Maggie stopped, then understood. She dropped her eyes to her feet.

"Don't ever look down, child. And don't look away."

But Maggie couldn't help it. The shame of her life was now even pervading her dreams.

"The innocent have no need to fear the light."

"I'm not innocent," Maggie said. "I'm anything but."

Her grandmother shook her head.

"If you were a poem, could you prevent those things that affected your rhyme?"

Maggie looked up, curious. Her grandmother had always had a way of asking her questions that caught her attention, or, more to the point, made her *pay* attention.

"If I were a poem? I don't understand."

"We are all written things, Maggie. All our lives, from

one hand to the next, we are written things."

"Who's to say how one is written, then?"

"You are," her grandmother replied, leaning forwards, opening her arms. She was teaching still, even here in heaven, or wherever they were.

"How?"

"If you were a poem, could you prevent those things that affected your rhyme?" her grandmother repeated, this time with insistence.

"Yes."

"Correct."

The boat did its dance on the water, right to left, left to right. Maggie could hear the air for the first time, and the magic of it distracted her for a moment.

"So that's where it comes from," she said aloud, "that sound inside a seashell?"

Her grandmother nodded slightly. "My little Maggie," she said. "You were always so aware of all the little things."

The light in Maggie's eyes went dark. "Not aware enough, it seems."

"If you were a poem ... ?" her grandmother prodded again.

Maggie thought for a second. "I could change myself, so that I *would* rhyme."

Her grandmother nodded. "That which affects, can be affected."

"To what end?"

"The only end that counts." She looked at Maggie, strands of her hair blowing across her face, the love in her eyes reaching out to her as she said the next word: "Salvation."

The tide began to grow stronger, rocking the boat a little harder, and Maggie's grandmother took note of it, as if it were a reminder of some sort.

"You must not blame yourself for your fate," she said, swallowing hard at the words. "A sin against you is not *your* sin."

"Is this . . . like . . . purgatory or something?"

Her grandmother turned her head to the side, as if listening to someone else.

"You can't tell me that either?"

"This place is not any of those things defined by man or religion."

"Then what?" Maggie pleaded. "What's going on? Why do I keep coming here?"

"Because one cannot be re-written until one has been fully read."

It was as if her grandmother had punched her in the stomach.

"I know all there is to know now."

Her grandmother looked at her solemnly, as if pained by what she had to say next.

"No, child. Not yet. You know only that you are broken, Maggie." She paused and took a breath. Her breath smelled of chocolate. "That is a big step, but not the final one."

Maggie looked at her grandmother curiously.

"A soul is like a bone, child. One can know there is a break, but it must be seen before it can be properly set, and set before it can properly heal."

"I don't want to know any more of it."

"Just because a life is altered, doesn't mean it can't be steered back on course."

"What? I have a choice?"

"We all have choices. Only we can make them."

"No. This isn't fair. Too much is going on here. Can't I just stay with you?"

"This place is not where I am to stay. Only where I have waited."

"Waited?"

"For you."

"Why?"

Her grandmother paused a moment before speaking again. "I couldn't help you there," she said with a sigh, "so I chose to help you here."

They were silent together, then grandmother and granddaughter, love across two generations, held firm in a place beyond imagination.

"But there are rules, and now I have to go."

"What? No!" Maggie cried.

Her grandmother held her index finger to her lips, the act alone sending a wave of calm through Maggie.

"No tears, my child," she said as her image began to fade.

"*Quod vide?*" See this thing? She waved her hand across the boat.

"Yes."

"You must take it the rest of the way, on your own."

"How?" Maggie asked, stunned, looking out across the waters.

A stern look came across her grandmother's face. She waved her hand across the expanse of water all around them. "*Mare clausem.*" Closed sea.

She was fading further, almost transparent now, a light from within her glowing amber, like honey, and as her color was lost, her density gave way.

She reached out, and with the tips of her fingers she touched Maggie on the chest, right above her heart, smiling softly with a nod. "*Mare liberum.*" Open sea.

Then she was gone.

Maggie floated on the water, through a day, and a night, and another day. The sea around her changing shades, different hues of blue coalescing into soft shades of purple as a sun that could not be seen rose and set, illumined and darkened. After a while, she felt them, out there, just out of the reach of her mind, floating on the tides, some of them in the streams that led to the rivers, and others on the rivers that led to this sea, all of them, other people, lost and afloat. She realized that here, on a daily basis, the outcome of billions upon billions of lives intersected, some sane, some insane, and death was not a door that separated the two.

No.

Quite the contrary.

It was the door that swung between them.

CHAPTER FIFTY-FOUR

SHE HEARD HER cell phone ringing faintly in the distance, somewhere in her room, but her efforts to awaken were handicapped. She was in a deep sleep, deep as she'd ever been in, and to make matters worse, she didn't want to awaken. Not ever.

The ringing stopped. She sighed, closing her eyes, trying to go back. But then the cell phone began ringing again.

She tried to make herself remember why she was supposed to care about a phone ringing. There was a call coming, an important call, but she didn't know why or from who. She opened her eyes and blinked back the weight of her eyelids.

The phone continued ringing.

The room she awoke in was strange to her, until she turned her head and saw the station guide for the TV sitting there on the nightstand, a folded cardboard pyramid embossed with the ugly "B" logo of the hotel. She shook instantly back into the moment.

She was in Washington DC. She had followed Michael

here.

Michael was calling.

He had Julie.

She sat up, looking for the phone. It was on the floor, next to her jeans.

On the fifth and final ring before voice mail would pick up, she answered.

"H-h-hello," she said, sitting on the floor quickly.

"This is becoming a habit. Why no answer the last two hours, Maggie?"

"Wha . . . ?' she said, rubbing at her eyes. "Wha . . . ?"

"Maggie?"

"Yes."

"It's me."

"I know," she said, looking at the alarm clock on the nightstand, unable to believe what her eyes were telling her; it was a quarter past four in the afternoon.

How did that happen?

"What have you been doing?" he asked.

"Sleeping," she said, unable to explain any further.

Perhaps it was the lost sound in her voice, but he seemed to believe her.

"Good. Beauty rest is important."

Maggie remembered her grandfather again, a sick feeling washing over her. That heartsick feeling that awakens to a new day, after something terrible has happened, a new day that you would rather take a pass on.

Oh my God, I'm done. I'm totally done, she thought.

"Are you listening to me?" he asked impatiently.

"Yes. Shit. Yes. What?" she replied, annoyed.

"Your dress will be ready soon. Do you remember where to go?"

Surprisingly, it came to her instantly: *Playa's.*

"Yes."

She stood up, running her free hand through her hair, using the palm to press at the crick that was twisting in the back of her neck.

"It's paid for," he said. "Go in for your fitting, and wait for my call."

"Where are we going?"

"Never mind," he said. "I will tell you that when you have the dress. Don't be late."

"I'll get it!"

"You don't sound well, Maggie," he said, sounding concerned.

Her head was immersed in a fog. "I'm fine. Fine. I just gotta wake up."

"Okay. I'm sorry you've been through so much," he said, "but it's almost over now. I love you."

He sounded like he did when they were dating, as if she were his girlfriend again, as if comforting her when she was not feeling well was something that he was still allowed to do.

"I'll get the dress, and I'll wait for your call," she said, cutting him off, tired of playing his games.

He hung up in her ear.

She looked around the room, the stuffy furniture exacerbating her sense of feeling out of place. The bed was a mess, the sheet and comforter almost entirely on the floor, one corner of the mattress sheet pulled out of place. It apparently had been a rough night's sleep.

She still felt dirty, and a hot shower sounded good.

CHAPTER FIFTY-FIVE

AFTER HER SHOWER, she dried her hair and checked the TV menu. Someone had charged her card for a second day. This was not the type of place where the staff hassled the guests, and if anything, assumptions were made that extra charges could easily be afforded. Whatever. She managed to sneak in her dirty clothes out through the hotel lobby and back out to her car to fetch her bag, not seeing the man at the front desk from the night before.

She laughed at the sight of another ticket on her car. She was making this city rich. Once she made it back to her room she changed into fresh clothes; a pair of black yoga pants and a t-shirt, with a heavy red sweatshirt. Then she left, anxious to get on with things.

Twenty minutes later she was standing at the front door of Playa's, its window display a series of fall fashion gowns, their logo made of metal sculpted letters and painted a deep rust on a sign mounted over the entrance.

She took a deep breath. *This is nuts. All of it.*

And none of it is within your control. Yet.

She opened the door and walked to the front counter, where a tall red-headed woman waited in a green business dress, her lips full and glossed.

"May I help you?" she asked, her eyes greeting Maggie with warmth after a polite glance at her yoga pants.

"Yes," Maggie asked, "I think so. My name is Maggie. Maggie Kincaid."

The woman looked down instantly to a small scheduler on her desk.

"Yes. Ms. Kincaid, you're here for your dress and a treatment?"

"Yeah. I guess so. I mean, I knew about the dress, but . . . a treatment?"

"Sorry. Just a nickname we use. A massage first, then your hair and nails, and finally makeup. Your husband has arranged for the full 'treatment,' as it were."

Maggie was taken aback. Husband? She should have seen this coming. And you don't get a gown and go to a formal ball without being all fixed up. She noticed the redhead looking disappointed, as if she had expected Maggie to be more excited about this news.

"Wow," Maggie said, covering her tracks. "I'm shocked. I had no idea."

"He must love you very much," she said.

Maggie froze at the suggestion before making a decision.

"I think I'll skip the massage, though," she said.

Because I don't want anyone touching me right now.

"Oh? That's too bad," the woman said, looking back to her scheduler. "Are you sure?"

"Yes. Thanks anyway."

"Okay . . . welllll . . . let me tell Lynette, the masseuse we had scheduled for you today, that you will be skipping your appointment. Instead, we'll get your fitting underway, then get to the rest. Is that okay?"

Maggie smiled curtly. "Yes."

The redhead retreated through a sheer curtain to her right, the word "OFFICE" stenciled over it in some sort of flower-ridden type. Maggie noticed there were two other curtains in the corner of the store. One read "Spa" and the other "Salon." It appeared that Playa's was quite the boutique.

She was surrounded by dresses, most of which would have been beautiful to her eyes at any other time in her life, but not now. Now she simply dreaded finding out which one he'd chosen for her.

Before long the redhead returned with two women who evidently handled the alterations part of the visit. They ushered Maggie into a changing room and then brought in her gown. It was a soft shade of aqua, dusted with tints of blue that shimmered as the gown moved from side to side. She noticed that the material was satin, with a soft cotton liner, and that the gown cut off just above the breast line and midway across the shoulder bone; both there and at the sleeves it was trimmed with fine strips of lace.

He had remembered that aqua was her favorite color. She did her best to feign happiness to spare herself from any silly questions or an awkward atmosphere, both of which she didn't have the energy to deal with. All she could think of was getting it all over with.

After the dress was fitted it was whisked away to another part of the store, and Maggie was escorted to the salon. The hairdresser awaiting her was a Filipina woman in her late twenties named Mimi, who cooed and poked at Maggie's hair and made suggestions on how she thought it would look best. Maggie relented at every turn. She could not have cared less. Over an hour later her hair had been styled in a fashionable bun at the back of her head, interwoven with subtle strands of colored beads of blue and aqua, to match her dress.

After that she received both a French manicure and pedicure by an older woman named Donna, who kept telling her how lucky she was, how all the girls remembered her husband when he came into the store to order her dress, and how he was so handsome. Maggie wanted to ask her if she, or Mimi, or any of the rest of them wanted him, because they sure as hell could have him, but she bit her tongue.

Her makeup was the final touch, done by a girl who had the same skin tone as Maggie and therefore suggested a light touch on the foundation and blush, with an emphasis given to the eyes. Again, Maggie agreed with whatever was suggested, the time going by amazingly fast it seemed, because she was in such a daze of self-denial.

When the makeup was done, she shared the spotlight with two other women who were there, overhearing that one of them was going to a Georgetown ball at the Billsburrow Estates and the other to the Naval Academy Ball in Maryland.

Maggie waited the entire time for her cell phone to ring, so she would at last know where she would be heading for the night, but it never did. When the staff asked her, she honestly told them that it was a surprise. They, of course, thought this was all the more romantic and exciting.

Finally she was brought to the dressing room and given her dress, which she put on, looking into the mirror with mild surprise. She looked good. But it was a brilliant facade.

Beneath its surface she was reminded of her grandmother. She had said there was more to know, but Maggie couldn't imagine it. She could feel "it," whatever it was, moving through the back of her mind, like a caretaker on his rounds; one door to the next, locking one or unlocking the other, jiggling the knobs as he went.

Next, they brought her a pair of closed-toed heels, size seven, that were aqua as well.

They had saved the best for last. The redhead, full of glee, handed her a small beige box wrapped with a blue ribbon. Inside were a pair of diamond earrings and a diamond-studded necklace.

Just when I didn't think it could get any worse, Maggie thought.

"Oh, my . . ." was all she could manage. *They will talk about this for months to come,* she thought, *about that wet noodle that ruined their Romeo's string of surprises. Robbed of their ability to live vicariously through me, they'll now be hard pressed to forget me.*

She almost laughed at the look on all their faces. A collective "That's it?"

"I apologize, but I was expecting a call and . . ."

The redhead beamed unexpectedly. "Oh! Of course, I should've known." She turned to the other ladies. "Someone has the jitters. Is this your first Georgetown ball?" she asked, winking at Mimi.

"Y-yes. Yes, it is," Maggie replied.

"Oh, you poor dear. Well . . . let Mimi and I give you a few pointers while we wait for your limo," she said, shooing the other ladies off.

Limo? Maggie thought.

What followed next was like having two incarnations of Mrs. Catherly there with her at the same time, one a little older than Maggie, the other a little younger. But these were the aristocratic Mrs. Catherlys, the DC elite manifestations of her. They still dealt with womanly advice and etiquette issues, but with a harsher slant.

To make it worse, it appeared she was headed to a fund raising ball that was going to be holding court to a number of first-term senators and congressmen, a few of who were quite handsome and single, and this struck Maggie as the most amazing twist of all: they had just finished giving her a makeover, an expensive gown and a dream set of jewelry, all from a person they thought to be her handsome husband, and now they'd gone from giggling over marriage romance to discussing the actual possibility of illicit affairs with powerful people. How it happened all the time. How no one could blame her, being as beautiful as she was, if something happened, if she opted to "trade up" a bit. It reminded Maggie of all those Proustian writings of the French aristocracy, how it was never enough to have enough.

She heard a horn honking mercifully at the sidewalk. Her limo had arrived.

She left the shop both relieved and disgusted, the driver opening the back door of the limo, her bag in one hand—with the gun inside—and a small silk purse that had been handed to her by the redhead as she exited the store in the other.

She held her breath, wondering if Michael would be seated in the limo near the door or on the opposite bench.

But inside there was no one.

CHAPTER FIFTY-SIX

AT EIGHT O'CLOCK sharp the limo pulled through two giant gates at the base of a steep hill. A sign just to the left of the guard shack that followed read "Georgetown Oaks Country Club." After a brief stop, a guard motioned with a wave for the limo to go on. A short drive on a cobblestone driveway followed, and just in the distance she saw a large building. No doubt this was the main hall of the club

On the way there, with the privacy window up, she struggled with where to hide the gun. She'd been dressed in a pair of hose and garter belts—the girls at the dress shop cooing about how sexy the night that awaited her would be, like a "second wedding night" they laughed—but the garments were useless because they would not support the gun at all. There was also no place in her dress to stuff or hide it, so she had been forced to jam it into the purse that was given her, which was small and barely had any room. It looked awkward, and if she wore it on her arm the way it was meant to be worn, it was going to hang heavy and at an odd angle.

She didn't know what to do, but being separated from

her gun was not going to happen again, especially now, when she knew she would need it. She decided that she would simply hold the purse at her side, partially wrapped in one of the folds of the gown, and hope for the best.

Her nerves were shot and her hands were shaking. Badly. As the limo pulled into line behind a few others, she stole the moment to pour a drink from the decanter of scotch sitting just inside a rack next to one of the doors. She drank it warm. A half glass, straight down.

This is it! It's here. I can feel it. It all happens here.

Without warning, in her mind's eye she saw her grandfather, a pen between his fingers, sitting at his desk and looking out the pair of French doors he had in his den. He was calling out to her.

"Magggieee . . . Magggieee."

She blinked the memory away, and cleared her throat.

Where did THAT come from?

She pulled herself together as the limo came to a full stop and the driver got out. He circled to the passenger side of the car and opened her door, offering his hand to assist her.

Maggie looked at her bag.

"You won't need that," he said. "I'll be waiting for you until the end of the evening." He smiled.

She got out of the limo and immediately did as she had rehearsed in her mind; taking her purse, she tucked it into one of the folds of her dress, pretending to pull it up a bit, as if she were walking over a puddle. They were at the base of the golf course area, which was lined on one side by a number of mansions in the distance, delineated from the country club property by a short four-foot fence.

She walked up to the other guests who were entering, the sounds of conversation spilling out from the building into the cold night air. The snow from the night before had passed, but the chill it left behind was brutal, and sharp enough to cut to the bone.

Typical man, she thought. *He went the whole nine yards. The tenth yard being a shawl, or fur or coat of some sort to keep me from freezing my ass off.*

They entered through a set of large oak doors into a small entryway, which held a sign that read "Austin Medical's Lung Cancer Fund Raiser, 2017."

She remembered that Michael's mother died of lung cancer.

Another set of double doors awaited, and it was only after coming through these doors and taking a good dozen steps that she finally saw him.

He stood with his eyes locked on her, all cleaned up now and freshly shaven. She'd forgotten how handsome he was, somehow, in only catching glimpses of him in various states of disarray over the years. But his eyes were still a piercing blue, his cheekbones strong and his chin firm. As she had suspected, he had lost the weightlifter's build somewhat, but this only made him look thinner in his tuxedo and somehow fitter, his shoulders now more in proportion to his waist.

He stood in the center of a large room, a banquet hall and dance floor beyond, a party orchestra currently playing the fading strands of an old Nat King Cole tune she recognized immediately: "Stardust." A quote by Tolstoy came to her like a stray note from one of the flutes. "Music is the shorthand of emotion."

And that's what was welling up in her; a nor'easter of emotions, waves of them, as she saw him standing before her, one hand tucked in the pants pocket of his tuxedo, the other holding a drink. He gazed at her with eyes cloaked in sadness, as if his heart were breaking all over again.

She simply stared back at him, unsure what to do next. Terrified and yet full of resolve.

He approached her confidently, stopping just before he invaded her personal space.

Maggie felt as if she were covered in a plastic cocoon of unreality. How was any of this happening? And yet, how long had she waited for it?

They stood there, arrested by each other, until he finally leaned over and kissed her, firm and full, on the lips. Maggie held her head steady, refusing to tilt it to either side when his fingers slid under her chin, encouraging her to kiss him back.

She remembered having the same feeling in her grandfather's den one day, as the image of him seated in his chair again washed over her without warning while Michael was kissing her. She'd been terrified to approach her grandfather, and yet, a part of her now so utterly defeated and abused, she remembered also wanting to hurry things along, to just get it over with.

Michael pulled his lips away for a brief second, then kissed her again, nudging her chin more firmly to the side this time, but Maggie's eyes were wide open, staring through his head, back to that den, so many years ago. She was almost thankful when Michael slid the tip of his tongue gently between her lips, because it brought her back to the here and now with a snap.

She pulled her head away and took a half step back.

Shit! What's going on! I can't ... lose it ... now, dammit! Not now.

"Okay, baby," he said, "I'm sorry. I'm rushing things. I have just ... damn, I've just missed you so much."

"Michael, what are we doing here?"

He smiled. "Come with me, I'll get you a drink."

"I don't want a drink," she said, feeling the weight of the gun in her purse, her hand still pressed to her hip.

"Well," he said, finishing the drink he had in his hand with a chug, "I do."

He walked to the bar. Maggie followed.

CHAPTER FIFTY-SEVEN

"JD ON THE ROCKS, please," he said to the bartender.

"And for you, ma'am?" the bartender asked, looking to Maggie.

"I don't—" Maggie began.

"She'll have a glass of Chablis, please," Michael cut in.

As the bartender got their drinks, Michael leaned on the counter and looked sideways at Maggie.

"Your sister is doing fine," he said softly.

"So you say."

"I was never going to hurt her." He chuckled, as if this were all some sort of April Fool's joke.

"You mean, like not smack her around!?" Maggie snapped, her voice barely still a whisper.

Amazingly, he laughed.

She thought of pulling the gun out right there and splattering his brains all across the mirror behind the bar.

"Relax," he said. "She's okay."

Maggie could barely disguise her shock.

Seeing he had not convinced her, he added, "I mean it."

Maggie sighed. "Michael, don't play games anymore. Are you serious?"

"Yes. I would never hurt Julie."

"No?" she said, remembering her sister's voice on the tapes and how she'd looked in the text pic.

He seemed to read her mind. "Okay," he relented, "I'll rephrase that. I would never hurt her *seriously.*"

Maggie's eyes began to tear up, half in pure relief, half in rage. "You . . ." She stopped herself, catching the quick glare he gave her as the bartender returned to them with their drinks.

"Thank you," Michael said, taking the drinks and handing Maggie her glass of wine. She used her left hand to grab it, her right hand still holding her purse.

He looked at her solemnly. "Can I ask you something, Maggie?"

"Yes."

"Did you ever love me? I mean, for real?"

She caught her breath. "You know I did."

He nodded, then looked at the ground and shook his head. "Then why did you make me take it to this level?"

"Are you kidding me, Michael? This is *my* fault?"

Again, a quick snippet of that den came to her, and her grandfather, the words like broken glass. *This is all your fault. You're a bad girl.*

Michael took her by the arm to a corner of the banquet room, where they stood with their drinks and took turns looking at everyone on the dance floor.

"Drink," he said.

She barely sipped at her wine, because the buzz from the scotch she drank in the limo was now coming on strong.

"Are we going to sit?" she asked.

"No. I don't want to make small talk with some asshole

at the table."

"How did you get an invitation to this place?"

"It wasn't hard. My mother left quite a bit of money to this organization."

He took a drink and was silent for a few moments, as if trying to work up his courage to ask her something. "Then . . . who was it?"

"What?" Maggie asked, confused.

"Who was it that stole you away from me, Maggie?"

Not again.

"Nobody, Michael. Nobody stole me away from you."

"You're still going to stick with the stupid-ass dream excuse," he said bitterly.

"Michael. It sounds crazy, I know. But it's just that I felt . . . It doesn't matter *how* I felt it, I just felt that it wasn't going to be the best thing for me. For either of us."

"Thanks for adding me in there at the end."

"Michael, do you actually think—" and she wisely stopped herself from saying what she was going to say next. Another breakup speech was not what this was about. No. She had to give him what he wanted. Sincerely this time, like a good liar would. At least until she knew where he was hiding Julie. "I understand how much you love me now. I do," she said.

He swirled the ice cubes around in his drink and looked at her closely.

"I never did before. I never got it. But now I do . . . and I realize . . ." She inhaled for effect. "That I can still love you too, if you'll give me another chance."

He nodded solemnly, as if he'd been waiting to hear those words for years.

She held her breath, waiting for him to make the next

move. But he simply stared out over the dance floor, contemplating something.

They stood there together, quietly, as the band finished one song and began another, while he finished his drink. When he looked at her next she noticed his eyes were watery, as if that whole time he'd been holding back his tears. "I haven't seen you, up this close, in over five years, ya know?"

She nodded, looking him in the eye and seeing the caged trepidation there. The vulnerability. The pain.

"I guess you'll never understand it, but I just couldn't let go of you. I tried. But I couldn't. You're just too damn special, Maggie. I mean that. And each time I told myself to move on? It felt like the biggest surrender of my life, like I was giving up on everything I had or could ever want."

The room, though loud, felt quiet. She felt angry at him and sad for him at the same time. When she spoke she could barely whisper her reply. "I'm sorry, Michael."

He took a deep breath and then exhaled even more deeply. "I want to dance with you."

If he touches that purse and feels it . . .

There's no way you can risk dancing with him while holding the purse.

But, she wasn't worried about that. Because she had him now. She knew it. Not in a conceited way, but in a matter-of-fact way.

There was a vacant table by the dance floor. She smiled awkwardly at him. "Okay. I'd like that, too. Just let me put my purse down."

She walked over and placed the purse on the table, noticing an old man seated at another table with his back to her, his hair pure white.

Again, a flash in her mind. Her grandfather's hair had

been the exact same shade that day: pure white. But his intentions had been of another shade. She had walked up to the desk, her small voice asking what it was that he wanted, her big heart already squeezed by the knowledge of what it was. And he turned his chair slightly to the record player and put the needle to the vinyl. Cochella in E-Flat Major. As always.

Michael's hand went around her wrist, shocking her from her memory.

She trembled. Her mind was now working by its own clock, and it was terrifying her.

That was close, Maggie. Too close. You froze while putting the purse down. That had to have looked suspicious.

But Michael, seemingly overjoyed with the words she'd just spoken to him, hadn't seemed to notice. He took her hand and walked her onto the floor, where they began to dance.

He held her at a respectful distance as they began, coming in a little closer with each move until he leaned over and buried his head in her hair.

His chest rose softly against hers and then retreated in a long and full sigh.

"Do you think we could have been happy together, Maggie?" he asked.

"Yes," she lied, "I do now. Maybe we can still be happy."

"So much time has passed. And I've made a mess, now. Can you forgive me for everything? Your cat? This whole thing?" he asked nervously.

Keep reeling him in. Gently. Make it realistic.

"I won't lie, Michael. It's been pretty bad, but I think so."

"I can always buy you a new cat, right?"

She was glad he could not see her. She remembered

Zossima's little face and grimaced with hatred. "Yeah," she answered softly.

The music played around them, and Maggie followed his lead.

"You know, Maggie, I don't think I will ever understand why you did this to me. To us."

"Michael . . . can we stop talking about the past? Can't we . . ."

"Shh. I know." He breathed in deeply again as his hands encircled her waist and he began to sway. "Just one dance and a little talk, to help me clear this all up in my head."

He pulled her closer and leaned his head against hers, and almost wearily said something she could not believe. "Please?"

She stopped resisting then, in spite of herself, torn by the sorrow in his plea, despite everything that he'd done all these years.

The music slowly proceeded, and other couples swirled around them on the dance floor. Maggie noticed all the pretty colors of the ladies' gowns: bone white, a pastel pink, a watered-down mustard. All glittery, some with trim down the edges or frilly hemlines, others with lace sleeves and shoulder cuffs, each cut and styled to match the prospective flair of each dress. Soon a blend of colors surrounded them, broken up by the stark blacks and whites of all the men in their tuxedos.

"I wanted you to come here today to see what I had hoped for," he said.

She closed her eyes.

"Look at them all, Maggie, all around us. All these people, for the most part happy. Most of them married for decades, some of them newlyweds, others maybe just dating, but all of them in love, Maggie."

She opened her eyes and looked around; going beyond all the pretty dresses to the women who were wearing them, their hair styled so elegantly, pearls and diamonds on their ears and at their necks. She noticed that most of them were smiling, but not all. One lady with gray hair danced in her husband's arms and looked horribly sad, her lipstick stark red against her over-powdered face. To Maggie it seemed as if the dance were forced, the woman engaged perhaps in the mourning of her youth, or worse, the memory of her husband's infidelities. Maggie remembered something her aunt Mini had told her once; that all men cheat, and if she were lucky she would find one than only did so with his eyes.

Michael was right, most everyone seemed happy. But to Maggie, "seemed" was the operative word.

CHAPTER FIFTY-EIGHT

"WAS what I wanted so bad?" he asked.

She held her breath for a moment, hoping he didn't really want an answer. His continued silence said that he did.

"Michael, does it matter anymore?"

"Yes. It does. Because I can still remember it all so well."

"I can too Michael, but . . ."

He squeezed her waist harder, his grip as firm as his word. "No 'buts' tonight, Maggie, I'm too tired for those now."

He swung her gently around to his left, her face now to the bandstand, all the musicians in white tuxedos gently playing their notes, their music pages before them in diligent display. Music. It was what it was: a gateway to another place, all the time. At home, all one had to do was push play, but here it was different in an oddly magical way, because the "play" part was in the hands, and wrists, the instruments and the will of others.

"I did all of this so you would see," he said, startling her from her trance.

She bit her lip. *Buy time, buy time.* "See what?"

"What it's been like to be me, all these years."

"How?"

He then proceeded to list it all out so coldly that it was obvious he'd rehearsed it many times. "Your cat? So you would know what it feels like to lose someone you love, unexpectedly and unfairly. Your sister? To know what it's like to lose someone and want them back, desperately. The trick in the meadow? To know what it feels like to get your hopes up, all for nothing."

She was speechless.

He sighed. "Do you remember that night in Portland? When we went to that bed and breakfast on the shore, to whale watch?"

She closed her eyes again, not wanting to see anymore, not this place nor the one he was trying to remind her of. To no avail. The Inn by The Sea, trimmed blue with soft yellow paint, swimming in a rolling wave of fog, was cast immediately into her memory and then reflected, like a photo negative, stark against the inside of her eyelids. "Yes. Yes, I do."

"I remember that night because that was when I decided, without a shadow of a doubt, that your kiss was the only one I would ever need, for the rest of my life," and he said this with a remorseful chuckle, a grieving man's chuckle, a man who has chosen the laugh in lieu of the tears.

He pressed against her and she could now smell his cologne and his hair. He was still using the same shampoo.

"Michael . . ." she said gently, trying to stop him.

"No. Please let me finish. I want to say this. It's so important."

He swung her around again, her back to the bandstand now, the song not ending yet, perhaps never going to end, the strings of the violins muted and soft. The piano softly

327

dipping from the background to the foreground. Ivory notes across a canvas of melody.

"I couldn't kiss you enough that night, and that's when I realized I wanted to marry you. That, if you would let me, I could spend my whole life kissing you. Maybe then, with all those years, I could manage to kiss you enough. I loved you so much, Maggie."

He nuzzled his lips against her neck, his tongue dipping slowly out to taste her, his nose dragging gently across her jawline. She began to tremble.

"I wondered what it would be like to watch you grow old, and I saw you, Maggie, I saw you in my mind with our children on your lap, and then our grandchildren on your lap. I saw you grow frail as I grew bald and I figured maybe, just maybe, if God would grant me one final wish on my deathbed? It would be to do the impossible before I died, to kiss something no one else could ever kiss."

He brought his mouth up to her ear, his breath sending chills over her and raising goosebumps on her arms.

"I wanted to kiss your soul, Maggie. I wanted to kiss the 'you' that only God gets to see."

He nipped gently at her ear.

"But you're lying to me tonight, aren't you?"

He squeezed her sides and ribs, hard, startling her.

"N-no. No, I'm not."

"Yes you are. And you had to go and fuck all those other men after me, too. Didn't you?"

His voice grew deep as the orchestra climbed the scales, the ghostly sounds of the clarinets crying out as the saxophones surrendered the high ground, and the song filled up the room like a sonic wind.

He bit down hard on her ear, drawing blood. She gasped, the pain shooting directly to her brain, tears welling in her eyes.

Petrified, she couldn't move.

"And now . . . do you have any idea what I *want* to do now, my love?" he mumbled into her ear.

She began to cry. "N-n-no."

"I want to punch my hand through your chest and through your heart and rip your spine out from back to front, you thankless . . . loveless . . . cruel . . . bitch!"

He spat the final word. She screamed and pushed away from him. Stumbling backwards, she lost her balance and fell to the floor. There were gasps from the people near them, everyone unsure what had happened.

But Maggie noticed one lady, in a soft green velvet gown, who'd evidently been close enough to hear Michael's final few words, whispered as they were with just enough anger to carry. She pulled her husband off the dance floor, all the while glancing over her shoulder in fear at Michael.

The band kept playing and most everyone who was not immediately adjacent to them continued dancing, the full appreciation of what was going on with the lady in the aqua dress and her handsome, dark-haired date losing its affect one layer of the crowd at a time, almost in tumbling ripples. Those ten feet away not seeing her as having flung herself from her partner as much as having just fallen, those fifteen feet away thinking she'd had perhaps too many drinks, and those twenty feet or more away utterly oblivious to the fact that she had fallen at all. Perception was everything. And nothing.

Michael towered over her, looking down. She touched her ear and looked at her hand, the red of her own blood stark against the white of her fingers, even in the half light of the dance floor. Another lady, having seen Maggie's gesture, motioned for her husband to look at Maggie's ear.

Maggie could feel blood trickling down her neck and damming against her diamond necklace.

Michael spun around and disappeared into the crowd as another woman bent over to help Maggie up, plucking a tissue that had been tucked in her bosom as she shook her head and gasped. "What the hell happened?" she asked.

Maggie's shock dissipated immediately the moment the tissue touched her ear, when the pain finally ebbed through.

He was getting away.

No!

She pushed the woman away and rushed to the table to fetch her purse before dashing back across the dance floor in the direction that Michael had fled, her vision lost in the sea of tuxedos all dancing and intermingling, at once looking similar to his and then different when assembled against the shape of the wearer's body or the color of his hair, the advantage of height distinction lost in the depth of the room, the targets moving as they were from right to left, back to front, in a dance to a song that Maggie feared would never end.

If he gets away, Julie is dead. And she knew that to be true. Utterly.

Stymieing the panic in her chest she glanced to the back of the hall and, in the blink of an eye, caught his figure exiting out a pair of glass double doors that led to the patio.

Stopping quickly, she reached down and pulled off her high heels and then bolted to the doors. She squeezed her bag, feeling for her gun; it was still there. Reaching the door she pushed at it with both hands, dropping a shoe in the process. The doors having flung open, she now had a clear view of the golf course outside, its rolling green hills accented by the glaring lights of the dance hall. She saw him, running towards the parking lot.

"Michael!" she screamed, chasing after him across the cold lawn, the grass immediately soaking her stockinged feet.

She ran across the golf course and into the parking lot. Having expected him to be heading for a car, she was surprised to catch sight of him some fifty feet ahead, on the other side of the parking lot and swinging his leg over a low brick wall, climbing over it to the curb and street on the other side.

Shit. Where is he going?

He was headed into a residential area.

He must've parked his car over there, on the street.

She ran across the lot, bits of gravel digging into her feet, biting at her arches. It didn't matter. Nothing mattered but catching him. He couldn't get to a car. He'd get away and she knew it.

Reaching the wall, it dawned her that he might be lying in wait on the other side somewhere. She slowed, but only slightly, rotating the one shoe she had left so that the stiletto pointed out now, begging for an eye.

She saw him just up the street. To her amazement, he ran half a dozen houses further and then took the stairs up to the front door of one of the homes, disappearing inside.

What the hell?

She followed quickly.

Someone left their door open?

If a home had a front door, it most likely had a back door.

He's using it as an escape route!

A burst of adrenaline coursed through her body as she bolted for the house.

CHAPTER FIFTY-NINE

WHEN SHE REACHED THE HOUSE, the door was still half open. There was a hall light on, just inside. She took the steps two by two, bolting through the door and across a small area rug, her mind trying to guess at where the back door might be.

And that was when his hand closed around her throat.

In her haste to get in, she'd glanced around at the inside of the house a split second too late, and a split second was all it took. He came from behind her, his left hand gripping her neck, his right hand seizing hers, squeezing her wrist so hard the pain splayed her fingers wide open, forcing her to relinquish her grip on her purse, which thudded to the floor.

In sheer panic, she swung the stiletto tip backwards so hard that when it missed him it struck the wall and broke off.

He dragged her forwards into a living room and slammed the door hard behind her as she struggled. Her eyes bulged in their sockets and darted around, trying to fix his position and distance. Finally, she was able to turn her head a bit and get a look at him. She wished she hadn't.

He was to her right, his chin sticking out in a grotesque display of effort as he struggled to get a grip on her, his upper lip curled back, exposing his teeth in an odd way; even though he was the one on the offensive, he looked like a cornered dog. His eyes were like charcoal, a flat black so deep they did not seem to be of this world. They were jealous, hateful eyes and in them she could see only death.

Her hands were flailing around like probes on the ends of her arms, smacking the wall and at the air. A weapon. She needed a weapon. Her right hand swiped out and clipped at a collection of tiny glass animals that were arranged on a small table in the entryway. They scattered and shattered, sounding like breaking Christmas bulbs.

He descended upon her like a shroud, bearing down on her with all his weight, and she stumbled to keep her balance, alternating her hands to support herself against the wall or the furniture as he swung her around and around. She couldn't breath and the world was growing hazy.

My God, he's lost it. I knew it. Jesus, what now? The answer came to her like a car backfiring in the middle of the night: she had nothing left now but her nails, her freshly manicured nails.

She spun and dug at his face, her fingers doing a soldier march from his cheeks to his eyes, gouging at them.

She didn't realize how out of air she was until he relinquished his grip on her throat, grabbing at his eyes as he backed away. He was screaming at her but she couldn't hear him. All she could hear was her own pulse pounding in her ears, like he had squeezed too much blood into her head.

But she could read his lips some though, and there were disgusting things on them. Spewed words of his imaginings of what she'd done with other men, and let them do to her.

She screamed, but even that sounded muffled, and it dawned on her that they could both scream all they wanted to and still not be heard here. This was not an escape route, it was a trap. This was Michael's house, or a family house of some sort.

Panic, fear and terror all beat up on her at once. *What now?* she thought.

The purse was on the floor, at the base of an old wood credenza, too far away to reach.

"You miserable bitch! I'm going to kill you!" he screamed.

And if there was any slight hope left in her mind, any iota of faith that somehow she could talk or reason her way out of this thing with him, it was gone at that moment.

She hobbled over a small ottoman and darted towards a dining table, hoping to use it as a divider between them, feeling one of his hands on her right shoulder for a second before she shrugged it off. She could make it. She knew she could.

They had watched football games together when they'd first started dating. She hated football but wanted to please him, so she'd tried to learn the rules. Because of this, when she felt his full weight against her back, launching her much too quickly towards the table and the chairs that surrounded it, the word *clipping* immediately came to her mind.

The absurdity of this thought, coupled with the sheer terror in her heart, caused her to catch a laugh in her throat and fight back tears at the same time.

She was flying now, arms splayed out in front of her to cushion her descent. His hands were clawing at the back of her head. She fell hard, face-first to the floor, and skidded into the base of the table. He flipped her over and—like little

334

Johnny Kelso in the third grade who'd gotten her in a school yard pin for refusing to call him her boyfriend—he sat squarely on her chest and stomach, forcing the air from her lungs. He tried to grab her arms and pin them down, but she was struggling so much and moving her arms so fast that he couldn't get them down.

Oh, God. Please no! This is it. I'm going to die! Please God, no God, please, please.

She became hysterical, crying and begging and screaming for mercy. But it was no good, no use. He was kissing her now, on her neck and face, her tears smearing across his cheeks.

She looked into his chest, avoiding his maddening face, and began to claw at his neck. His hands came forwards in a flash, his reach much longer than hers, and cupped her cheeks. He was saying things again, crude things about other men and the pain he felt. Then he began to viciously slam the back of her head against the hardwood floor.

Out of the corner of her eye she saw that there, beneath the dining table, was a wooden spoon that had been knocked off the table as they'd fallen into it.

It was while trying to gauge her ability to reach the spoon that she felt his hands around her throat again.

Terror, bundled tight in her chest, sprung immediately into every corner of her body. Her hand lunged at the spoon, once, twice . . . missing it by inches. On her third try her fourth finger briefly scraped over it.

Her energy was draining quickly.

She sucked for air and, desperation overcoming her, looked back into his eyes.

He was looking through her now, as if she weren't even there anymore. The enormity of the hatred in those eyes drew her away from them and to the rest of his face. The final act of a dying person, she looked to her murderer for comfort. The human instinct to reach out having nowhere else to go at that final moment, she wanted to see something there to comfort her, but there wasn't.

For it was not *this* face that had kissed her hand and looked so adoringly upon her at one time, it was not *these* eyes that had widened in anticipation when they had first made love.

She thought she had been clawing at his throat but realized now that she'd made deep gouges in his face. Blood was tricking down her fingers and over the top of her wrists. This person, this thing, was no one and nothing she had ever known. She wanted so badly to love him once, wanted so much for things to be better, inside herself, but she should've known better.

Sometimes you can never get past the past.

Maggie was not just tired now, but tired of life.

But for Julie's sake, she could not surrender.

She made a final lunge for the spoon, twisting her pinned body at the waist, which shifted his weight just enough for her reach to succeed. Her fingers grabbed it and immediately spun it around, the handle now like a wooden knife.

She stabbed with all her might at his Adam's apple.

He gasped and choked, falling backwards.

She rolled and stood up.

Seeing a kitchen door not ten feet away, she ran to it. His hand grabbed at her ankle.

A knife. Get to a knife.

The door was an old fashioned one that swung both ways, and upon realizing this, an odd thought occurred to Maggie, one borne of all the horror movies she'd ever watched in which no one, none of the air-headed girls or muscle-bound guys, ever thinks to double immediately back through a freshly closed door when being chased by the killer. Ever. It seemed so obvious . . .

That it might just work.

She spun around as soon as she was completely into the kitchen, figuring he would be right behind her, and threw her entire weight back against the door, hoping to catch him just as he was trying to run in.

She felt the satisfying thud of his head and heard the crunch of the bone in his nose as she did so, the door being almost ripped from its hinges at the combined torque of the two of them colliding against it at the same time.

She was much lighter than he was, but it didn't matter— she was braced and on the offensive, and he was completely unaware of what was coming. The door froze dead in place as he bounced off it and backwards, screaming.

CHAPTER SIXTY

MAGGIE CONTINUED THROUGH the door just in time to see him tumbling backwards.

She advanced, refusing to lose the offensive, picked up a chair and swung it at him. He grabbed at it with one hand, missing, missing again, his other hand trying to shield his nose, blood pouring from it and spilling down his tuxedo, before he finally managed to clasp it.

He cried out and rammed the chair into her body, pushing her backwards.

She felt her back being sliced open by shards of glass as she was thrust into the glass doors of a hutch that was behind the dining table, plates and glasses breaking over her head and spilling down all around her.

But, incredibly, Michael didn't continue his counter-attack. Instead he fled back through the living room and up the stairs to the second floor.

He's hurt. You hurt him bad!

Maggie pushed herself gingerly out of the cabinet, feeling the warmth of her own blood spilling down the small of her back and across her buttocks.

But there was no time for that. For the blood. Or the pain.

She envisioned him coming back down the stairs, this time with a hatchet or baseball bat.

Provoked by these thoughts, she scrambled back out through the living room and headed towards her purse, afraid she would never reach it in time, expecting him to come down the stairs . . .

Hurry, Maggie! HURRY!

You're not going to make it. You're not.

Seeing the purse, she slid in her ball gown like a baseball player across the polished hard wood floor of the entryway, her hands scooping at the purse, the stairway off to her left, her fingers fumbling at the snap and then grabbing at the gun.

It was stuck, jammed into the fabric too tightly.

Shit!

She heard herself screaming, louder, with each passing second.

He's coming!

She wrestled it loose, sure in her heart that it was too late.

She spun around and, catching a glimpse of something moving just off to her right, she squeezed off two shots. They cut into the wall near the base of the stairs.

But her eyes had obviously been playing tricks on her.

He wasn't there. He hadn't come back down the stairs.

She had her gun, though. The scales were a little more balanced. Her joy and confidence at finally being armed gave her an idea, and raised a taunt to her throat.

"You'd *better* run, Michael," she called mockingly. "I've got four more bullets, all with your name on them."

It was risky. Julie could be up there. But she could do nothing about that but try to keep his mind focused on her. Taunting would help. His male ego simply wouldn't be able to resist it.

She ascended the stairs cautiously. The top of the stairway was dark.

The first floor was little more than a bathroom and two small bedrooms, one of which had been turned into a sewing room. She hit the light switch in the hall, which completely illuminated the bathroom right across from it. The shower curtain to the tub was open, and the rest of the bathroom was clear. She immediately shut the bathroom door, eliminating it as an entrance or exit point.

She took two steps to the bedroom door and removed his element of surprise by slamming that door shut as well. If he were in there he would have to open it to come out, and she would hear him do that. She moved to clear the sewing room, her gun firmly in front of her.

She crept down the hall, the sewing room partly lit from the hall light. She could see an old-model Singer, white with polished silver tabs, and a few large thread spools on a nearby table.

Slowly, Maggie. Take it easy.

She went through the door of the sewing room ready to shoot anything that moved, reaching to turn on the light switch as she entered. He was standing about six feet away, in the corner. She rotated and fired at him, realizing too late that it wasn't him at all, but instead a headless sewing dummy. The bullet ripped directly into its chest, the force slamming it against a wall and toppling it.

Dammit!

The rest of the room was also clear. His only other hiding place would've been the closet, if the doors hadn't been removed long ago to make room for shelving bays for rolls of fabric.

She turned immediately back to the closed bedroom door.

We know where he is now.

And again, her mind became stuck like an antique type-writer, three or four adjacent letters jamming into one, the grease between them too dry to separate them.

Her grandfather's den. Again.

We know where he is now, we know what he wants.

Cochella in E-Flat Major filled the room and weighed in the air. He sat back in the chair, his hand dropping off to the side, beckoning her. Grandmother was gone. She had to leave on short notice for the remainder of the day to help a friend. Maggie's father would be there, by three in the after-noon, to pick her up. That was a long time. So long. His hand, beckoning. Like he had all the time in the world.

No! No. Stop that. Stop thinking of that shit. Focus.

She kicked in the bedroom door. It was an old door, and an old jamb, and it gave way with startling ease. The room was dark, except for one corner, where faint light from a hole in the ceiling was casting down. She stepped to the side, al-lowing more of the light from the hall to spill into the room. It looked clear at the entrance. She moved forwards cau-tiously before reaching in to flip the switch. Nothing. The room remained dark. But she could vaguely see that the light from the hole in the ceiling was casting down onto a set of folding stairs.

"No!" he screamed.

She rotated and fired two shots blindly into the room, one to her left and the other to the right.

She heard him laughing from above her, at the top of the folding stairs somewhere.

An attic. It was an attic.

Oh, man, man, man, man, man . . .

She moved slowly into the room when she heard him calling softly from above.

"Hey, baby," he said. "Why not come join the party?"

She was frozen with fear, but forced herself to ascend the stairs to the attic at a measured pace, the wood of each step creaking slightly with each footfall. Making it to the top stair, she leaned back against the wall.

The attic was lit by only a few lanterns that had been placed in the corners of the room, creating a breeding ground of shadows that cast themselves in every direction.

Wait. Wait. Let your eyes adjust.

Her body was so tense that she could feel herself to the minutest detail: her lungs expanding and collapsing, her heart vibrating rapidly, her pupils enlarging, sifting and separating the darkness in front of her, casting objects in different shades of gray and charcoal and pitch black.

This must be how dogs see things, she thought.

As the room began to unlock itself and objects began to reveal themselves, she scanned her head from side to side; an old reclining chair was to her left and against the wall, a large oak cabinet stacked next to it, and over-spilling bags of clothes and rags were strewn about. Along the wall was a dresser, about fifteen feet away, which obstructed her view of what was beyond it. The room appeared to be about thirty feet deep or so, but with all the junk stacked against the remaining walls—boxes and rolls of wrapping paper, wine cases and what looked to be a plastic Christmas tree, covered in dust and standing in the corner nearest her—it was hard to tell for sure.

Then a voice came out of the darkness, startling her so badly she almost screamed.

"He's behind the dresser, Mags."

Julie. It was Julie's voice. Weak and faint.

"You dumb whore!"

Michael's surprised voice, so close that Maggie couldn't believe it.

CHAPTER SIXTY-ONE

JULIE SCREAMED, and Maggie, having no choice now but to take her sister's word that he was where she said he was, took two quick steps to her left to increase her line of vision behind the dresser.

He stood with a knife in his hand, partially turned away from Maggie and towards Julie, who was lying on a sleeping bag on the floor, her hands and feet bound with dirty rope. Maggie immediately lost her breath at the sight of her sister's face, looking up in horror at the towering figure above her.

"Get away from her," Maggie said.

Michael froze. Rotating his body to follow his head, like a machine, he turned slowly to face Maggie.

"You should have gagged me better, you dumb bastard," Julie screamed at him defiantly.

Maggie noticed a small sock with silver duct tape on the end, sitting just below Julie's chin.

Julie broke into tears, a soft weeping that broke a levy in Maggie's heart and gave way to a flood of rage. She looked back at Michael. The lantern directly behind him left his face totally in the dark now, just a hulking shadow levitating there in the attic air.

"You have one left," he said.

"What?" Maggie said.

"One bullet. That's all, Maggie. I've been counting."

Maggie held her breath, her hands shaking, and blinked.

"Shoot him, Maggie. Please. Shoot him," Julie pleaded.

"First Julie's gag, Michael, and now this. You're running out of luck."

He feigned a swift motion to his right.

Maggie aimed with confidence and pulled the trigger, the bullet striking the edge of the dresser before ricocheting into his shoulder.

"Shit!" he screamed, grabbing his shoulder with his free hand.

He stepped back a few feet, his teeth bared, and bit down on his lower lip.

Julie's face melted in shock. Maggie had missed him.

For a brief moment, the three of them seemed to reflect on the situation in its entirety. Maggie noticed Julie glancing repeatedly between the two of them and then around the room, in total panic now, as if she were looking for a weapon of some sort, even though that instinct seemed to be totally useless, her limbs tied as they were.

"Almost time to die now, my love?" Michael mocked.

Maggie lowered and rotated the gun, as if to use it as a blunt instrument to bludgeon him with when he got within range. "Not yet Michael."

Julie locked eyes with Maggie. Maggie saw in them their own diction, their own vocabulary. *Oh my God,* they said. *Oh my God.*

Maggie couldn't help herself. She looked Julie quickly over from head to toe. All her clothes were still on. Maybe he hadn't touched her yet.

"Your sister can't help you, Maggie," he said, taking another step forwards.

"You better not have laid a single hand on her, you bastard," Maggie said.

Michael stopped, and then smiled.

"How sweet. Really. Quite touching. She's a feisty one. And I've noticed she has a real nice ass. But no, not yet, not until I'm done with you. Then I'll see what she looks like. You know, Maggie, what I mean? With her legs spread wide and her eyes rolled back?"

He took another step forwards as silence took the room in the palm of its hand.

"Poor Maggie. All those magical bullets, and only one got to me." He smiled again, his arm dropping now, the hand holding the knife dancing, ready to do its work and carve her up.

Maggie waited for what was to come, wanting him to step from the shadows so she could see his face.

"Jesus, Maggie, *run*!" Julie screamed.

"No, Jules," Maggie said. "No more running."

Michael smiled and marched towards her.

When he was six feet away she brought up the gun and pulled the trigger three times, the blare erupting through the attic, making Julie flinch and Maggie jump.

The bullets struck Michael's chest and began to do their work.

Knocked backwards, his body recoiling from the impact, he dropped the knife, a mixture of shock and anger interlocking in his features.

"Did I say four Michael?" Maggie asked, her voice now

cold and hollow. "Or was it fourteen?"

She advanced two steps.

"Or was it twelve?"

"What?" was all he could say.

"Are you thinking about that gun in my apartment, the one you left on my pillow? The .38? Ah. Okay. Now *that* gun only shoots six. But I didn't bring *that* gun Michael, I brought *this* gun."

She paused to catch her breath, fighting the tears in her eyes, not wanting them to affect her aim but helpless to them nonetheless as she looked down the barrel of the gun, its cold blue steel and etched .22 reflecting the lamplight.

"This is my daddy's gun," Maggie said, the words like a magic spell cast across the room, a vindication of her only hero: the only man who ever loved her pure.

"Ten in the clip, Michael." She took a step forwards. "One in the chamber."

She pulled the trigger two more times. The bullets struck him in the stomach. He stumbled backwards, his feet betraying him as he backpedaled out of control, his face a mask of horror that brought joy to Maggie's heart.

All his fear, right back at him.

He fell against the attic window, shattering it, his eyes growing even wider with the anticipation of the fall. Instinctively he shot both arms out to his sides, his hands splayed in a backwards grip, his fingers curled to cling at anything, one catching the old matted drapes that hung there, the other an unbroken pane of the window. One foot partially on the floor, the other wedged against the inside ledge, he hung there like a scarecrow, bleeding at the edges and down the middle.

She had one more bullet.

But she couldn't use that one.

That one was for herself, when this was all over.

What he said next amazed her. "The police will be coming for you. Doing all this, right after getting out of jail? You're done for." He chuckled as blood spilled out his mouth, then he twisted his face to mock her. "No one will ever believe you."

The last of his words destroyed her.

Maggie's legs went numb. She began to tremble all over. "No one will ever believe you," she whispered.

How many times had her grandfather said that to her, all those days after church when he had eagerly reached up her skirt in the den, his fingers rubbing her thighs, excited by the fact that her body wasn't ready for these things yet, by the fact that he was "dirtying her up?"

Her world began to slide away from her again.

Don't. Not now. NO!

Her mind, like wax, was melting beneath the searing heat of another memory.

CHAPTER SIXTY-TWO

SHE SAW THE DEN unfold around her, enveloping the attic, saw herself cradled in her grandfather's arms, her face buried in his chest, his hand holding it there to muffle her cries, her legs splayed across his lap, her skirt pulled up, the den door shut and locked, her grandmother gone for the day, her father not due until three, on that final day. That's right.

It was the last time.

He knew I was moving away. He knew this would be his last chance.

She was crying, uncontrollably now, heavy sobs ratcheting up and out of her throat.

She heard Julie from somewhere far away, screaming for her. "Maggie! Maggie!"

Too late, Jules, I'm too far gone now. I got him already, though. You'll be safe. I'm in Pappy's den now. What was that?

"Maggie! What are you doing!?"

Oh, I'm just reading, Jules. Books are good. Books take you away from things, ya know? Far, far away.

"Maggie! Snap out of it!"

In books, I only see what I want to see.

And in her mind the den became a kaleidoscope of the seasons: spring to winter, winter to fall, fall to summer. Time was passing, she realized. Backwards. To all the years before that final day. And the nightmare still wasn't over. *It kept going. Oh God, Pappy, why so long? Didn't you ever get bored of me?* And the answer came to her as quickly as she asked it. No, he didn't.

And it was good for you, Jules . . . that he didn't. I unintentionally kept him away from you.

"Maggieeeeee!"

From my "bestest."

Then came the worst Sunday of all, just before her parents had suddenly decided to move away and Daddy got his job transfer. Before it would all be okay again.

Maggie felt her hands on her face pulling at her skin, spreading her eyes. She didn't want to see or remember or feel any of it.

He'd been worse to her that day than ever. He'd made her bleed. And in his thick voice, as he had hurriedly cleaned her with a tissue, he assured her that it would be alright. What had he said? She felt nauseated at the memory. He had actually tried to comfort her, hadn't he? Tried to educate her . . . explain to her what it was, in her, that had given way so painfully . . . and how it was a "good thing."

He said it all with a smile, but a worried smile, as if there was now a serious risk of getting caught, of evidence being left behind, a spot of blood on her dress perhaps, or a pain that would not subside, pain that she would tell her mother about or need to go to the doctor for.

He spoke again to her. Something horrible. What was it he said to her? *What* was it?

"It's okay, Maggie. You get to make a wish now," he said.

Oh . . . my . . . God. You sick, sick man.

Then he'd cradled her tightly in his arms, letting her cry into his shoulder and insisting that she could make a wish, that it was a good thing, trying somehow in his feigned excitement to turn it all into a magical moment, like a nightmare turned into a fairytale.

And when she finally stopped crying, and told him that she'd made her wish, he had demanded to know what it was, asking her over and over again.

But she wouldn't tell him.

Because something in her even at that young age was convinced that letting him take the wish from her would be an even worse thing than what he'd just done, the child in her clinging superstitiously to the belief that by telling him her wish, it could never come true.

"What did you wish for, Maggie?"

The past exploded . . .

Had these last words come to her from outside of herself? From Michael?

. . . bringing her back to the attic.

Maggie blinked. Michael was looking at her dead in the eye, both feet now planted on the floor, his left arm folded across his chest, blood trickling from his mouth.

"You . . . keep babbling about a wish. What did you wish for, Maggie?" he asked again, frozen in place, glaring at her with a sickening smile.

"Maggie? Please. Kill him! Shoot him!" Julie cried hysterically. She begged her sister to come back to her, to come back to reality.

Inside Maggie, the inner workings of her mind turned in a finely tuned set of wheels and pulleys, like an expensive

351

antique watch, the second hand all that she was, the hour hand all that she would ever be, each sliding in a synchronicity of self.

Maggie smiled. "For love," she said softly, tears in her eyes. "I wished for love."

Of course she had.

Maggie wondered what girl ever in the world had not lost her innocence without that same hopeful, naïve wish to be loved and loved forever, feeling that what they gave, or what was taken from them, was something so precious as to deserve the reverence, respect and tenderness shown through the reciprocity of just that: love.

At ten, in the arms of a monster, she could never wish for his love, could not contrast it against the affection of a lover, could not even fathom or plunder the real depths of what love was or was supposed to be. All she knew was that in the books she read it was always spoken of as something really, really special, so she'd done like any child would do; she had placed her wish for it in something that could keep it safe.

Where the wish could stay in suspended animation. Like the deer. Like the cabin.

Until one day, she could fully understand it.

She had placed her wish in the snow globe.

There on the bookcase.

The sacred hiding place of a little girl's dream.

She looked at Michael and then beyond him, to the shattered window and the night sky.

He saw the intent in her eyes. "Don't do it, Maggie," he said.

The time for talk was over. Maggie rushed forwards, planting both hands in the center of his chest and pushing hard.

Launched backwards, his fingers sliding through her hair, he flew through the window and out into the black of night, tumbling in his dark tuxedo down to the ground, where he landed on his head, the rest of his body following until he crumpled onto himself like a human accordion with a crunch of bone.

Maggie dropped to her knees, the dark night sky above her, Julie's weeping behind her, the gun still in her hand.

Only one thing left to do.

The cold steel of the gun now matched everything: the cold of the night air and the cold on her skin. So many nights, sleepless or otherwise, alone and wishing for something, for someone. No more lonely nights. No more books to read.

I'm so tired, Grandmother, she thought. *So tired of it all.*

She wondered what it would feel like, the bullet going into her brain. It was a small bullet; maybe it wouldn't hurt so much. But hadn't her father said something about them bouncing around, these small lead things? There would be some pain, yes, but then it would be over and she would be in that other place, on the island, where it was all so peaceful. Where the air smelled like cinnamon and she would sit on the shore and watch the tides roll in.

No more pain. Not there. No more bad memories and no more . . .

"Maggie?"

Julie.

Maggie blinked, not realizing she'd closed her eyes.

"Maggie, I'm so cold," she said.

She turned her head to look at Julie, sitting there on the floor, still bound. She would die up here unless someone found her. But with all the screaming and gunshots, some-one had already called the police. There were sirens coming. Lots of them. Still, she balanced there, between the love of that heaven that was not quite heaven, and the love of her sister, unable to appease both.

She thought of the snow globe again, and this helped her choose. She realized that she had picked it up that day, as a child, and put it back down again. But she had never let it go.

Her entire life, she had never let go.

But now, at last, she could.

CHAPTER SIXTY-THREE

SHE AWOKE SITTING on the golden shore of the island, her toes digging into the sand and feeling the trapped warmth beneath, just a few degrees hotter than the surface.

The sea was still and deep purple now, small swells tipping at its surface in slices of baby blue, the waves crashing in a dazzling white and yellow froth, not twenty feet away.

She sat for a few moments and drew circles in the sand with her fingers before noticing a brown stick cutting lines in the sand next to her.

She looked up, and blinked.

The Walrus Lady sat next to her in a light beige gown, her hair combed back in a bun, the grays all gone, as if they'd never existed.

"Hello, Maggie," she said, happily.

"Madeline? What are you doing here?"

"I finally escaped that miserable insomnia and fell asleep," she replied, her lips in a slight smile as she looked across the ocean.

"How long do you get to visit me before you wake up

again?"

Madeline looked at Maggie and put a hand on Maggie's knee. "You misunderstand, child."

Maggie squinted at her.

"This is a sleep that lasts forever. There's no going back," Madeline said, a mixture of both happiness and sadness in her expression.

"You mean . . . ?"

"Yes."

Maggie felt the spray from a wave cast over them, its mist cool but not cold. She could taste it on the air and it was like sugar, not salt.

"Why?"

"It is done, that's why," Madeline said with a swift nod, as if a hammer had just been put to a nail somewhere.

"What's done?" Maggie asked. Every visit to this place, it seemed, was made of questions and confusion.

"Him, and all he wrought," she answered, looking back and forth across the shore, the light glimmering in the sand seeming to catch her fascination.

Maggie said nothing, sensing that Madeline intended to continue.

"Kincaid," she finally said, pulling her lips together before looking deep into Maggie's eyes. "I never knew his last name," she said. "Only his first: Henry."

"What are you talking about? Do you—" and Maggie stopped cold.

Madeline touched her hand and shared her truth.

The man in the barn, just after the war. When Madeline had been just a girl. Henry. He'd raped her that day.

Maggie's mouth dropped in sudden realization as she looked at Madeline in disbelief.

"Your grandfather was a laborer, Maggie. He migrated

from Ireland to England with his parents before they came to America. It was him that day. Do you understand?"

"Oh, Madeline . . ." Maggie said, reaching out to grab both of the old woman's hands.

"Don't you see, child? In us, his evil came full circle; I was his first, and you were his last."

Maggie put her hand to her face in shock. She thought of his tombstone on the day they'd buried him, his name etched in the marble: Henry Kincaid. It was true.

Seeing that Maggie was still speechless, Madeline pushed on. "His evil was destined either to be cleansed or reborn. That is how evil works, you see, like bacteria. To survive it must spread. But, unlike real bacteria, it does not spread by being shared. No. Evil spreads by those things in life that are left within us, to fester."

"I never knew . . ." Maggie said.

"No. How could you have? I was the strange woman across the street, that's all. Someone you watched and nothing more. It's what we all do—watch. And in so doing, we forget."

"But that we were put together, on the same street . . ." Maggie interjected.

"At those chosen intersections of our lives?" Madeline added, nodding firmly.

"Fate?" Maggie blurted.

Madeline shook her head with a knowing smile. She was part of something now, and Maggie was not.

"It's what we all do, Maggie; we watch. And in so doing, we forget that we're also being watched. There are so many forces at work, Maggie. Every day, in every twist of every second in our lives. Fate is little more than a 'guess' at what it truly is."

"Then . . . why?" Maggie asked.

"Prior to Henry, there was Henry's father, who never abused the boy in the same way as he would grow to abuse us, but in other ways that would make it possible for him to be the cruel creature he became. Beatings and lashings, of his mother and his sisters."

"Oh my God."

"Yes. It's how he came to objectify us, as women. We were little more than farm animals, you see. As his father took the rod to one, so he could take the rod to the other. There was no difference."

"But it *was* different . . ."

"Yes. It was. That's how evil works. It's a shape shifter. It has to be." She shuddered, then looked up to the sky and beyond it. "To remain hidden from what can see it, expose it and destroy it. So it transforms, because if a man can beat a woman until she begs for mercy, so too can another rape her, all to deny the same." She sighed heavily.

Maggie sat in silence, dumbfounded.

"Where the father drew the line, the son simply extended it," Madeline said. She picked up the stick she'd been drawing in the sand with earlier and tossed it into the waves. As it hit the water, Maggie was astonished to see it transform in a flicker of light from a stick to a fish, its tail fin flapping for just a second in the air before it burrowed into the sea and disappeared.

Another memory, set free, Maggie thought. Something clicked.

She realized at long last what this place really was: heaven abridged. A plane where lost souls and buried memories came to dwell, the former held down by the hand of God, the latter by the hand of man, a refuge place for things that would not, or could not, leave, either because they didn't want to or because they weren't ready to.

She noticed Madeline looking at her intently, almost with pride. She would be leaving soon. Maggie could sense it.

"But grandmother never said anything about . . ." Maggie continued, buying time.

"He never hit her. That's what I mean about different forces at work. He'd already developed a taste for another form of abuse."

"*Quid pro quo*," Maggie said.

"Yes. *Quid pro quo*. This thing, for that. Until the circle can be made smaller."

"We are here together," Maggie said.

"I'm sorry that he ever happened in your life, child."

Maggie grabbed her hand. "I'm sorry that he happened in yours."

The old woman stood up, pulling Maggie up with her.

"I have to go now, Maggie."

"No."

"I have to. It is my time."

"Madeline, I'm sorry it took so long for this all to end. All the days and nights you lived with this . . ."

Madeline smiled and squeezed her hand gently, and then said something Maggie would never forget. "It's okay, dear. It was just my life."

"*Quo vadis?*" Where are you going? Maggie asked.

"Where I have to go," Madeline answered, the smallest hint of sadness in her voice drowned out now by what sounded very much like a little girl's glee to be going someplace special, someplace so exciting.

"I'm going to miss you," Maggie said, choking back her emotions.

"Not for long. It will all pass so quickly, child, so enjoy your life. Go find love. Real love. It's out there, I promise.

And remember . . . we'll be watching."

Maggie knew who else she was referring to: her grandmother.

Madeline pulled away and began to fade, that special, white glow coming over her.

"Wait!" Maggie cried. "I want to know one thing before you go. Please. What's it like?"

"What?"

"Heaven?"

"Oh," Madeline replied. Then she broke out into a deep, full-bellied laugh. "You know I can't tell you that."

Maggie's heart sank.

Then she winked at Maggie and motioned with her head as if to say "lean in close." She was beginning to float, up and away, and it was all Maggie could do to get to her in time, Madeline's words barely a whisper across the air, but when they came, a smile broke across the entire divide of Maggie Kincaid's life.

"It's like a really good book," Madeline said, smiling.

Then the wind took her up a bit more into the air and she was gone, a memory given to the sky, not to the sea, and as such, a memory that was set free.

Maggie repeated the words in her head as she stood on the shore, feeling the sea and its tides pulling her back to her life. In her mind, it all came together with a resounding sigh.

How many hours had she spent in her favorite reading chair, all those years, searching and looking for it?

Heaven was like a really good book.

Of course it was.

With the perfect ending.

She came to on her knees, the stillness of the attic broken only by Julie's whimpers. She lay curled up on the floor nearby. Maggie crawled over to her and pulled the rope around her feet and hands off. Julie let out cries of relief and they embraced, rocking back and forth. The sirens were getting closer. That was okay. They'd get here when they got here.

Maggie smiled. It would all be okay. Thank God. It would. She was finally free of all the shame and fear. Now, at last, she could write her own story.

In it, there would be meandering descriptions of the future, where you could get lost on all the paths of possibility. There would be scenes of hope and love, and, yes, pains and setbacks too, because all the best stories have both.

And she was sure, beyond a shadow of a doubt, that it would be epic.

EPILOGUE

IT WAS A SUNNY DAY in Los Angeles, four months later, when Maggie pushed a few stray hairs behind her ear and walked into the beige building at the corner of Forth and Boylston, her stomach swimming with jitters.

The move to LA had been of a different sort. For the first time she was going someplace, not fleeing there, and that made all the difference in the world. Rooming with Julie was fun, but at some point Maggie knew she'd have to get a job and find her own place. Her job interview today was the first step on that path.

The lobby entrance was painted mint-green and there were plants in three of the four corners. A small coffee table, old and rickety, sat in front of four dark-green upholstered chairs that were along the wall. There was a reception desk directly opposite the chairs that had thick glass in front of it, with a metal circle that had slanted grooves to speak through.

A black woman in a purple blouse with thick glasses and graying hair looked up from the other side of the glass. "Can

362

I help you?"

"Yes. Hi. My name is Maggie Kincaid. I'm here for—"

"The job interview, yes?"

Maggie nodded and smiled politely, feeling incredibly shy for some reason.

The woman stood, looked around the lobby as if to make sure that Maggie was alone, and motioned to a door next to the counter as she buzzed Maggie in.

"My name's Yvonne," the woman said, shaking hands with Maggie over the small counter on the other side of the door. "Evelyn's out in the courtyard right now, but I'll call her and let her know that you're here. In the meantime, here are a few more forms we need you to fill out, okay?"

"Sure," Maggie replied.

As she stood at the counter and filled the papers, she was struck by the quiet busyness of the place. It was a fairly large office, with multiple cubicles. A few women walked by hurriedly with a number of brown files, and nearby a short man in a blue plaid shirt and jeans was struggling with a large copy machine that had jammed.

A short time later, a small voice spoke from behind her. "Maggie?"

She turned to find a short Asian woman with a bob haircut in a white cotton shirt, beige chinos and black flats. She looked to be in her mid-forties, with crow's feet dabbing her eyes, which were almond shaped and inquisitive.

"Yes. Evelyn?" Maggie replied.

The woman smiled gently and nodded as she motioned Maggie into an office down the hall, where they sat and made small talk for a bit before getting into all the usual job questions and answers. At the end of the interview Evelyn leaned back and nodded. "Well. Normally we'd have another interview, one with a board member, as they like to have a say in matters. But we're insanely busy right now and, quite frankly, I think you'd be perfect for the job."

"Wow. That's great to hear," Maggie said with a smile.

"When can you start?"

"Well, to be honest with you, I'm pretty bored these days. So the sooner the better."

"Really? That's great."

The office door was half closed. There was a light rap on the door jamb. It was Yvonne, smiling nervously. "I'm sorry, but we just had a shipment of clothes arrive an hour early. I've got to run to the dock out back to make sure they get offloaded correctly and there's no one to cover the phones."

"Oh. No problem. We're done here and—"

"I could cover them," Maggie said boldly, wondering if she'd lost her mind. But she wasn't lying. She really was bored. Julie's new job had her working non-stop, and Maggie felt that if she spent one more hour alone in the apartment or wandering the neighborhood, she might go crazy.

The two women looked at each other and chuckled.

"Well," Evelyn said, with a playful shrug. "It's not the job I hired her for, obviously. But she's gotta cut her teeth sooner or later. And I've got a conference call I've gotta jump on."

"Okay . . ." Yvonne said. "Seat of the pants it is, then! It won't be for long and you can just take messages."

On the way down the hall Maggie got the run down. Most calls came in mid-morning, when the "clients" were able to get free. All of them were high maintenance, but in the best of ways because they were almost always at the point of being completely overwhelmed by the time they called. Patience was crucial, as was an ability to listen. Yvonne showed her the phone system, which was child's play compared to the one at her receptionist job in New

York, and then ducked away.

Maggie was a little stunned to be seated at the very counter that a little while before she had seen for the first time. The desktop before her was a collage of papers, reports and Post-It notes, broken up only by a stapler and a half dozen Bic pens. A sticker with speed dial codes for the police, fire, ambulance and hospital numbers was taped on the wall over the phone.

Being at the desk made everything more real, and Maggie was suddenly nervous.

She was telling herself that it was just going to be for ten minutes and to calm down when the phone rang and her heart jumped. Then she realized it was okay. She could do this. Looking at the business card Yvonne had left her, Maggie rehearsed the name quickly and then answered the phone.

"Eden Hill Women's Shelter," she said.

Then? She listened as the woman on the other end of the line began to tell her story. As a soon-to-be "assistant case worker" here, Maggie would have to get good at listening. At sharing. At helping others overcome, as she was now. And though she knew some people would say that here she was again, with her MBA, doing a job she was way overqualified for, Maggie knew better.

For her, this job was perfect.

Thank you for reading THE SNOW GLOBE. I'd be grateful if you would take a couple of minutes to leave a review. It only needs to be one or two sentences, and it really does help other readers decide if they'd enjoy the book.

Read on for a special preview of ONE IN A MILLION, book one in the Millionth Trilogy by Tony Faggioli.

SPECIAL PREVIEW OF
ONE IN A MILLION

CHAPTER ONE

STANDING IN THE bathroom of his hotel room, the sweat of lust glistening on his chest in the mirror before him, Kyle Fasano realized he had done a terrible thing. Her lipstick was smeared on his neck. He could still feel her hands on both his temples, pulling at his hair, urging him on, silently begging for something far more than the deed itself could ever provide.

He heard her stirring in the bed. He'd waited until she'd fallen asleep, her breathing soft and level, before he slid her arm from his chest and snuck to the bathroom. He still couldn't believe he'd done it. A twenty-three-year-old, the most ogled girl at the company the last two months, and he landed her. Or more likely, she landed him. He knew his intentions, but really, this had always hinged on hers. Even when they decided to get a room a few hours earlier, the look in her eye, the hesitation, and yet... a faint smile betrayed a subtle hint of determination.

What had he done? It was all a mess. He could keep getting laid, screw up his whole life for a kid who would grow weary of him soon enough, or he could stop it all now and risk ending up in Richard or Jerry's office on Monday with a stack of sexual harassment paperwork to square up.

He wiped his face with a hand towel and took a leak, aiming for the inside of the bowl. He didn't want to wake her. If he did, she might want to go again, and he would. There was no stopping it now, this lust that had sparked the first time he'd laid eyes on her and inflamed over drinks after everyone else bailed at the end of happy hour. That was right before the jokes about getting a room started. Just kidding around, just a little joke.

He looked in the mirror again, seeing the punch line.

He couldn't breathe. It were as if the lust was a living thing, sucking up the air in his lungs and suffocating his heart.

He remembered his grandmother when he was all of fourteen, lecturing him on the Bible while she chopped vegetables for dinner, telling him in her stern Catholic voice that all sins were forgivable save one: adultery. She told him that her best friend once died on the operating table and had been brought back to life, and she'd claimed to see, to her horror, that hell was filled with adulterers. "That is one sin you don't get past, Kyle. Remember that."

How absurd. He was only fourteen. How in the world did he have any idea what adultery was, or marriage for that matter, in any real sense? Now, as an adult, he wished he'd been old enough to ask the obvious questions that day, the ones that might've gotten him slapped upside the head. Exactly how did your friend know all this if she hadn't done that very deed herself? Was it some sort of whorish act of infidelity with the butcher in the deli just after closing, or had she simply fulfilled a cliché and been seduced by the mailman, turning to her rosary in a sense of shame that would haunt her the rest of her life?

What was it, Grandma? And by the way, it wasn't you, was it, Grandma?

His conscience was beginning to dig and bite at him like a cornered rat. He was starting to care again, just a bit, just enough to make it feel wrong, and the feeling was incomplete, as if there was more guilt to come, a ton of it actually, but just not right now.

God, what have I done? I'm so sorry.

The irony of the prayer, lonely and brief as it was, was not lost on him. As if any God, Almighty or otherwise, was interested in bailing out a thirty-eight-year-old man who had just broken his marriage vows, tossed the security of his children to the wind, and, oh yeah, in many ways just taken advantage of somebody's loving daughter.

The gears in his mind turned and rang like a cash register tabulating the price that would have to be paid for this night. He chuckled. He hated being in sales; everything came down to the math: the commissions, the residuals, the losses.

After turning on the cold water, he splashed his face, trying to wash her smell off his lips, that sweet smell of sin and victory that comes from getting a girl to do something against her better judgment, after she's done pretending that she doesn't want it too. His shoulders felt tight. Standing naked on the marble floor made the cold air around him seem more intense and he began to shiver, causing the shadows cast by the lights over the mirrors to move across his body in eerie patterns.

He thought of his wife, Tamara, and as swiftly as her face came to mind he banished it. No. Not here. Not now.

Not with the smell of another woman's perfume all over him and that deep red lipstick still smeared there on his neck like blood from the marriage he'd just murdered.

Tamara was never anyone's fool and never would be. She would never tolerate this. Not even to protect the kids. Well... maybe. That would be the only card left to play. But what did it matter? He didn't care anymore, right? That's right. Who cares? Screw it.

Perfect word. You screwed her and now you've screwed yourself, all in a few short hours of your life. Great job, champ.

He had to leave. The urge to get out of the hotel room struck him as surely as the urge that had gotten him into it. His breathing became even more labored as his lust morphed into anxiety, and he mocked himself for probably being on the edge of a heart attack.

That's what you get for banging a kid nearly half your age. She had so much energy. You could barely keep up, and now, well, how about a big laugh at the idiot who goes into cardiac arrest in a hotel room with another woman on the night of his wife's thirty-sixth birthday?

He forced himself to concentrate. Deep breaths in, deeper breaths out—but even then they were barely more than puffs. He remembered football in high school, the game against Mater Dei when the wind was knocked out of him. Coach Pete standing over him like a stone golem, screaming at him to breathe, because he had cost them a time out. Coach Pete was the biggest bastard he ever knew, and sure enough here he was again, all these years later, a mirage on the bathroom wall, screaming at him again, "Kyle, you little priss, don't you black out on me! Breathe, dammit!"

He did, barely, clawing air down his throat in desperate

gulps.

Again, it hit him: he'd really done this. He had. Worse still it was dawning on him that, like it or not, he *did* care. He did. Hearts would be broken by this, and lives, all for a college-style lay.

He thought of his daughter, Janie, ten years old, and her soft brown hair, and what it would feel like to read her bedtime stories only on every-other-weekend visits.

Nausea stirred his stomach, and he grabbed a towel. First he couldn't get air in, and now he could feel vomit trying to come out. He willed the urge away and scrambled toward the bedroom. He would get his clothes, quietly, and like a low life piece of shit, he'd sneak out of here before she woke up. Later it was going to be bad, when he'd have to see her again at work, but now, this moment, was more than he could take.

As he stepped from the half-light of the bathroom back into the bedroom, he heard her before he could see her. It was an odd sound, half-murmur and half-whisper. His lack of vision as his eyes adjusted to the darkness seemed to heighten his sense of hearing. He could barely see her outline; she was sitting at the foot of the bed, slightly hunched over.

"I've done what you want, what you want, done what you want, want..."

He froze. Was she on her phone? Had this whole thing been some sort of setup? How? Why?

Her voice was changing, the words now gone, and then she began a soft chant of some kind. He felt hairs across his entire body rustle to some sort of primal attention, as if an unknown danger had just joined them in the room. But that was ridiculous.

He stood there for a good fifteen seconds, naked and exposed, trying to get his head around what was happening.

Adrenaline poured into his bloodstream. The breathing problems? Subsiding rapidly. The nausea? Gone.

Jesus! What do I do?

Something was very wrong here, in a very bad way. Something told him that he would be the stupidest man alive to make a sound, to yell at her or try to snap her out of it—whatever "it" was that she was doing. What the hell? Was she a head case? She had never seemed like one. Was she on drugs? Possibly.

But if the explanation was as simple as some bad X, then why was there an irrational command from somewhere deep in his mind telling him to consider every move he made next very, very carefully? It was as if he was being introduced to an instinct he never knew he had and it was telling him, point blank, not only to avoid disturbing her but to run, naked, right out of the room.

The whispered chant, intonations from deep in her chest, continued as he willed himself to move forwards, to the chair where his shirt was tossed. He did so slowly, to avoid making any sound on the carpet.

Shirt in hand, he grabbed his shoes and looked for his socks.

As he moved to the side of the bed, closer to her now, her chant subsided, and again she began to speak. "I know, I know, I know, I know, I know." The two words were like rocks skipping across a lake, slippery and fast, plunking between each pause. She shook and her hands fidgeted in her lap, the fingers strumming one another uncontrollably.

Screw the socks. He could do without his jacket too. Then his stomach dropped.

His pants lay on the floor, opposite the corner of the bed where she sat but still far too close to her for comfort.

He actually decided to go without the pants, as crazy as that sounded, before realizing that his cash and keys were in the pockets.

Shit. She's probably got Tourette's or something, Kyle. Just let it go. Snap your fingers and she'll come around.

As if in response to this thought, the girl he knew as Caitlyn went completely silent.

Are you kidding me?

Not a word. Not a sound. And the silence was far worse than the chant.

He dropped to one knee and half-scooted to the pants. The bed was a nice big California king. She was a little thing, easy to bounce around, and oh what fun that had been a hundred years ago, before this moment. But still... at five foot four or so, her at one corner and he at the other, she couldn't possibly reach him.

Yes. That's the good salesman. Do the math.

But that same new instinct was telling him that she wasn't human anymore.

That's ridiculous! She's hopped up on speed or something. That's it. She's just tripping.

He was losing it. Barely able to stifle the panic in his body, he edged closer to his pants, realizing that he would have to take his eyes off her for just a second to reach down below the bed, sacrificing his line of vision.

He grabbed the pants and immediately looked up. She was staring directly at him, her chin out and her head tilted at an odd angle.

The room, his heart, time, and the heavenly host above, all stopped. Frozen.

"You weren't supposed to see, supposed to see, supposed to see..." she said. Her words, deep and guttural, were nowhere near as chilling as her eyes. They were now pure black orbs.

Again, he pleaded. Oh God, please, get me out of here.

She stood, but even this movement, from sitting to standing, was jilted and inhuman, a cross between a mime and a puppet, the joints in her knees popping loudly.

It was time to go. Period.

He moved toward the door, and she smiled.

Here he was in this horribly unreal situation, in a hotel room with a woman who was not his wife, and a part of him was still clinging desperately to the notion that he could get out of this clean somehow. But her smile proved how pathetic that idea was and how desperate he had become; it was the same level of warped desperation that makes an animal stuck in a trap believe that it can still get away if it just chews a little flesh off its leg, right around the edges, just a little at a time, then just a little bit more.

"Was I good, Kyle?" she asked, and the words came out with a half-click at the back of her throat. She moved towards him, bringing her arms out at her sides like a gunslinger, her fingers splayed as though she was in some sort of primal attack mode.

He couldn't speak.

She *wasn't* human. It was obvious now. She wasn't. It made no sense, and deep down inside, way deep down, he hoped that he was the one who was tripping, some weird brain convulsion caused by too much rum and the Viagra he'd snuck earlier at the bar.

Yes. This whole thing had been very much premeditated, hadn't it? Right down to the pill he'd taken to bang her better. He was no innocent husband seduced by the office harlot. He had planned it all out, very carefully. Like a suicide.

"What do I do, do I do, do I do?" she asked, speaking to the floor now, caught in a conversation with someone or something else, momentarily distracted.

He saw his moment and took it. In three quick strides he sidestepped to the door and opened it so he could escape. He didn't take his eyes off her for a moment, his hand still on the door handle, his peripheral vision guiding him.

She looked up. "Kill him." She said it matter-of-factly, as if she were ordering a scoop of ice cream, before those horrible black eyes went wide with rage and those fingers with their French-tip nails came forwards to stab and claw the soul right out of him.

She charged the door with a scream as he stepped out into the hall and slammed it shut behind him. He heard her thud against it loudly on the other side. That too was abnormal. A human being would've slowed down upon seeing the door being closed in their face, but like a feral cat or a rabid dog she had charged directly into it.

He fled down the hall, nearly naked and with clothes in hand, closing the thirty feet to the elevator.

She banged and screamed from inside the room as if she couldn't get out, the sounds echoing down the hall, and he realized that she might not be able to, that the difficulty of using those claws to open that door might be the only thing saving him right now.

But still, what *was* human in her, if anything, might figure it out any second now. Then she would be out and after him.

He had no time to waste. Making it to the elevator he pushed the call button, and to his relief the doors opened immediately. There was no one inside. Finally: a moment of luck in this whole mess.

He jumped in and punched the "close" button repeatedly. He held his breath as the doors shut agonizingly slowly, certain that she would appear in the opening before they fully closed.

When the doors finally came together and the elevator began its descent, he exhaled deeply, still in a state of shock.

Oh God. What just happened? God, please, just help me. Get me out of this.

He had twenty-two floors to get himself dressed and he managed it, but just barely, and only because there were no stops along the way. The elevator opened and he was out into the lobby at a quick clip. Passing the front desk, he nodded curtly at the smartly dressed employee on duty, thankful it was a man for some reason.

When the front doors of the hotel opened and the crisp night air outside spilled over him, he began to reason with himself. This was all a bad dream. Yes. He was brilliant enough to have had an affair with a closet crack addict who was up there in that room right now in some sort of drug induced hallucination. That's all it was. He just had to get to his car and—

"Kyle Fasano?"

The voice was deep, authoritative, and came from somewhere to his right.

This *had* been a setup. He *was* going to get scammed somehow.

He turned to face a tall man with a gray face, who was in a gray suit and wore a gray hat that sat evenly over his white hair.

"This is not a scam, Kyle," the man said, his face full of pity.

Had this guy just replied to his thoughts? No. That was impossible.

I must've spoken aloud without realizing it.

"No, you didn't," The Gray Man said.

Kyle hadn't buttoned his shirt up all the way, and the cold air bit at his chest as the night came to a standstill.

"What is this?" Kyle finally asked.

"You've been asking for God's help, haven't you?"

"What?"

"Yes, a number of times, actually, in the last few minutes."

"What are you talking about?"

"You know, Kyle, I actually feel a bit sorry for you, I'll admit it," The Gray Man said.

"Why?"

"Because God has heard you. But I'm not sure you're going to like His answer."

*****

Buy Now!
One In A Million (Book 1 of "The Millionth Trilogy"
Go to: https://tonyfaggioli.com/books/

ACKNOWLEDGMENTS

The Snow Globe began as a short story fifteen years ago in a Creative Writing class I took at Pasadena City College in California, when I decided to return to writing after a decade away. I owe a special thank you to Dr. Howard Hertz, who always offered wise counsel and heartfelt encouragement.

After that, I received unwavering support from my Novel Critique Group. Ruthless readers who've become great friends, they helped me turn a ten-page short story into a full book. From there, it was my awesome editor, Sophie Playle, who was then able to help me flesh out the real story I was trying to tell in the real way that I was trying to tell it. This is my fourth book with her and I couldn't be more grateful.

A big salute also goes out to all the members of Team One, my beta readers group, who were beyond generous with their time and efforts, and my author's assistant, Jennifer Oliver of Sidekick Jenn, for her caring advice and for formatting this book for publication.

Last, but not least, I want to thank my wife Maxime for her love and guidance, my son Anthony for his enthusiasm for Dad's dream-chasing, and my daughter Sophia, who just this week at school picked me as her "Personal Hero" for a class project because "My Daddy writes books!"

ABOUT THE AUTHOR

Tony Faggioli was born in Pittsburgh, Pennsylvania. He graduated from the University of Southern California, where he majored in Public Administration and was chosen to intern at The White House. After college, he transitioned to corporate America before deciding to start his own business. One day, he realized that nothing brought him anywhere near the amount of joy as the writing he did from grade school all the way through high school. So, at age 35, he returned to school and rekindled his passion. He's now written four novels and begun his fifth. He's married, with two children, and lives in Los Angeles, California.

VISIT HIS WEBSITE TO SIGN UP FOR HIS NEWS-LETTER AT:
https://tonyfaggioli.com
And be the first to know about new releases and special events!

For more information, connect with Tony on:

TWITTER: @steelertony

FACEBOOK: https://facebook.com/tfaggioli

WEBSITE: http://tonyfaggioli.com

MORE BOOKS BY TONY FAGGIOLI

<u>One In A Million (Book 1 of "The Millionth Trilogy")</u>
Kyle Fasano has it all: a good job, a loving family and a house on the hill. Still, it's not enough. Risking it all, he has a fling with a woman from the office. But Kyle is about to learn that with every choice, there are consequences, and sometimes there can be hell to pay. Literally.

<u>A Million to One (Book 2 of "The Millionth Trilogy")</u>
There's hell...and there's hell on Earth. And Kyle Fasano is about to discover that there are some demons that you never see coming.

<u>One Plus One (Book 3 of "The Millionth Trilogy")</u>
Sometimes the war for your soul can only be won by defiance. Kyle Fasano will never give up. Because love is a promise. You just have to believe.

Made in the USA
Lexington, KY
11 May 2018